EVERY MOTHER'S FEAR

JOANNA WARRINGTON

DISCLAIMER AND BACKGROUND

I am dedicating this book to an incredible lady, my employer, Mrs Lorraine Mercer, MBE. Lorraine was born in 1961. Her mother was one of thousands of women who took the drug thalidomide to alleviate morning sickness during pregnancy. As a result, Lorraine was born with limb damage. Because of her life, I was inspired to write a story centred around the thalidomide tragedy. Lorraine has led a rich and rewarding life and through every difficult situation she's faced her sense of humour and fun shines through. She is an amazing artist, she enjoys carriage riding and she was recently awarded an MBE for her charity work.

The thalidomide disaster was one of the blackest episodes in medical history with devastating consequences for thousands of families across the world. Developed in the 1950s by the West German pharmaceutical company Chemie Grunenthal, it was released to the world as a wonder drug, rigorously marketed and sold in forty-six countries under different brand names. Testing failed because the drug was released for distribution before sufficient time had elapsed to collate and connect information and to monitor the possibility of long-term side effects. It was used to treat a range of medical conditions and was in particular a mild sleeping pill. It was supposedly safe for pregnant women, who took it to alleviate morning sickness. During patenting and testing scientists found it was practically impossible to achieve a deadly overdose of the drug and animal tests didn't include looking at the effects of it during pregnancy. By the late 1950s doctors were concerned about the possibility of side effects as a growing number of babies were being born with deformities. Thalidomide caused thousands of children worldwide to be born with malformed limbs and the drug was taken off the market late in 1961.

There was a protracted criminal trial in Germany and in Britain a newspaper campaign during the 1960s and 1970s. They forced Grünenthal and its British licensee, the Distillers Company, to financially support victims of the drug. It led to tougher testing and drug approval procedures in many countries, including the United States and the United Kingdom.

Thalidomide has its place in the medical world; it's still out there and is used as a treatment for leprosy and bone cancer. Its use is heavily regulated, to prevent a repeat of the tragedy it caused during the last century.

Every Mother's Fear is a fictional story based on actual events. The story of how Chemie Grunenthal came to manufacture the drug and the part played by Distillers is widely known and in the public domain and has been written about and discussed in TV dramas such as *Call The Midwife,* therefore I have decided to use the correct company names in this story. The characters in Distillers and in Grunenthal, however and the board meeting and court scenes, the views, opinions and personal backgrounds of the characters are a product of my imagination and elaboration and how I imagine things might have been at the time.

The founders of Grunenthal were members of the Nazi party. Documents unearthed by Dr Martin Johnson, director of

The Thalidomide Trust suggest that the drug was tested on prisoners in concentration camps, by Third Reich scientists during the Second World War and that it was created as an antidote to nerve toxins including sarin.

The characters in this story are fictitious. Any resemblance to actual persons, living or dead, is coincidental. The story reflects situations and experiences families and thalidomide survivors might have faced and my heart goes out to them and their continued campaign for justice.

Thalidomide is associated in the public mind with limb defects. While these account for the majority of cases any organ of the body could be affected resulting in a multitude of related conditions. Fascinating research revealed that the specific damage to an individual depended on which day during gestation the mother took the pill. This could be pinpointed with accuracy.

I would like to thank Dr Ruth Blue for her help with this project, for answering my questions and for inviting me to The Thalidomide Society AGM. It was wonderful to talk to some of the survivors and to hear about the ongoing issues facing them and the struggles they have faced over the past fifty odd years. They have been the subject of much scrutiny and media attention, and this has taken its toll. They have a unique and exclusive bond and it is this strength and determination that has kept them going. They have led diverse lives. It was a very moving and sobering experience for me, but out of this tragedy and their adversity it was lovely to see so much positivity, camaraderie, laughter and fun among friends who have known each other for the best part of their lives.

CHAPTERS

Content

1

GERMANY, DECEMBER 1958

Heinz, former chief chemical expert to Adolf Hitler paces his office, having just opened a letter that he finds alarming. The letter contains a damning report about the drug his company makes: thalidomide. It's not the first negative report he's received about thalidomide. But it is proving to be as popular and lucrative as aspirin and a cure for many illnesses, and the company has big plans for it. In West Germany alone more than a million people are taking contergan, the German brand name for thalidomide. It's the best sedative on the market.

Heinz's mahogany desk is part of a recent refit because the company is doing so well. Profits are rising month on month with projections for continued growth into the following year and much of that is due to contergan. Heinz and his family have moved house to a bigger property, with land on the edge of town and his wife has become used to this lavish lifestyle. With very little effort or actual hard work he's become a millionaire in a matter of months. He's a senior partner in the company and his father is proud of him. He's spent years making this happen. Life hasn't been easy for so many

Germans since the end of the war and the West German job market has been flooded with skilled professional workers from East Germany. Heinz is lucky. Working for a successful pharmaceutical company brings hope for a brighter, more prosperous future for Heinz and his family.

Heinz twirls the ends of his moustache pondering the letter and picks up the phone on his desk. He calls his secretary to ask her to arrange an urgent board meeting. They'll fight this and come up with a plan.

Two hours later the board of directors sit around the table. They are a group of talented scientists, but Heinz is aware that to some cynical outsiders they are a rogue's gallery of wanted and convicted Nazis; mass murderers who practised their science as medical roulette in notorious death camps like Auschwitz. One of them was the chief concentration camp doctor and another developed a drug-laced protein sausage that was tested on concentration camp prisoners, killing many. Frank Otto was a brilliant, charismatic and charming chemist who developed the nerve gas sarin. Otto served eight years in prison after the war and he is a great asset to Grunenthal. Heinz is in awe of his team but admires Frank the most. Frank is the Head of Pathology and was a leading proponent of the Nazi racial programme, working with the SS on its population policy during the war. He made the decision regarding who should live and who should die. With his team Heinz gained knowledge and skills developed during experimentation that the world condemns. Until it goes wrong and affects 'our people,' our people turn a blind eye to leaked stories and tales of atrocities; well it was in the name of war, wasn't it? Those brave people gave their lives for the good of others—but it was during the war and stuff happens, best not to think about it too much.

The board are divided in what they think about the report,

but he expects this and must bring them round to his way of thinking if they are to move forward.

'The letter is from a doctor in Dusseldorf,' Heinz tells the board meeting. 'He claims that ten of his patients, all of whom have been taking thalidomide for a year, have peripheral neuritis. He believes there is a connection between long-term use of thalidomide and this condition.' Heinz takes his glasses off to look at each person around the table. 'It's a serious illness and can occur anywhere in the body. It begins with a prickly feeling in the toes, followed by numbness and cold sensations. The numbness spreads leading to muscle cramps, lack of coordination and weakness in the limbs.'

Outside the window and beyond the brevity of the boardroom a cluster of attractive buildings over Stolberg sit snug in a green valley around a medieval castle on the outskirts of Aachen. The prosperous air of the town is in part due to the success of the company Heinz has helped to build. Grunenthal is a family firm founded in the last century and is the pillar of Aachen society and its philanthropy has included a new roof to the city's centuries old cathedral. People rely on the company for their livelihood and generations of families have worked here. The world is resting on Heinz's shoulders. He must protect thalidomide, for the sake of his town and the men and women who live and work here.

'I've had requests from doctors for it to be put on prescription,' the sales manager tells the meeting. 'So that it can be monitored.'

The marketing director gasps. 'That's got to be avoided at all cost. A substantial amount of our volume comes from over-the-counter sales. Our sales reps are going to have to warn doctors and pharmacists across Europe that they stand to lose a huge amount of money.'

'We can't turn a blind eye. There will be more reports of side effects,' another member says.

'Not necessarily. Arrange for more leaflets to go out to doctors in each country stating that thalidomide is non-toxic and completely safe. All they need is reassurance.' Heinz is willing to pay the marketing manager a vast salary—many times greater than he's currently getting in order to manage a good, effective marketing campaign. He will do whatever it takes to make thalidomide a success.

'What shall we reply?'

'We can assure you that such problems have not been brought to our attention before—or words to that effect.'

Some of the members are dumbfounded. They aren't fooled by this. There's a murmur of disagreement. They know it's not true, but they are in the minority. The prevailing thought on most of the members' minds is profit. It's difficult for them to shake off the way that they have been trained to think. They find it hard, in this new post-war world to dwell on suffering. There is a coldness and a level of detachment. They struggle to make their primary concern the patient.

'We can't just turn a blind eye,' one member says.

'We need a slogan.' Heinz has affected a bright tone to his voice. 'How about, we must succeed whatever the cost?'

Everybody smiles and nods apart from two people.

'But what are we going to do about the reports? We should order more clinical trials.'

'We've conducted enough tests and trials. The government doesn't require us to.'

'This is nothing more than a storm in a teacup,' the financial director says, with a smile into his cup. 'Please excuse the pun. It's been tested on rodents for Christ's sake. We've done all we can. '

'The world is hooked on barbiturates. Thalidomide is the only non-barbiturate sedative on the market. Some doctors are suggesting it could be used to alleviate morning sickness in pregnancy too,' the medical director says. 'Do you know how many babies are born worldwide every year? This new use for it could be massive. It gives people a few pins and needles, so what? The possibilities for this drug are endless and, in the meantime, I've got an eminent friend who could write a favourable report and get it published in medical journals across Europe.'

'Great idea. Good publicity is what we need. Right, well if that's all business concluded, can we close the meeting? I'm playing a round of golf this evening and need to practice my stroke,' Heinz says, feeling more positive.

The men chuckle.

2

SANDY, LONDON, 1960

Sandy whispers into Deirdre's ear, 'He's ogling me.'

'You think every fella in town fancies you.'

Sandy doesn't need to think it—she knows it. With blonde hair, blue eyes, long slender legs and a big bust she can have any man she wants.

'He could be looking at me,' Deirdre giggles.

'Maybe.' But Sandy thinks it unlikely. Deirdre's skin is the colour of semolina and her body's fleshy, like a figure in a Hogarth painting. She's wearing one of her grandma's knitted cardigans with pockets at the front filled with crumpled tissues because she always has a runny nose. With her dumpy legs and flat chest Deirdre rarely gets asked to dance. Sandy likes it that way. She doesn't have to compete for men's attention. Deirdre is perfect dancing company, even though Sandy refers to her as Dreary Deirdre behind her back.

All Sandy has to do is smile in a man's direction to make them want her. She knows she's attractive. It's evident in the way she stands, her posture screams confidence with her hands-on-hips attitude and it's in the way she flicks her hair from her face. Her dress reveals a hint of cleavage. Sandy looks forward to Saturday nights at the Cricklewood Palais.

'He might not come over and risk getting snubbed by one of your cruel put downs.'

'Who me?' Sandy laughs. She's renowned for her pithy knockbacks. 'I never humiliate them.'

The hall fills and the evening livens up. The band is a collection of middle-aged men in ill-fitted suits. Babbling girls in their hooped skirts with a flash of scarlet across their lips, stand to one side of the hall and wiry boys with Vaseline sculptured Tony Curtis hair wait in an unofficial mating ritual on the other. Each side of the room eyes up the talent on the other. Feet clatter on the maple floor. Cigarette smoke hangs in thick yellow banks. Sandy watches the men ask the women to dance, brought together under the slow swirl of the glitter ball. Everybody jokes that the weekly dance is a monkey parade. People mill around the room, laughing and enjoying themselves, couples jive to the beat of Bill Haley, not daring to join in themselves.

'He's just a damp chancer.'

'Could be a champ dancer.'

They lean into each other giggling. She's about to find out. The tall man with slicked-back hair carves a passageway through the crowd, stopping in front of her.

'What a stunning dress.'

His eyes trail over her like a finger over Braille.

'It's the colour of danger and I'm probably too dangerous for the likes of you.' She giggles and Deirdre throws her a warning glance as she extends an arm towards him to introduce herself.

'Does purple reflect the kind of woman you are then?' He asks Sandy.

There's a mischievous glint in his eye.

'I like to stand out from the crowd.'

'I'm Jasper and you?'

'Sandy.'

Part of her hopes her purple dress isn't garish, as if she's trying too hard but a part of her wants to be striking and to be noticed. In her job it's the way to be. If she doesn't spend hours in front of the mirror, preening her hair, polishing her nose and attending to crow's feet, how will she get the next modelling contract? Looks are everything and if she doesn't get asked to dance she considers herself a failure and mopes around the house the following day wondering where she's going wrong.

She gives him a twirl and he takes her hand and leads her away from Deirdre and into the crowd of dancers shuffling in steady steps across the floor, her friend gawps after them.

Sandy looks forward to the weekly dance, escaping the dull routine of her parents' lives, the rustle of her father's newspaper and the hum of her mother's new vac as she pushes it up and down the lounge, always dressed in her pinny and turban. Sandy wants more from life than her mother has achieved, marrying her husband at seventeen for a menial life of domestic drudgery and ditching the chance to join the Wrens and see the world. Sandy knows her parents aren't in love but she doesn't doubt they love each other in a safe and comforting way. Their sort of love is expressed in smiles across the kitchen table over roast lamb and gravy, apple pie and cups of tea. Sandy wants fireworks, racing hearts and physical – she blushes – desires.

Jasper is as light on his feet as Fred Astaire and they dance in sync as if they've been dancing partners for years, mirroring each other's moves, their faces hot and smiling.

She unfurls her hands above her head, like a flamenco dancer, declaring she needs a break. Out of breath and clammy they saunter to the bar.

'Your dress catches nicely under the light.' Propped at the bar, they sip shandies.

'Purple was invented by accident by a chemist called William Perkin. He found it when he was working on a treatment for malaria.'

She'd read it somewhere in one of her modelling books. She remembers useless pieces of information and can answer all the questions on *What's My Line?* But grasping the bigger picture is hard for Sandy and explains why she dropped out of school at the first opportunity.

'It makes me think of wisteria climbing up my grandma's house. I think it would make a great colour for a packet of cigarettes to purvey an element of danger.'

He shrugs. 'Cigarettes are fine. My doctor's always smoking, so it can't be that bad. Would you care for one?' He reaches into his pocket and pulls a cigarette out. She holds it between her lips while he lights a match for her. Their eyes meet as he smiles. *Yes, I've hooked him.*

'You like danger in your life then?' she asks seductively.

'Not particularly. I've just been to Cyprus. No more danger for me, thank you very much.'

'National Service?'

'Yes.'

'RAF? My dad was in the RAF during the war.'

'Sadly no. I fancied the RAF. I had the interview and the medical exam.' He looks down at his crotch, drawing Sandy's eyes to it. 'They pressed down there which was pretty embarrassing and they did all the usual tests. Anyway, on the way out of the building I banged into the fire extinguisher and it exploded and covered the captain.'

'No way.' Sandy's face went red with embarrassment.

'God's honest truth.' He laughs. 'There was spray everywhere. I received a letter a week later saying that I couldn't go into the RAF because of my eyesight.'

'There's nothing wrong with your eyesight. You spotted me from across the hall. So what did you do?'

'I joined the Royal Signals and hated it. I wrote to my Methodist preacher about the way we were treated. The officers ransacked our rooms at five in the morning because we hadn't made our beds properly with hospital corners. It wasn't all bad though. On Saturday afternoons we went to Paphos and played dominoes with the old Turks.'

Sandy likes the way they laugh long and easily, the first barriers of courtship broken down. He isn't the stiff and starchy civil-servant type of fella dressed in a tank top and tie that she's used to.

'Care for another dance?'

Remembering Deirdre, she is worried her friend is alone. Spotting her chatting to people she allows him to lead her onto the dance floor where feet pound the wooden boards to Elvis Presley's Big Hunk O' Love and girls scream. As he twirls her around she sees her reflection in the floor-to-ceiling mirror along the wall. Her hair has loosened from the French roll she's copied from the cover of *Seventeen* and her face is blotchy. Any ideas of being like Jean Shrimpton disappear. Soon her feet ache in her new winklepickers and she longs to be in Deirdre's frumpy sandals. Still she dances. She contorts her body in sensual moves as she tries to impress him. He's a natural on the dance floor, his hips and arms move to the beat and he stands out from the other men bobbing their heads, hoping to get noticed with the odd pervy move. People line the walls, too terrified to venture onto the floor in case they are mown down by the fast pace. The record slows and merges into Frankie Avalon *A Boy Without A Girl* and Jasper draws her into an embrace. They avoid stepping on each other's feet and he drapes his arm over her shoulder.

He whispers into her ear. 'I'm a boy without a girl. Home from National Service and lost. Are you a girl without a boy?'

All she can do is smile and enjoy the closeness of their bodies as they step in a circle, but the romantic moment is ruined by worrying about her hair that needs extra grips to hold it and her face that's blotchy and needs more powder. By the end of the record they are cheek to cheek even though they've just met. She can feel the warmth of his face against the heat of hers.

'I'll be back in a minute. Just nipping to the ladies.'

Sandy doesn't need the loo. She wants to check her hair and makeup. Gazing into the mirror she marvels at her reflection. The soft lighting in the vanity area enhances the tones of her skin to a beautiful salmon. She waves a blusher brush over her cheeks and turns to admire her perfect cheekbones; pursing her lips she applies a slash of lippy. Using a pencil around the edges she draws a fine line to give them a fuller appearance. She is stunning, if she does think so herself. The ice blue of her eyes can dazzle any man. The only thing that she hates are the dark circles under her eyes that make her look as if she hasn't slept in a fortnight. Covering them up is a daily battle and involves raw grated potato for two hours in the evening lying rigid on the bed so that it doesn't fall off. Potato has a natural bleaching agent to get rid of puffiness and lighten the skin. The following evening, she uses sliced cucumber. If she wasn't going out she'd alternate between potatoes and cucumbers and sometimes lemon drops and during the day, she'd reapply nude-coloured foundation, or when she sensed somebody was looking at her dark circles.

A toilet flushes and a cubicle door opens. Deirdre comes out and sidles up beside Sandy.

'You spend too much time in front of the mirror.'

And you don't, thinks Sandy, which is why you look a frump. Deirdre has taken her cardigan off to reveal a faded red dress, stitched by hand, the pattern chosen by her great aunt. It makes her bum look fat and she looks like a sack of potatoes. Poor old Deirdre, Sandy thinks, she has got to pull herself together if she wants to find a partner.

How's it going with that fella?'

Sandy puts an extra kirby grip in her hair. 'His name's Jasper. Yeah, he's alright. Not jealous are you?' If she cares about the way she looks, like I do, thinks Sandy, then maybe she'd stand a chance. But then again, Deirdre and all the other girls for that matter don't have my natural beauty. Some are even bordering on ugly. I have it all.

'Has he asked you out yet?'

'Not yet. But I'm not that bothered. I'm going travelling round Canada next year.'

'Not that idea again. You can't go on your own. Anything might happen. Don't you want to get hitched? I do. I don't want to end up on the shelf.'

'There's plenty of time for all that. My career comes first.'

Sandy snaps her bag shut and trots off to find Jasper.

LATER ON WHILE she's engrossed in a conversation with him, Deirdre appears at her side. Her voice is clipped and Sandy can tell from the look on her face that she is miffed at being ignored all evening.

'The last bus is leaving soon if you care to make your curfew.'

Sandy glances at her watch. It's twenty minutes until the last bus and still time for a dance before heading across the road to the bus stop. She's annoyed with Deirdre for interrupting the conversation and knows she's dragging her away deliberately. Sandy is about to tell Jasper about her new modelling contract with Revlon and how she got the job. Being spotted by a famous photographer in John Lewis while trying on lipstick always impresses men.

Deirdre taps her foot, the cue to go, forcing Sandy to stand up. She yanks her arm and Sandy says a flushed goodbye, telling Jasper she'll be at the dance next Saturday. And then he gets up and pulls her towards him to tell her that he's had a really nice evening. She knows he means it. She wants him to ask her out. Bloody Deirdre, she curses under her breath, cutting the evening short before he's had the chance to ask me.

They climb onto the top deck of the bus for a quick puff of a cigarette. With a roar and a belch of diesel fumes, the bus pulls away from the pavement and the evening is over. Sandy peers out of the misty window hoping to wave to Jasper who has followed them out into the cold night to make sure the bus arrives. She wipes the window with her sleeve but can't see him. He's vanished back into the warmth of the hall, probably to chat up another girl. A pang of sadness washes over her. He likes her, she's sure of that and she more than likes him.

It's going to be hard to sleep tonight for dreaming about the way he'd held her on the dance floor. She closes her eyes as the bus bumps along, recapturing the scent of Brylcreem and Imperial Leather.

3

RONA, BLACKPOOL, ENGLAND, 1960

'Come on, love, give a big push, I can see baby's head,' Rona coaxes.

'I'm exhausted.' Rona's exhausted too but doesn't show it. This has been the longest delivery in a while.

The woman gestures for Rona to take her hand and she squeezes it so hard Rona thinks she's cut off her circulation. She keeps her composure and resists the urge to wince or wipe her sweaty brow. Her skin prickles and she's desperate to scratch it. She hasn't sat down in hours, her feet are swollen and aching and the paper hat on her head itches. Her mouth is parched, the father-to-be could get her a glass of water but she's too polite to trouble the terrified young man standing beside the bed, about to become a father for the first time. Putting her own needs to one side, she shoots him a reassuring smile and focuses on delivering the baby.

The bedroom is cramped and airless. Rona clears her dry throat.

'Now pant Nancy, don't push, the baby's nearly out.'

As Rona watches the head emerge, the light over the bed grows brighter. The woman's blood-curdling screams and the man's voice fade into the distance and her head swims. Sensing she is going to faint she grabs a chair and sits down, reaching over the bed to help the baby into the world, determined she will see this through.

'Nurse you look terrible,' the man says and fetches a glass of water.

'I'll be fine in a moment.' Rona feels embarrassed and struggles to keep her composure. She's respected at the hospital for being one of the most experienced and dedicated nurses. She mustn't lose it, not now. She can hear Matron's voice in her head scolding her. She gulps in air to stop herself keeling over but the room is spinning. *This is the most important stage of the delivery process. This woman needs me to be strong and in control.*

Nancy's husband John is behind Rona, helping her drink a glass of lemon barley water. Rona can feel her blood sugar returning to normal and the room stops swimming. She stays sitting but is able to stretch over and deliver the baby and placenta while all the time wondering why she is feeling so ill. This isn't like her. She's used to long shifts and unsociable hours. It's all she knows. She's done this job for years, apart from dropping out for a year to help her mother look after her dying father. Rona is more than capable. A niggling thought loops around her head. *Could I be? Do I dare to imagine that I might be?* No, I won't be, she corrects herself and pushes the thought from her mind. There have been false alarms before and hopes dashed. I'm just very tired and overworked and I'm not getting any younger.

Rona wraps the baby in a towel and passes her to the mother, plumped up on a pillow.

'Thank you, Nurse, you've done a brilliant job. I thought for one awful moment...' The man gives Rona a broad smile, filled with a mixture of gratitude and relief. It's a look that she's grown accustomed to and it makes her job worthwhile. Rona takes the mother's hand and stifles a tear, feeling pride for the role she's played in making this couple's life complete.

'It all worked out in the end.' It was a home birth and they always caused Rona extra worry knowing that at any moment even the textbook and simplest births could go wrong.

John sits on the bed and rubs his wife's arm. 'You did the hard work love.' The mother always does the hard work. Rona is just the facilitator, but it is right that he should be lavishing his praise on his wife rather than her. 'And look what you've produced, our beautiful baby girl.'

'Yeah, I certainly did the hard bit,' the woman laughs. 'You did the easy bit.'

Rona smiles but inwardly feels a mixture of happiness and sadness at the word easy. It's never easy delivering babies, when life is held in the balance. She delivers them every day; it's a never-ending production line of gurgling, chirpy babies, all the end result of man's easy role nine months before.

'Nip over to the corner shop and get me a *Woman's Weekly*, will you?' Nancy asks John.

'And a bag of toffees?'

'There's some change in the bedside drawer.'

While John is gone Rona suggests taking the sheets off the bed to wash them and asks if she can make her a cup of tea. There is still a lot to do before she can return to the hospital but the time is disappearing and Rona needs to make the mother comfortable before she can leave. And first she has to check that the baby is able to feed.

Handing the mother a cuppa, Rona asks how she's feeling and if she needs some painkillers.

'I'm a bit sore down below and need some sleep but other than that.'

She lowers her voice and glances out of the window as if to check that her husband isn't on his way back. Then she leans her head towards Rona and fixes her eyes on her. They are glinting with anxiety and excitement. Rona senses she is part of a conspiracy. 'Can you keep a secret Nurse?'

Nothing surprises Rona in this work. Her job is colourful, that's why she loves it. She's used to expecting the unexpected, never assumes anything and has become unshockable.

Before she has the chance to answer, the mother is vomiting her secret. Tears and a hint of fear glisten in the mother's eyes. 'She's not his.'

Rona stares from the baby to the mother, speechless. She doesn't frown or show alarm, tut or sigh. Her face is professional, remaining calm in the face of the confession. But she can't control the blush spreading across her face as she prepares for the aftermath of the woman's confession.

'I'm not proud of what happened.'

'Well I...' Rona can't think how to finish the sentence. It's not supposed to be like this. They're supposed to be a loving, happy couple who've been trying for a baby for a long time—a deserving couple. The baby is a gift of their love, a miracle even. They have stopped being two people and are a picture frame of three people. Rona is generally good at putting her emotions into a box while she works because it's her job, but from nowhere disgust wells inside her. She realises that her own painful circumstances are spilling into her working day and affecting how she feels about her mothers.

'I went to a dance with a friend in town and got awfully drunk. I had one too many gins, you see. They don't call it Mother's Ruin for nothing. I had a one-night stand, that's all it was and just my luck I fell pregnant. Can you believe it?' She chuckles as if she's committed a minor misdemeanour like forgetting to cook her husband's dinner, while Rona gapes open-mouthed and tries not to shake her head.

'I couldn't believe it. I've never missed a period. We weren't even trying. We were waiting until the time was right and we had more money in the bank.'

Rona baulks but covers her thoughts with a comforting smile.

'I worked out the dates and realised that John couldn't be the father. He'd been away on a big job laying concrete in Manchester. Motorways are going up everywhere. You won't say anything, will you Nurse? I do love him.'

Rona pats her hand and gives her a smile. 'No, of course not. I can see that he loves you to bits. I wouldn't dream of interfering. Now we need to change these sheets before you can settle down to sleep. If you move over to one side I'll do it in stages.'

Rona feels dreadful for playing down the deceit but it isn't her place to judge even though she can't help but feel judgemental. She smooths the sheet trying to appear unperturbed, as if she's acting in a play. She is used to this, mothers seeking her reassurance and treating her as a confidante, but it's hard to be unmoved by their stories. Sometimes the biggest secrets are the ones you can only tell a stranger. Rona appreciates that. She doesn't have secrets of her own because having a secret often means telling a lie which always leads to getting caught. Rona is too honest. She's a good citizen and a pillar of society. She wonders if John suspects anything but loves his wife so much that he's prepared to keep her secret and raise another man's child and she wonders what that would be like.

The woman shifts up the bed wincing in pain.

'What made you go into nursing? It's not something I could do.'

Rona stands up, puts one hand on her aching back and thinks for a moment. She can hear her father's voice in her head. 'It's a natural job for women. Nursing is the best preparation for learning how to be a good wife and mother. If something ever happens to your husband, you'll have something to fall back on.' Her father had been the more powerful guide, he'd influenced every decision she'd made, he was her rock and support. She misses him so much.

'When I was nine my cousin was born and I loved cuddling and playing with her. I made cribs out of cardboard boxes and I took her for walks in her pram and I dressed her sometimes. My aunt was poorly soon after she was born you see. She had pleurisy and my uncle was called to war. He was away for long periods fighting in the army. My aunt relied on me to help out sometimes, but I didn't mind. I adore babies and then I had it in my mind that I'd become a midwife. I was fascinated by pregnancy. My aunt didn't talk about the pregnancy and so when Betty arrived it seemed like a miracle.'

'Do you have children of your own?'

Rona is changing a pillowcase. She stops, puts the pillow down, her heart in her throat, taken aback by the question. She bristles but knows the woman means no harm. Asking about her job is one thing but asking whether she has a family of her own is another. It's a weighty question, often asked so easily, so lightly, just an innocent remark but it hits like a nuclear weapon. Rona feels a twinge of the loss she always feels when asked if she's a mother and brushes away the thought that it might never happen.

'I'm too busy looking after other peoples' babies to have my own,' she laughs, unruffled. 'You mums do the work and I get to cuddle the little bundles.'

'You're so lucky. You've made the right choice. This little mite was foisted upon me. I'm scared of being a mum, but I've got to make the most of it. Yours sounds like the perfect situation and you're earning an income. We've got to live on one wage and it's going to be really hard.'

Rona pushes the pillow into the case with more force than she intends. Feathers flutter in the air. 'You don't regret her though, surely? She's beautiful.'

'She is and I love her to bits already but it'll take me a while to get used to the idea of being responsible for another human being and never sleeping again.'

Rona would love to be responsible for another human being.

John returns, complaining that it's cold outside. He's dragging urgently on a shifty cigarette, perhaps his real reason for nipping over to the shop so willingly, and Rona is glad when her work is done so that she can leave them to it.

4

SANDY

Sandy is paid double rate for modelling lingerie, it's like combat pay in the army. This Monday morning she has an interview with an agency. She stands naked in front of a full mirror checking her body for creases, bruises, cold sores and bags under the eyes.

She bathes and shampoos her hair with strawberry shampoo, giving it a glossy glow and a wonderful smell. She shaves under her arms, smoothes her legs and creams her body from top to toe. She does her toenails and fingernails. She scrutinises herself in her underwear, analysing every inch of her body. The photographer will be able to airbrush any tiny skin marks. She curses herself for not having a nude strapless bra and slips into a pair of long-line full panty hose in a nude shade, to make sure the re-toucher doesn't have any work to do. She opens her wardrobe and pulls out a spotted dress deciding that red is the colour of fever and blood and both a welcome and a warning. It's the perfect colour for her first meeting with the team because nobody would know that inside she was a quivering bag of nerves.

'It's not a big job,' her fat bloated agent told her. 'The client is a lingerie outfit that makes colour coordinated items – bras, matching slips, girdles and stockings. They want some big colour slides for a presentation and if you fit the bill you could feature in a national ad. It could be the break you're looking for. Make sure you get an early night. I'm counting on you babe.'

A wave of nerves turns her legs to jelly as she thinks about how important today is going to be. She's been avoiding her mother's spotted dick and treacle puddings and hasn't touched pastry because it makes her stomach swell until she looks pregnant. Photographers like a cinched-waist and a flat belly. The tinier the waist the better.

She boards the bus that will take her into central London. Her nerves jangle with excitement and worry about everything that can go wrong and she's terrified that the director will speak in technical lingo and she might not understand his instructions.

The offices are on the top floor of an obscure building on Charlotte Street and Sandy presses the intercom as if her whole life depends on how long she holds down the button.

She's intimidated by the gorgeous receptionist in stylish glasses and a tight pencil skirt, who waves her to a chair without a smile, as if she's one of the many candidates she's seen today. She hands her a form to fill in, with questions such as: Do you have any warts, children, moles, scars? She stares at them. The receptionist is busy banging away on her typewriter and is of no help. It's like a quiz—spot the odd one out. She wonders why they want to know if she has children. It takes a while for the penny to drop and for Sandy to realise that childbirth, like moles ruins the body. She shudders to think how dreadful that would be and how children would spell the end of her modelling career. No agent would cast their eyes over a saggy belly and stretch marks.

The posters around the room depict the models assigned to the company. The receptionist stops typing. The room is silent.

Sandy can feel her casting a cold eye on her, from the heel of her shoe to her hair roots. She feels as though she is waiting in a dental surgery and is about to have her mouth prodded. The paranoia is getting to her. The receptionist isn't interested in sizing her up, she's reading something on her desk.

'Mr Hillier is interviewing another lady, he won't be long. Can I take your portfolio?'

Sandy has beefed up her portfolio with some recent lingerie shots. The receptionist opens it and flicks through them.

'Nice pictures.'

A door opens and a model makes her exit. They size each other up like two lions in a standoff.

'He won't be a moment. He's got a few phone calls to make,' the receptionist says.

Sandy is ushered in. The receptionist puts her portfolio on his desk and leaves, closing the door behind her.

Mr Hillier doesn't shake her hand or stand up as she comes in. She is human fodder to fill the pages of magazines and make him a tidy profit. He sits at his desk, poring over the photographs in silence, flicking between pages with his chubby fingers. He's repulsive and Sandy isn't looking forward to taking her clothes off in front of him. He pauses, opens a drawer, takes out a Havana cigar and lights it. A plume of smoke drifts through the air, giving off a rich earthy smell, reminding her of fallen leaves and fresh cut grain.

'You do lingerie a lot?' he asks.

'No, this will be my first time. I've been modelling lipstick.'

He peers at her middle. She's been doing press ups every day to tighten her stomach muscles.

'You have to have a damn good figure to show off a girdle. You need the kind of body that doesn't need a girdle in order to get to pose in one.'

To survive in this industry Sandy needs thick rhino skin

and hasn't grown one. She's mortified. Even her father, whose words are often harsh would never insult a woman with that sort of comment. His hands are steepled on the desk and she feels self–conscious as he drinks in every detail of her face and waits for him to turn her down and send her on her way.

'Your look is out of date. I'm not sure I can use you for the shots I need.'

'They were taken a few months ago.'

'Things change fast in this game.'

What a waste of time, Sandy thinks and worries that this might be the end of her career. She imagines herself at the telephone exchange where most of her friends work in a repetitive, nine-to-five job that would drive her mad. Sitting around all day would make her belly sag and the pounds would pile on. She hates the idea of a dead-end job and not being able to use her beauty to make money. If this fat pig turns her away, there will be other contracts. She feels certain of it—but what if there aren't? What then?

'Okay,' he says, after dragging on his cigar. 'I'd like you to try this on.' He gives her a bra, a slip and a pair of stockings hose to wear and waves her towards a changing cubicle.

When she's put them on he asks her to turn round so that he can get a circular view.

'Your bottom looks too big.'

Sandy looks at her bottom in the full-length mirror. She likes her bottom. It's one of her best assets. It's peachy and pert, not saggy, like her mothers. Builders always wolf whistle from scaffolding and men digging up the road call out 'nice arse love.'

'That said you do have something about your look.'

He gives her a tiny bikini he wants her to try on. It's a good fit and a tasteful design, creating a deep cleavage.

'Now we're getting somewhere, that's far better. That's

exactly what I want in the slides and in the ad. It's up to the minute and the way things have got to be.'

He walks round touching her shoulders, waist and legs as though he's sizing her up for a fitting or inspecting her in a cattle market. She feels like a plastic mannequin being mishandled.

'All right. Take off the bra.'

'I beg your pardon?'

'Didn't the agent tell you? There's a bare top shot.'

'Well then I'm not doing it.' Sandy tries to sound diplomatic but she comes across as rude. She doesn't want to pose naked but her blunt response is going to lose her the deal.

'What if I just hold my hands over my bust?'

'No, that won't do. I know what I want. There are plenty of other models out there with a more flexible attitude.'

'It's not something I've done before.'

'There's a first time for everything.'

'I wouldn't want people I know to see the ads.'

'It's for the French market and won't air on tv in the UK.'

'Really? Can I think about it and get back to you?'

'I'm interviewing ten other girls today.' He flicks his hand dismissively as if waving a pesky fly from a meal. 'I'll easily fill it. If you want to take the contract I need a decision now.'

'What's the going rate?'

'Look darling if you're interested I'll make it worth your while. I'll pay double the rate that I would for modelling underwear.'

Dizzy with nerves and her stomach in freefall she leans against the frame of the changing room to steady herself. The director picks up on her anxiety.

'It might be best if I get someone else, it seems to be out of your comfort zone.'

Pound signs dangle in front of her eyes.

'I'll do it,' she says, surprising herself with the rash decision and her stomach groans in response.

'Good.' Mr Hillier's photographer, who has just come into the room, lifts his tripod with a Hasselblad camera fitted and adjusts the viewfinder.

'Come on then, take the bra off and lean against the wall. I haven't got all day.' He points to the black wall on the opposite side of the room. She doesn't like his manner. Taking her bra off in front of a stranger is a big deal. It's scary and she wants credit for her courage but she also wants to get it over with as quickly as possible.

'Loosen up and relax for God's sake.'

When he's finished setting up the camera he examines every aspect of her boobs as he stands next to her, as if they are a painting in an art gallery. She holds her breath, doesn't move, terrified that he is going to touch them and when he turns his attention back to the camera she exhales with relief.

An old piece of advice springs to mind. Fake it till you feel it. She smiles, relaxes into the role and ignores her pounding head and the butterflies dancing in her stomach. She follows his instructions but one thought takes precedence in her mind. I can go to Canada on the back of this. I'll save up. Visions of smoked salmon, maple syrup, craggy mountains, grizzly bears and wheat blowing like an endless sea flits through her mind. Several of her friends have trained as Norland nannies and secured positions in Canada. She's envious of them. Not because they are nannies and spend all day clearing up poo and puke and covering their ears. To Sandy being a nanny is the worst job a girl could do and is always so unappreciated. She has sensitive ears to the sound of screaming babies and a short fuse. She doesn't fancy going through all that fussy training and wearing a frumpy brown uniform, making girls look like lukewarm coffee, just to secure a passage to Canada. She hates kids and can't bear the idea of looking after spoilt rich brats all day long, even though they live in amazing houses with swimming pools and tennis courts overlooking lakes and mountains. But she does want to tour the country on a Greyhound bus and stay in luxury hotels, playing at being a glamorous English lady until the money runs out, forcing her to return to her parent's semi in Cricklewood.

SHE HEADS out of Tottenham Court Road station and into a side street where she finds a patisserie sandwiched between a shabby pub and an antique shop. The window is festooned with gateaux, delicate confectionary and flans filled with fruit and cream. Mindful of her weight and the need to keep her figure trim she isn't tempted by the array of treats, but is lured in by the traditional French charm, rangy wooden booths and Sorrentine tile work. A waitress in an orange apron with a thick and sexy French accent serves her. Transported to France in this tucked-away cafe, she thinks about the adverts that will soon be appearing in French magazines. *Did I really pose topless?* Not quite believing it, she pinches herself. The director said he would confirm everything in a week. It's a long time to wait. As she sips her coffee, absorbed in thoughts about Canada and jotting down some figures on a scrap of paper she doesn't notice the man staring at her from across the room. He comes over and interrupts her.

'Fancy seeing you here; mind if I join you?'

'Jasper! What a lovely surprise.'

'Not interrupting anything am I?'

'Not at all, sit down.' She folds the paper away, not wanting him to see her workings.

There is something graceful and well-bred about the way he folds his coat and puts it on the plastic seat beside him and there's something tantalising about the way he combs his hair from his face with his fingers in one brisk move. His eyes are a warm cornflower blue. While he places his newspaper and wallet on the table she imagines sitting in the back row of the pictures cuddled up to him.

'Why are you over this way?'

She'll have to tell him - but not everything. 'I've been for a photo shoot.'

'Nude?'

They laugh.

'No. Did I tell you that I'm a model? It was just bikinis and dresses, today. Sometimes it's hats, or lipstick. I'll do anything, within reason. Apart from itchy woollen hats during an August heatwave.'

'I'd love to see you in a bikini.'

She fidgets in her seat, unsure where the conversation is heading. 'No chance, I know your game.' She swiftly slays the blush, forming across her cheeks.

'Do you like swimming? We could go to the public baths?'

Mascara would dribble down her face and she'd need to wax her legs. He'd have to come up with a better idea for a first date. Picking up on her apprehension he says, 'I'll take that as a no then.'

He laughs and with a flick of his hand waves over the waitress. Sandy isn't sure about the risqué side to his banter, she's not used to men being so forward, but she can feel the tug of attraction between them.

'Two coffees please and a selection of your finest patisserie.'

'Not for me thanks.'

'Really? Not even a strawberry-and-cream flan? They're delicious.'

'I don't eat that kind of thing, nice as it is. I'd pile on the weight and never get a contract.'

'You've got a gorgeous figure. You don't need to worry.' Sandy is used to flattery and is relaxed enough with Jasper to refuse a cake, but with some people it was hard to say no, or she didn't want to be the only one not eating so she'd have to go to the loo afterwards to vomit.

'Oh I do. I only have to look at a cake and I put on a pound.'

'Does that mean I can't tempt you out for dinner?' He tilts his head to one side like a barn owl.

'Do you know anywhere that serves lettuce?' She laughs. 'I've been living on rabbit food for the last few months.'

'My mum's, but she drowns it in salad cream.'

'Maybe not. Do you like Wimpy Bars or a chop suey? I could break my diet for one night. As long as it doesn't become a habit.'

'I've not tried Chinese.'

'You're missing out. Chinese is delicious but a bit salty. It's so exotic. Deep fried seaweed or lemon chicken. Which do you fancy?'

'I think I'd rather not eat marine algae. I'll stick to a bowl of rice, it's safer and I'll take you to the cinema afterwards. *Ben Hur* will be out soon.'

'Sounds like a plan.'

They exchange a smile. He brushes a finger along her arm. It's an innocent action and fleeting but it's daring and forward of him. She hardly knows him. Electric current shoots through her and make her tingle. The waitress arrives with coffee and a strawberry tart for him and it's his turn to blush as he pulls his hand away like a naughty schoolboy.

'What are you doing with yourself now that you're back from Cyprus?

'I'm back in my old job at an engineering firm. I hate it. I want to get into journalism but I need a lucky break. While I was in Cyprus, a few of us mentioned to the sergeant that we wanted to go to Jerusalem for a few days. We caught a plane from Nicosia. We went to Nazareth, Bethlehem and Jerico. I took a boat-load of photos, but lost the slides. When I got home, I wrote an article and gave a talk on Jerusalem at the

Methodist Church. They were impressed and suggested I send an article to the local paper. It got published.'

'That's amazing.'

'Every morning at work I went to the loo with the *Daily Telegraph* to look for jobs. One day someone had *The Daily Mail*, a paper I can't stand. I borrowed it, took it to the loo and there was an advert for a journalist with the *Manchester Evening News* in the science section. I've got an interview, in a few weeks.'

'So if you get it you'll be moving to Manchester? It's cold and always rains up there.'

Sandy doesn't want to put a damper on his plans and the comment comes out without thinking. Her mind lurches between excitement and hope for his new career and her own crushing disappointment. Her insides are folding in on themselves. She likes him and hasn't felt this way about a man for a long time. She sits up and smiles her enthusiasm and encourages him with kind words— all the time reminding herself of her own career plans and dreams and not to get too drawn in. They can have fun but it's not going anywhere.

She takes a sip of coffee.

'If you get the job what would you write about, besides donkeys, camels, olive trees, minarets and domes?' He's painted a beautiful picture of Jerusalem. She holds the vision in her head of the city with its tiny winding roads, eastern music and Arabs carrying carcasses on their backs and dirty children begging.

He sits back and doesn't answer immediately. 'I'll be writing about any news to do with science and medicine.'

'But what would you really like to write about, if you could? Is there something, beyond your travels during National Service that you want the world to know?'

'Let me tell you a story.'

She sits forward, cradling her cup even though it's finished.

He's intriguing, she thinks and has the power to captivate with his stories, all told in an animated way.

'On the sixteenth of July in nineteen forty-five in a desolate part of New Mexico a group of scientists and military personnel watched in horror, as the landscape was lit by a burning light several times the intensity of the sun. As the mushroom cloud towered in the sky one of the scientists said, "I am the death who takes everything away, the destroyer of worlds." The destructive power of nuclear energy was known to us from the beginning.'

'And what's that got to do with anything?'

'In the last twenty years we've made enormous progress in the discovery and introduction of new drugs and yet legislation is not keeping pace with the progress. Doesn't that worry you?'

'Sorry, you've lost me.'

'While I was in Jerusalem, I read Aldous Huxley's, *Brave New World*. It's a warning of the dangers of runaway science and technology. It's an eye opener and made me think about the way our society is going. In the future, and I can see it beginning now, we'll enjoy lifelong bliss and happiness because of designer drugs. There will be a utopian wonder drug to take away any negative thought you have. In fact, pain and discomfort will be a thing of the past. The medical profession will drive us into a sterile world where all we have to do is pop a pill to be happy—or buy more consumer goods.'

'I suppose after years of war and countries fighting each other the goal has to be a happier world.'

'Yes, but doctors are dishing out pills like confetti at a wedding. I'd interview MPs and I'd write an article arguing the case for a committee to be set up on safety within the drugs industry. We need legislation to review all new medicines being released into the market for their safety. I'd also lobby for better licensing concerning new medicines. We need greater regulation, medicines must be tested and trialled for their safety, which doesn't happen. And there needs to be a system for reporting adverse reactions. It's not good enough to sign in medicines coming from other countries like West Germany. We trust their pharmaceutical companies bringing the medicine and accept that we will be safe without conducting our own clinical trials. We need to look into the addictiveness of drugs. In the wrong hands Heroin is harmful, we all know that, which is why it was outlawed in America years ago—but not here. The government needs to ban its manufacture, import and export. Some of these are a disaster waiting to happen.'

'I think my mum takes something to stop her getting anxious.'

'What does she take?'

'No idea, but she swears by them. I think they help her sleep.'

'Doctors dish them out like candy. They're a quick fix and it saves them having to find the root cause of the problems.'

'Doctors wouldn't prescribe them if they weren't fine.'

'We don't know that. There isn't enough research. Every painted line on the autobahns in West Germany are controlled by regulations, but no proper guidelines exist to ensure safe and efficient protection of the millions of German drug consumers. Pre-clinical animal tests are only recommended indirectly. The clinical testing of drugs is the dark side of medicine. There is no proper control of pharmaceutical products. German law doesn't require specialised drugs to be tested and then they come over here. No guidelines for testing drugs exist in West Germany. Severe damage could be inflicted by poorly tested medicine.'

Sandy glances at her watch. She's meeting a friend in Oxford Street in an hour's time, to hunt for a new dress for a dance and since he stopped talking about her, the conversation has got tedious.

'Sorry, I'm boring you now. Medicine is my pet subject. Do

you have any long-term ambitions beside meeting a handsome man and getting married?'

She bristles. 'I don't plan to get married for a few years.'

'You'll be over the hill by then.'

'I'm not buying into this fear of being left on the shelf, there's too much to do before I settle down.'

But Sandy does buy into the fear, whipped up by her mother's constant reminders, but she tries to put it to the back of her mind. She doesn't want to rush into marriage and domesticity even though, at nineteen already—the body clock is ticking.

'Like what?'

'I want to go to Canada for a year. I'm saving.'

'Who are you going with?'

'Nobody.'

'You're not travelling on your own, surely?'

'Yes, what's wrong with that?'

'You need a chaperone, missy.'

'You offering?'

He laughs. 'I wish. Some of us have to work.'

Jasper checks the time, pushes his cup to the side of the table and stands up. A wave of disappointment crashes over her. She's surprised at how much she is enjoying his company —even if some of his conversation is dull—and she would like him to stay longer, despite the new dress.

'I'd better get back to work, it's been good chatting though. So nice that I've lost track of the time. Thursday for the pictures?'

'Yes, sounds good.' She smiles at him, enjoying the flicker of warmth in her belly that sparks when she thinks about seeing him again.

She scribbles her address on a scrap of paper and they arrange a time and then he goes, leaving her to gather her bag and thoughts.

. . .

JASPER RAPS on the door ten minutes early. Sandy's mother flies to answer it, duster in hand, like an eager child waiting for the postman to bring birthday presents. Her father lurks behind her, his newspaper folded under his arm.

'Pleased to meet you Mr and Mrs Lambert.'

Sandy's father hesitates before shaking the hand extended in front of him. Her mother doesn't shake it which doesn't surprise Sandy as she has no manners when it suits her. She makes a fuss of wiping her hands on her apron as if she's been under a car bonnet and they are thick with grease.

'Shouldn't you be getting off?' Mrs Lambert scowls. 'Sandy needs to get back by eleven so you'd better be on your way, if you're going.'

Sandy doesn't question why. It's always better to bite her tongue and accept what her mother says. In any case she doesn't want a confrontation in front of Jasper; she'd only be made to look stupid. She can't wait to get away, anything to escape home. Life in their home is dull. The only form of entertainment allowed is the wireless, but even that is restricted to the News on the Home Service, Woman's Hour, which her mum listens to every afternoon and church services. Once, when Sandy bravely suggested they get a television set her mum had gone scarlet with rage and declared that she would have no new-fangled devices under her roof.

5

RONA

Rona's shoes squeak along the echoing hospital corridor. The red lino stretches ahead and she feels the stirrings of a migraine. She longs for a day off but they are short-staffed and so she hasn't booked annual leave in months. Most days Bill is home long before her, making a start on the dinner because there is always one more thing to do at work, another bedpan to scrub, a urine sample to take, or a mum who needs a chat.

The smell of carbolic makes her feel queasy and she wrinkles her nose as she passes the toilets, wondering why she has a heightened sense of smell. *Could I be?* It's a classic symptom. She brushes the thought away before she allows herself to be excited.

The bedpans have been stacked on the shelf haphazardly. This is all she needs, she was only passing the sluice on her way out. One or two nurses aren't pulling their weight and again it's left to her to sort the mess out before Matron comes in and blames everybody. She can hear Matron's words in her head reminding the nurses that running a hospital isn't just about caring— it's about cleanliness and attention to detail. Rona takes the pans from the shelf, polishes them with a cloth so that they gleam and stacks them properly before sterilising the sink. Her shift finished an hour ago and she still has notes to write. She visualises Bill taking her dinner out of the oven and putting it in the bin. Poor man. She feels guilty for not being the wife he deserves. He works hard as a builder, continuing the family firm that his grandfather set up. For several years three generations have worked together, but now it's just Bill running the show and waiting for the day when he can hand it over to his son.

Rona longs to give Bill a son to continue the firm. A boy would make his life complete. He'd promised his grandfather he'd steer a son into the trade rather than sell it to strangers; he'd hate handing over everything they've worked so hard to achieve. In her haste to get home she nearly bumps into Peggy, one of the expectant mums on the ward. Peggy is crying.

'Peggy love what's wrong?'

'Nurse, I'm glad to see you. Have you just come on duty?'

'No, not exactly.'

'Sister Agnes was cross because I didn't want my dinner. I don't like meat pie and mash. I'm not hungry. I did tell her but she doesn't listen. I hate her sharp tone. Just ignore me it's my hormones. I hope baby isn't too much longer.'

'She's just anxious to get your diabetes under control. They'll make you some toast and a nice cup of tea if you ask. Would you like that?'

'They're so busy I'd have to wait ages.'

'Tell you what,' Rona glances at her watch and stifles a sigh, 'I'll make it for you.'

'Oh would you Nurse, thank you so much.'

'It's no trouble.'

Rona gets home two hours late and goes through to the tiny

kitchen of their Victorian mid-terraced house. She looks forward to coming home to Bill and telling him about her day, but she hates this house. As soon as she turns the key in the door her heart sinks. It's fusty and outdated with cornices along the tops of walls, high ceilings and coloured glass in the front door. Old sash windows make the rooms draughty. The house encapsulates the pain she holds inside, a dull pain that never goes away. They've done a lot of work to update the house. The latest spate of work involved lobbing the fireplace in a skip and Bill has pinned a piece of hardboard to the wall to cover the empty space. But no matter what improvements they make to the house her spirits never lift. It reminds her of her grandma's day, the only difference is Rona doesn't scrub the doorstep with a donkey stone or chat to neighbours outside. They inherited the house. Rona wants to move away from Blackpool and live in one of the new concrete high rises going up across London. She dreams of living at the top and gazing at the twinkly skyline, watching life go by and all without the burden of a garden.

'Alright love?'

She tries to sound cheerful to avoid another row about the long hours she works. She hears the rustle of his paper, *The Daily Herald* as he folds it away and she hangs her coat up.

'You're working too long at that place, love. They won't thank you for it.'

His bald head looks polished and shines under the bare light bulb that hangs from the ceiling. She leans down and kisses it. 'Don't start.'

Bill sighs. 'There's a cottage pie in the oven. It might be a bit burned on the top. I didn't want to chuck it.'

'It'll be wonderful. I'm starving.' Bill is a good man. His job is demanding and he still cooks the dinner. She opens the oven door. The heat slaps her. She tilts her steamed glasses to see inside, takes out the burned pie but doesn't say anything. She's grateful to come home to a hot dinner and she's lucky to have a husband that cooks at all. Her friends' husbands don't go anywhere near the kitchen, but Bill is different, he mucks in. He is one in a million and will make a wonderful dad, one day.

'Did you book that week off?'

'We're so short staffed at the moment I daren't.'

'You are entitled to some holiday, love. It's ridiculous. We desperately need a break. I was looking forward to going to St Ives.'

'A holiday isn't going to make the problem go away.'

'It might help.'

'I hope you're not working all hours to take your mind off it love.'

'No,' Rona says emphatically, but there's an element of truth to it that hasn't occurred to her. It's hard to pull away at the end of the day. The hospital, despite its sanitised environment, the blinding white walls and the iron beds in rows, feels safe and protective. The sound of a baby crying, flowers, the smell of powder and mother's milk gives her a measure of comfort and props her up. When she leaves the hospital though and joins the queue for the bus, the feelings disappear and all she is left with is an aching sadness.

Rona chews through the dry gristle and they sit in silence. With the gulf between them Bill goes back to his paper.

He doesn't settle and fidgets in his chair, and puts the paper down. She knows what he is going to ask.

'This morning you were saying...'

'Just leave it. I don't know yet.'

'You seemed hopeful.'

She had been hopeful and deep down still is, but tiredness envelops. She longs for sleep to take over, smothering the sadness of her inability to conceive. It has been ongoing for three years, the endless waiting, wondering and hoping. The false alarms, the preparations in her mind, dashed away in an instant.

She stands at the Belfast sink. Enjoying the warmth of the soapy water on her cracked hands Rona stares at her reflection in the window. She doesn't want to be reminded of the toll that it's taking on her. The window rattles as if it's responding to her pain. The woman staring at her looks like day-old porridge, dark circles and deep lines are etched around her eyes. Wispy strands of hair escape from the bun on top of her head. 'I look like a horror movie.'

'Leave that till the morning, love. *The Goon Show* is on the wireless in a tick.'

Rona isn't in the mood for comedy and listening to Bill snort with laughter. She wants to tuck up in bed with her Daphne du Maurier novel and a hot water bottle, drift into a nice sleep and wake up refreshed for her next shift. It's going to be another busy few days because several mothers are due to give birth. Rona turns to face Bill. She takes her time drying her hands on the towel and rubbing her fingers. Years of using strong disinfectants at work have made them red and chapped and they burn angrily.

'Come and sit down. I've hardly seen you all week.'

'Don't nag me.'

'You need to relax.'

'Fine chance of that.'

'You're home now.'

I'm just nipping to the lav.'

He stands in the doorway, his arm outstretched. She pushes past him and into the hallway.

Rona sits on the toilet. The voices of Peter Sellers, Spike Milligan and Harry Secombe filter through from the lounge. 'This is the BBC home service, but please don't take it too hard.' Her lower back aches and she feels a dragging sensation across her abdomen. She leans forward nursing her belly. *I've been on my feet all day, of course my body aches. Or could this be it, she wonders, the first symptoms?* It had started this way before.

Cymbals clash, then a trumpet, a tambourine, chickens. 'We've added the sound of chickens for those living in rural districts.'

Rona sniggers. Maybe she will join Bill on the settee, rather than rush to bed. Bill is already in snorting mode.

She pulls some toilet paper from its holder and reaches down to wipe herself, enjoying the antics of the three men on the wireless. She doesn't notice the telltale rusty stain on her knickers. She pulls them up, turns to flush the toilet and sees that the water is crimson. Her knees soften, she holds onto the cold tiled wall as the 'hit by a truck' feeling returns. This is like a game of snakes and ladders and she is on the losing side. The snake has dragged her back to the first square while all the lucky pregnant women stare down from the tops of ladders, triumphant. It's another set-back and another month to wait.

6

SANDY

Sandy spends hours getting ready for their second date and thinking about what to wear, aspiring to be like her fashion icon, Audrey Hepburn. They are only going to the cinema but it's important that she makes a good impression. She changes her outfit several times before deciding on the European look, a pair of blue Italian-looking Capri pants that end at mid-calf with a slit on each side. She puts on a white Spanish cummerbund and pulls shirts from her wardrobe settling on a nautical look, a Roman shirt with light and dark-blue stripes. The effect achieved is 'holidaying in the Italian Riviera' and she twirls round in front of the mirror until she's satisfied. A white bolero jacket thrown across the shoulder and a splash of Chanel number five and she is ready.

Her parents lurk in the lounge, near the net-curtained window. Her dad is polishing his shoes to spit-shiny military style. He aims to polish until they are a mirror to shave in and he likes the blue sky reflected in them as he marches down the street. Her mum, still in her pinny stands at the mantel mirror applying lipstick. She purses her lips and preens her hair with her fingers before picking up the duster for one last flick around the mantel and coffee table.

'Come away from the window. Can't you just act normal for once and sit down? I'm only going to the cinema with him. He won't want to come in and chat with you two. It's not as if he's about to ask for my hand in marriage. It's so embarrassing when you hover at the window.'

'Well it's about time you did get married. You're nearly twenty for goodness sake. Your mother and I were married at eighteen.'

'Yes, I don't know what it is with your generation. If you found a man on a good wage you wouldn't need a career and as for this idea about swanning round Canada, honestly love, I don't know why you can't settle for a simple, happy life.' Her mum smirks. Canada has become a big issue between them.

'I am going to Canada and nobody can stop me.'

'What was the point in us spending a fortune on elocution lessons for you to waste time and money on a stupid dream to travel the world? I can't abide feckless ways. You need a direction in your life.'

Sandy had elocution lessons throughout her teen years, to ensure she didn't 'pick up common,' as her mum called it and she had deportment lessons to improve her posture. She knew their game. Their intention wasn't to propel her into a good career but into finding the right sort of eligible man to marry.

Her dad twiddles with his moustache. 'What did you say this chap does for a living?'

'He's got an interview with a newspaper in a few weeks. He wants to be a journalist.'

'I doubt he'll earn enough to support you on that. Not unless he makes it. Few do,' he says with strange malice.

'Who said he's going to support me?' She can't wait for Jasper to arrive to get the first couple of minutes with her parents out the way. It's stressful enough going on a date but she doesn't need this as well.

'Has he got a Rover? There's a chap just pulled up,' her dad says picking up a cigar to quell his nerves.

Her mother is at the window twitching the nets. 'My goodness love. He must be loaded.'

'It's probably his friend's car. He said he was borrowing a car for the evening. Drop the net Mum.'

Sandy rushes upstairs to check her hair. Peering out of the landing window she likes Jasper's confident swagger as he skips up the steps with his hands in his pockets. His knock rings through the house like shots and Sandy hurries downstairs to open it, her dad bellowing from behind not to let the cold in, he pays the bills and nobody gives a stuff. His face brightens when he sees Jasper, holding a bunch of flowers and a bottle of wine. Her dad is good at putting on airs and graces and making it look as though he's a welcoming host, taking the wine with a surprised look on his face. Her mum stands behind, the demure sweet wife with a bright though plastic smile on her face as she takes the flowers bought for her, her condescending, egotistical thoughts are kept well hidden.

Sandy has forgotten Jasper's good looks and debonair clothing. He's wearing a cashmere jumper, corduroys and suede shoes. There's something polished and well-bred about him and her parents have clearly picked up on this because they welcome him into the lounge. His self-assured, sophisticated aura is out of place in the grey staidness of their lounge and Sandy flinches. There's no awkwardness as she expected, and beyond the pleasantries her dad asks him about his National Service and he regales stories about his time in Cyprus. In no time at all it's as if he's known them for years. It's a comfortable atmosphere and Sandy knows that her parents like him and will be rooting for them to see each other again.

She looks at her watch, coughs in Jasper's direction and they exchange a look that says we really must go now.

'We better get on.' Jasper stands, holding out his hand. 'It's been a pleasure to meet you both properly.'

7

RONA

Rona hears the door slam in the familiar way and, before Bill has struggled out of his coat he appears at the kitchen doorway. 'Guess what? Mavis is expecting.'

Bill always calls into The Red Lion for a swift one before Sunday lunch, while Rona prepares the lunch listening to *The Archers*. She's finished peeling the spuds and is about to toss them into the pan but the words jar and grind in her chest. Pretending to be distracted, she stabs a potato out of sheer frustration. He's next to her, a cloud of beery breath and a purple-veined nose, drawing her into his arms. Bill's a tall man and radiates a huge presence. She could disappear in the comfort and protection of his arms and the subtle fragrance of his day-old aftershave mingling with body odour, sends her spiralling back to the first time they met. He always greets her like a love-able Labrador with a sloppy kiss and a brush of stubble. He is a better husband than many, despite her mother's objections when they'd announced their engagement seven years ago. He works hard and doesn't spend all his earnings on booze. He can turn his hand to anything around the house and is attentive, often bringing flowers or chocolates home. He's interested in how her day has been. She couldn't have wished for a better man and loves him with all her heart.

'Mavis is expecting.'

'I heard you the first time.'

'I didn't want you to hear it from anyone else.'

'And what difference would that make?'

'It wasn't easy for me, love, surrounded by my mates slapping me on the back saying, "Isn't it wonderful that Mavis is pregnant and can't wait to wet the baby's head. Isn't it brilliant? You must be so thrilled?" As if it was my wife pregnant rather than Reg's. And suddenly I think they realised, because they were glancing at one another and backing off in embarrassment. The lads have twigged that we're having a bit of - you know - trouble.'

Rona sighs. 'They were just happy for you to be an uncle again. People don't think. They're all tactless.' Her head screams bitch. How long had Rona and Bill been trying for a baby? Three years at least. And wasn't it bad enough that Rona's sister Amy was pregnant again—for the fourth time, as if to add insult to injury.

'Bastard. He spills his magic baby-making potion inside her inner-thigh and hey presto she's up the bloody duff. They make it look as easy as blending gravy in a saucepan. Talking of which are you ready for me to carve the meat?'

'I'll call you when I'm ready. Take the weight of your feet.'

Normally Bill carved the turkey but Rona wants him out of the kitchen, so that she can digest the news on her own.

She takes the meat from the oven and puts it on the counter. Tears spring to her eyes and she dabs them with a hanky. She grabs a knife from the drawer and hacks at the bird, dumping heavy slabs of meat onto their plates. She puts the knife down, her gut dull with resentment for Mavis, the bloody baby machine who churns them out like strings of sausages.

'I was going to carve that.' He looks hurt, as if this is grossly unfair, like a bob-a-job scout turned away on the doorstep.

'Can we adopt?'

Bill slices into the meat with extra force and licks his fingers. There is a moment of dithery throat clearing. 'Can't we just wait and see?'

Rona sees the wall of resistance. Convincing him isn't going to be easy. 'That's what you always say. I've waited three years. I don't want to wait any longer. We need to put our names down. Get the process started.'

'I'm not sure it's the right time.'

'It won't happen immediately. I've heard it can take months, by which time you never know, I might be pregnant. Look at it as a back-up plan.'

'But you're not looking at it like that. You're looking at it as a rescue package.'

They take their plates to the table. Irritation spirals inside her and lingers as they eat beneath a cloud of tension that will burst at some point. He finishes first, wiping his mouth with the back of his hand and emitting a loud burp of satisfaction.

'Just admit it Bill.' She keeps her voice calm even though her heart hammers in her chest. 'You don't want to adopt.' She spears a carrot.

He dithers before he answers, buying time. 'I'm sorry, Rona.' She knows that he feels her pain but has his own thoughts on adoption and he isn't going to budge.

'At least think about it,' she pleads, scraping back her chair. 'We've got nothing to lose by putting our names down.'

He squeezes his face with his hand and is torn by the need to make her happy but he's never going to share her enthusiasm. Beads of sweat form on his brow. 'I'd end up resenting it because it wouldn't be mine and then I'd screw everything up.'

'You don't know that. It doesn't always work like that. Some-

times parents have problems bonding with their natural children. We've got so much love to give.'

'You have Rona. I'm not sure I have.'

Rona clears the plates, taking them to the sink. She takes
the apple pie to the table and cuts him a large slice, dolloping
custard on top. 'The way to a man's heart is through his stomach,' she can hear her mother remind her. 'You're sure to win
his affections.' The apples are Bramley, his favourite, the crust
sweet and flaky but after one mouthful he's had enough.

'I don't want to adopt. Don't try to persuade me.' She knows
she's pushed him too far. 'My mind's made up.' His spoon sinks
into the gooey mess and he nudges the bowl away as if it has
transformed into his worst pudding. He lights a cigarette and
ambles down to his shed in the corner of the garden, beyond a
small patch of vegetables. It's his escape, the place where he
goes to get out of her hair.

Rona loves apple pie but has lost her appetite. She waits for
his words to sink in before getting to her feet, too stunned to
move. They were final, she knows that and nothing is going to
make him change his mind. She feels like a caged bird, the key
lost with no way of escaping the prison of childlessness that she
has found herself in through sheer rotten luck.

As she rinses the plates, wraps the remains of the turkey in
foil, wipes splashes of gravy from the table and sweeps the bits
from the floor, her thoughts centre on what will happen now.
His words are cruel and selfish but she doesn't want to think
badly of him. By the same token she can't accept that this is the
end of the road. She's longed for a baby for so long. She isn't
going to give up on the dream. He's closed the last option open
to us, God willing. She understands that you enter marriage, in
sickness and in health, for better for worse, for richer, for
poorer and of course she can't leave him. Where would she go?
Going back to her mum, with her tail between her legs isn't an
option. She couldn't bear hearing her mum say, 'Well I told you

so,' and 'We gave you a grammar school education so that doors would open, but marrying a builder was the path you chose, Rona.'

She takes her marriage vows seriously and Bill has done nothing wrong. He hasn't slept with another woman, beaten her or done any other wicked deed. He's a solid provider and even though she hates the dreary house they live in, at least they own it, with no mortgage. But does this mean she has to accept his feelings? Maybe, if she tries hard enough she can find a way of convincing him, somehow.

Rona's head burns with a headache as she mulls over how she's going to do it. Bill is a stubborn man. When he has set views it's hard to budge him.

8

SANDY

Sandy and Jasper take the train to Brighton. It's early May. Jasper's interview has been deferred because of unforeseen circumstances at the newspaper. They mooch around the labyrinth of tiny streets and browse in and out of shops filled with bric-a-brac and knick knacks. It's a maze of Aladdin's caves and music fills the salty air.

Jasper swings Sandy's hand along the sea front. The sky is as thick and grey as spat-out chewing gum, the clouds full of unshed rain and the sea's choppy and dark pewter. Fighting the wind Sandy ties a scarf around her head. They gorge on fish and chips wrapped in newspaper and afterwards watch the fat seagulls feast on leftovers.

They chat about their childhood and future dreams. Jasper's eyes light up when Sandy talks more about her plans to travel round Canada. She can see in his expression and the way his body is tilted towards her that he is interested and not plodding through motions of politeness. He doesn't dismiss her ambition like her parents and friends do but asks questions and rides on her enthusiasm. It's refreshing and hearing herself talk she feels keener than ever that it is the right thing to do.

But at the same time she finds his enthusiasm unnerving and disappointing. If he is keen on her, then surely he wouldn't be excited for her because it means they have no future together.

A row of anglers fish from the West Pier and a family brew tea on a meths stove.

'My mum used to live down here,' he says after a while. 'One evening during the war she was supposed to be going to the cinema with a new fella but cancelled at the last minute. The cinema was bombed and people were killed that evening.' His voice trails away and his face is grave. 'The whole course of your life can change in an instant.' He snaps his fingers.

Sandy tosses chips towards a seagull. 'Yes, we should be grateful for every second of our lives. That's why Canada is so important. I don't want to get caught up with life and forget my dreams. I'm determined not to end up like my mum.'

'It's terrible to think all this could have been blown away. I often wonder what it would have been like if the Nazis had occupied Britain.' Jasper is in contemplative mood.

'We've already had two wars this century. What if the Cold War between the West and Russia develops into a third world war?'

'I don't want to have to think about another war. I'm just back from National Service. It's bad enough replaying the horrors in your mind, never mind being in the middle of it all.'

'Sorry, war's the last thing you want to think about.'

'Yes.' He takes a pebble and throws it into the sea. She wonders what horrors he is replaying in his mind and conjures up a pageant of possible scenes. They watch the pebble skim, creating patterns across the water. He stands up. 'Brighton is your oyster. We need to live. "We've never had it so good," Harold Macmillan told us, remember? We can dine, dance, go the theatre, let me show you a good time, let's make merry.'

'I'd like to sit here, doing not much and seeing what happens.'

He sits down. 'And what if this happens?' he whispers and plants a gentle kiss on her lips. 'You're really beautiful. Has anybody ever told you that?'

Plenty of people she wants to reply, because it is the truth but she doesn't want to come across as vain and big-headed. Skimming over the question she thanks him for the compliment. Their shiny lips, after the greasy batter meet properly. He smells of salt, fags and Brylcreem but she doesn't care and is swept away in the moment.

Conscious of the row of old people lining the beach even though many of them are snoozing under caps and knotted hankies she pulls away, so that they are inches apart. They are getting to know each other's faces, every crease and curve and seconds seem like minutes, each wondering where things could lead.

'We should find somewhere private,' he whispers, weaving his fingers into hers.

'You're naughty.'

'We could check into a hotel as Mr and Mrs Smith. What do you think?'

She can't tell whether he's joking. 'I'm not easy, if that's what you think.' She wraps her arms around her legs in defence.

'Course not. You're lovely. I'm just teasing, going back to what we said earlier about making the most of life.'

'Come on, let's go and explore.'

They wend their way through the Pavilion Park, unaware of where the path is leading, ambling along, carried away in their chatter. They call into a pub. She has a whiskey sour and he a beer. They carry on up the London Road and into the Co-op department store. They trail their way through clothes rails and he pulls things out and drags her over to the changing rooms with an armful of clothes, ordering her to change. Each time she comes out of the changing room for his opinion she finds him leaning against the wall smiling and admiring her as if she is a princess. She's never had this sort of treatment before and it is like being placed on a pedestal. She feels truly appreciated.

The counter is piled with a blouse, a bra, a dress and matching shoes. Sandy can't believe her luck in finding such a generous man and knows that her friends will be envious. He counts a wad of notes.

By the evening as they trudge back up the hill to the station with sore feet and laden with bags, Sandy feels as though she is falling through feathers, light and carefree and dizzy with love. All thoughts of Canada are put to the back of her mind—what was the appeal again? All she wants to do is to spend every moment with this wonderful man who's made her laugh by feeding her with strawberry ice cream at the end of the West Pier.

As they enter the station concourse there are no trains and a chalkboard announces that all trains to London are cancelled.

'What are we going to do?' Sandy is close to tears and knows that her parents will worry. They don't have a phone so she'll have to call her auntie who lives nearby to relay the message to them.

Jasper puts an arm around her. 'We'll just have to look for a hotel.'

'We could find the coach station.' Sandy doesn't like the idea of staying over, even if he is a true gentleman and books two single rooms. She has no wash things, makeup or clothes, it's unthinkable. A wonderful day turns to disaster in a flash.

'Really?' He drops the bags on the pavement feigning defeat.

'Hotel then,' she sighs. 'But don't think you're going to get your wicked way with me.'

He smiles. 'Now was I thinking that?'

They head from the station towards the sea, stumbling on a nondescript hotel along a small street running adjacent to the seafront.

Before Sandy has the chance to ask for two single rooms Jasper is striding up to the reception and giving the names Mr and Mrs Smith to the shapeless landlady. She takes out a dusty ledger from under the counter. They sidle up a narrow staircase to a half landing where they find their room.

Opening the door, the smell of damp hits them. Faded, peeling wallpaper adorns the walls and a grimy net curtain covers a small window, opening onto a flat roof with a maze of central heating and drainage pipes.

'No sea view?'

Jasper stands behind her, his hands on her shoulders. 'If you crane your neck you can just about catch a slither of blue sky.'

They fall onto the bed giggling, making jokes about the landlady and the room and they laugh again when they discover they are lying on a double eiderdown hiding two single beds pushed together.

Jasper stretches his arm over Sandy to read the notice on the bedside cabinet.

'Do not change the linen.'

'My goodness, does that mean they don't bother to wash the sheets? We'll be scratching ourselves to death by the morning.'

'I can start scratching you now if you're already itching. Oh God, don't move I can see a bedbug crawling in your hair. The place is infested.'

Jasper takes a thread of her hair and pretends to concentrate, while Sandy complains about having to wash her hair again.

'Only kidding.'

'You tease.'

They roll around on the bed, tickling each other and pretending to find bed bugs until they collapse breathless. Their clammy faces touch and they kiss, long and hard and for Sandy it feels all-consuming and overwhelming. In their frenzy they pull away to take their clothes off and despite Sandy's good intentions not to go all the way, she throws caution to the wind, letting the strong urge in her body rule her head. They are like two children devouring an ice cream sundae, their bodies entwined as they kiss each other's necks, moving lower down and exploring their sensitive parts.

Jasper is on top of her, guiding himself in with his hand.

'Stop.' The electrical current sparking inside Sandy's body is fizzling as reality hits. 'This isn't such a great idea. We should use something. It's too risky.'

Jasper gets up and fumbles in his pockets and wallet for a small silver packet, tossing his trousers across the room when he can't find one.

'Thought I had one.' He stands with his legs apart, running his hands through his hair. He's losing his erection.

'Maybe we should get dressed.'

'Oh well, I don't like doing it with a johnny on. It's like going to bed with your socks on.'

Sandy doesn't have an opinion.

He leans down and kisses her on the forehead. 'I love you. I want to feel every part of you, properly.'

The words hang in the air like the sweet smell of roses in a summer garden, making Sandy feel warm and appreciated.

'But it's too risky.' She's aware of how small her voice is.

'I'll withdraw, just before.'

She chews her lip in thought.

Something within her collapses and she goes all small. 'I don't suppose it happens first time anyway.' She doesn't know whether she's trying to convince him or herself, as she hovers above two opposing camps, wondering whether to give in.

He kisses her breasts, taking a nipple into his mouth and his hand moves around her groin, before slipping a finger inside her. She groans. There is something deeply sensual about the way he touches her.

'You're very wet.'

'You're turning me on again.'

The worry she feels dissipates in a cloud of lust. He eases his way in, gently moving up and down. Her legs are wrapped around his back, her hands pressed on his bottom, helping him to go deeper and then he stops, panting, his hot face pressing against hers. 'We should take it out, in case you come.'

'I'm really sorry, I already have.'

'You promised me you'd withdraw.'

'It just happened. I had no control. It's you. You shouldn't be so damn sexy.' He laughs. 'You encouraged me. You'll be fine, don't worry. Have a hot bath. The water will flush it out.'

9

RONA

I t's a perfect late autumn day. A bank of mist hangs in the air like a shroud waiting to part into a cloudless day. Rona loves pottering in the garden on days like this, breathing the earthy perfume of late summer: the fungus, rotten blackberries, sour apples mashed on the ground and damp leaves.

It's the weekend and she isn't due at the hospital until the evening. Bill usually works for part of the weekend, but he's said that he needs to nip out to the shops for work items.

The ground crackles under her boots. The night has brought an early frost and there's a sparkle to the lawn. Digging her fork into the ground she sucks in the fresh air, light-headed with the sense of release from the sadness that envelops her. Is this it? She wonders. Will I spend the rest of my life feeling bereaved? It is an odd emotion, given that nobody has died. It's a dull, heavy ache and it never goes away.

Several weeks have passed since their chat about adoption and Rona hasn't found the courage to bring it up again. She senses an unwillingness in Bill to open up and say how he feels. It isn't manly and she can't imagine her father discussing such issues with her mother.

There is a palpable atmosphere between them that wasn't there before the conversation. It is as if Bill knows how let down Rona feels about his decision but he is treading on egg shells around her. It's easier for him to pretend that the conversation never happened. Rona hopes that in time he'll change his mind. If he loves her enough he'll want to make her happy.

She loves being outdoors. As a child she was always badgering her mother to let her play outside. Rona's mother has chosen to stay in the house where she's raised Rona and her two sisters, Amy and Rachel, despite her husband's death and the difficulties of managing the place. She can't bring herself to move, even though it's far too big for one. It holds precious memories spanning more than forty years. It's a posh house, built at the turn of the century. Roses frame the doorway and clematis tumbles over the walls and the roof is thatched, making it look as though it should have been built in Devon rather than Blackpool. A riot of colour in the front garden beckons visitors in. Rona imagines her own children enjoying the house and garden as much as she had, counting to twenty in a game of hide and seek behind the yew, playing croquet on the lawn and laughing on the tree swing her father made years ago. But it is not to be. She finds it hard being with her nieces and nephews and feeling left out, pining for children of her own who could enjoy the same experience.

Rona rakes the lawn of fallen leaves, mushy apples and dead growth from the borders, piling them into a wheelbarrow. She takes her gloves off and heads to the warmth of the kitchen to bake scones for tea. She's rubbing flour into butter when Bill arrives, beaming at her from the kitchen doorway with his hands behind his back.

'What are you so pleased with yourself for Bill Murphy?'

Rona wipes her floury hands and on tiptoes kisses him. They have known each over for ten years but the spark is still there.

'You're hiding something.'

They laugh as she wrestles with him. It's a cardboard box with holes in and he holds it above his head, out of reach while she jumps to grab it, like an excited child.

'Careful, let me put it on the table first.'

A scratching sound comes from the inside as he sets it on the table. He pulls out a chair for her to sit down while he carefully cuts the tape securing the edges. A snowy white kitten with a tortoise shell tail is nestled in torn newspaper and when Rona sees it she gasps in delight. In its unfamiliar setting it meows pitifully. Rona scoops him up and cuddles him under her chin.

'I'm not sure what its purpose is but I know you've always wanted one.'

She puts it back in the box and hugs Bill. When they were first married she'd pleaded for a cat, but he hadn't been keen. He knows that she was denied a pet as a child. Her parents weren't animal loving. She'd nagged them to buy a dog, a hamster, a guinea pig, a rabbit, a tortoise, any pet would have made her happy, even a humble goldfish from a funfair.

'Of course, there's a purpose. It's something to hold and care for.'

'That's what I thought, love. You've been so unhappy lately.'

He's like an open book. She knows exactly why he's bought the kitten, it's to salvage his own guilt because he refuses to adopt a baby. Rona wrestles with how she feels about it. She doesn't want to wallow in hurt and pity and the feeling of being let down. This isn't her. She can swallow pride and wrestle with negative thoughts, rising above them and doing the best to get on with life, blessed with all the positive things, like a happy relationship, a husband who cares and will do anything for her. Except for one thing– he won't adopt but it doesn't matter because she has him and is grateful for that, at least.

They go into the lounge and Rona puts the kitten on her

knee, stroking its soft fur, listening to it purr, all the time trying to convince herself that she can be happy with a cat instead.

10

SANDY

A few weeks after Brighton, Sandy and her parents come down with a sickness bug, which they blame on a pork pie from the local butchers, which has a dodgy reputation. Her parents recover within a few days but Sandy is unable to keep anything down for five days. Nausea kicks in so aggressively that it feels as if she's been poisoned. She vows never to touch pork pies again. The thought of them makes her retch.

When the sickness doesn't go away she goes to the doctor who feels her stomach and diagnoses gastroenteritis. All she can do is lie motionless in bed, waiting to get better. She lies there crying, sleeping, being sick and wincing at the slightest noise. She can't bear it when her mum comes in with a glass of water and sits on the bed, making it rock.

She wakes one day feeling better, energised to press on and secure her next modelling contract. She hasn't received a response to the photo shoot with Mr Hillier. He'd told her not to expect an immediate answer but this is getting ridiculous. She's left a couple of messages. With no answer, she heads over to his West End studio and buzzes the intercom at the bottom of the stairs. As far as she's concerned they are wasting her time and she is growing irate. She wants an answer and it's rude that they have taken so long to get back to her.

The scowling receptionist guards Mr Hillier like a Doberman and peers at Sandy as if she's something the cat's dragged in. She agrees to wait until Mr Hillier is free and after an hour his door opens and he ushers her in. He pours himself a glass of rum, picks up a smouldering Havana cigar from an ashtray and leans back in his swivel chair. There's an aura of trouble around him. The room smells of an old barnyard mixed with a seedy bar in the tropics.

'I've been up to my eyes in boobs.'

Sandy feels herself shrivel into the chair. 'Were my photos suitable?'

'Sorry dear but I need firm boobs.'

'What about the shots in the bikini?' Her boobs are firm. He's talking rubbish.

'I'm not shooting plain Jane types and your style isn't right.'

'Well how do I make my looks right?' Sandy keeps her cool but it's hard given this attitude. 'I'm very keen. I want to do well.'

He doesn't reply but strokes his moustache, with two fingers, starting from under his nose, outward towards the corner of his mouth. She feels like an animal behind bars in a zoo waiting for him to throw her a banana.

'I think you could do with losing a few pounds. Come back when you've lost a stone.'

'A whole stone?'

Her heart sinks. She's always been so careful with food, sticking to salads and fruit but lately she's put on weight, which doesn't make sense given the past weeks' sickness. Her trousers are tight around the middle and she needs to rein things in and be firmer with Jasper. It isn't his career at stake. She'd let things slip, giving in when he'd suggested fish and chips on the beach and ice cream and calorie-laden lasagnes in West End restaurants. It has to stop, otherwise it will be hard to shed.

She gets up and thanks him, picking up her portfolio from his desk.

He grabs at her hands. 'Do you do any hand work?'

Desperate to get the money together for Canada Sandy is ready for anything. Sumu wrestling, dog grooming or a crocheting contest. She's game.

Sandy tells him that she's done nail varnish. She's not considered that there might be a whole contingent of models who do nothing but close-up photographs showing flawless hands in a variety of situations.

'I'd like to have one of our producers give his opinion on your hands and you can come back to me in a few months when you've lost weight. I might be interested then. Be warned. It can be as gruelling and intense. You have to be prepared to hold your hands in the same position for hours at a time. And it doesn't pay as well.'

He buzzes another office. She is directed to the next floor and they examine her hands and explain that hands are pigeonholed into types. The housewife hand has short nails and no polish. The horror character hand is chapped and wrinkled.

They call her hands beauty hands because she has slim fingers, long nails and supple wrists and she is sent away with instructions about how to prepare them in the lead up to the shoot. She is warned about the dangers of water retention and medical changes, like pregnancy that might cause her to have pudgy fingers. It's another area of her body that she will have to monitor and take care of.

Sandy goes home and over the coming days she soaks her hands in cold cream and lotion and wears gloves at night. She tells her mother she can't do the washing up and she wears rubber gloves in the bath so they don't wrinkle and she gives up using soap. Her hands are the most precious part of her body, because they are earning her money. In the meantime she eats a strict diet, skipping breakfast and having crisp bread and cucumber for lunch and a light consommé soup for dinner.

SANDY AND JASPER are walking back to the tube after seeing *The Mousetrap* at the theatre, when he drops a bombshell into the conversation. Sandy stops walking, nearly bumping into the couple behind them, oblivious to the crowd of people rushing along the pavement under umbrellas in the drizzling evening rain.

She drops his hand. 'Why didn't you tell me earlier?'

'I've been building up to telling you. I've known for a few days, but couldn't find the right time.'

His words sting.

'That's great news.' She tries to sound happy for him. He's been offered the job in Manchester. Her voice is flat and it's hard to hide the hurt.

'Hey you'll be off to Canada soon.'

'Great.'

'It's what you've wanted for ages. It's your dream remember.'

'Yeah but...'

'I'll come back to London and visit you.'

He's offering crumbs, a pick-me-up and put me down type of relationship. She isn't convinced they work.

'Oh, don't bother.'

He grabs her arm.

'Hey this isn't the end of us. I'm not walking out on you.'

'You are. That's exactly what you're doing. I'm pleased for you, but once you're up there and busy working, you won't be giving me a second thought.'

'You've always known my plans. I haven't kept anything a

secret from you and we've always known that we were heading in opposite directions. I could ask you to come with me, but I'm not ready to settle down and neither are you.'

The word marriage lies between them, too delicate to be touched.

'How would you know? We've never talked about it. You don't know what I think.'

'Oh come on Sandy, you hate the idea of marriage and kids.'

He's right but she isn't going to admit it. 'I've never specifically said that.'

They move to the edge of the pavement huddled under her spotted umbrella. He pushes his damp hair from his forehead. Drops of rain are dripping onto his copy of the *Municipal Journal*, tucked under his arm, making the black type illegible.

She half expects him to propose, right there on the pavement, to make a point or call her bluff. Part of her wants him to, to prove how much he cares but it's more through a feeling of conquest and triumph than any desire to commit. She feels worthless and this is a new feeling. She's used to men putting her first and getting her own way and doesn't like this new experience of being put in her place. Jasper is offering her morsels and it riles her. A snatched weekend here and there when he can find the time to ride down to London on his scooter, just isn't good enough.

'Let's just see what happens. I need to put my career first.'

But Sandy isn't going to be strung along and have the terms of their relationship dictated to with everything on his terms. A thread of anger shoots through her. He's a selfish man and doesn't love her enough because if he did he'd be looking for a job in London, not moving halfway across the country. She makes fists in her pockets and storms ahead, leaving him to scurry after her. Salty tears prick in the corners of her eyes. Never before has she felt so humiliated. At the top of the steps to the underground he catches up with her and yanks her arm.

'Let's find a cafe. We need to talk.'

They head into a nearby cafe and the waiter guides them to a table and takes their order.

'We've only just had a coffee. I'll be walking on the ceiling with too much caffeine at this rate,' she grumbles.

He takes her hands.

'I don't want to lose you Sandy. But you're making this really hard.'

'I don't want a relationship that's just going to drift along.'

The next ten minutes pass in an awkward silence. He continues to hold her hands, rubbing them as though it's enough to make things better. She pulls away and dabs her eyes with a napkin.

'Maybe it's time to move on. I feel torn but all I can think about is starting this new job. This is my big break.'

'So you keep reminding me.'

'Don't be like that. Even if this isn't going anywhere we've had some good times together haven't we?'

He has a cheeky grin on his face.

'Oh I know what you're thinking about. The night in Brighton?' She smiles but she's only going through the motions. So that's all she's been to him, a sexual conquest?

'Well you've got to admit it was very dirty.'

'That's insulting. I'd rather you described it as loving.'

'We were naughty though. It will always be our secret.' He squeezes her hands, a smutty look on his face and she takes them away and picks up her bag to go.

THE CONVERSATION SWITCHES to cheerful things as they make their way back to Sandy's house, but it feels strained. There's a forced politeness between them and the easy humour they shared is replaced by a starchy stiffness, as if they are newly acquainted neighbours. They stand outside Sandy's house under the blazing light of a street lamp, like orphans who have lost everything—including each other. They feel wretched but there's nothing more to say. She turns to go without saying goodbye and before she reaches the bottom step he grabs her in an embrace. She tries to say something but somewhere in mid-sentence he shuts her up with a kiss. They kiss frantically. But it's a parting kiss, a last flush, clinging together like lost souls at sea, in danger of being swept away by a large wave.

11

RONA

Rona can't get enough of Bill. She works long hours, they both do and sometimes days go by when they are passing ships in the night. She's tired and sore, but it doesn't put her off. Even though they've been trying for three years her determination to get pregnant hasn't waned and although she loves the kitten and it keeps her entertained, it isn't a surrogate baby.

She wants him inside her all the time when she's ovulating. She plans her life around the small window of opportunity, often swapping shifts and cancelling friends and family. She'll do anything to engineer sexy-time with Bill, giving the best chance to succeed.

Rona stands in front of the mirror dressed in a red bra and knickers. She spends all her spare cash on sexy underwear from department stores, to keep things alive and fresh and make him desire her, but it's contrived. She feels devious and dirty. Her natural default is to put on a winceyette nighty flowing to the floor with buttons to the neck, bed socks and her hair in curlers.

'Just putting the cat out. Do you want a cup of Ovaltine?' Bill calls up.

Their life is full of little passion squashing routines. It's the same routine each night. If Rona isn't on a shift they always go to bed after the ten o' clock news. Rona heads up first putting the electric fire on to warm the room while they undress. It's a relationship based on routine, habit and dependence.

Rona brushes her hair and sprays her neck with a new scent. The underwear is extravagant and out of place and belongs on a prostitute. She wants to feel sexy but she hates her body. She's ashamed of it. The lingerie hasn't done what it's supposed to. Hearing Bill's feet on the stairs she grabs her dressing gown to hide behind.

'You smell nice love.' Bill kisses her neck and slips a hand into her gown cupping her breast. The gown falls to the floor.

'Wow, red.'

Embarrassment and shame flood her body. They don't earn much. She shouldn't be splashing out on pricey undies. Under normal circumstances she wouldn't have bothered.

Warm calloused fingers trail inside her thighs. They feel like the brush of sandpaper. 'Do you want me?'

'Yes.' But she wants him because it's the right time of the month, not because she wants to enjoy sex. Sex is a chore and a burden. It's part of the marriage contract that has to be endured to keep her husband happy and stop him straying. As he kisses her breasts her brain spins to another place containing all the mixed emotions she's feeling. He pushes her onto the bed and the poshest, most expensive knickers and bra she has ever owned are disposed of and flung to the floor like pieces of litter.

He's a heavy man and it's uncomfortable to be underneath him, but she learns to get used to his crushing weight, knowing that it's the best position for conception and feels deeper. She relaxes, pushing her anxiety away. It doesn't hurt as much when she's relaxed. He drives into her, whining with pleasure as she stares at the cracked ceiling. She feels his belly tighten, hard as a board and goes into spasm. Getting pregnant is an intricate science and she imagines that her ovaries are lost planets somewhere in the universe of her complicated solar system.

Thankfully the sex only lasts a few minutes and then he rolls off and within minutes is snoring peacefully beside her, leaving her to cradle her belly, hoping and wondering. But something inside her feels broken.

12

SANDY

Jasper doesn't leave a forwarding address and Sandy hasn't suggested writing. She's sad that she's thrown the relationship away—as if a relationship is disposable, like a tin can. But he hasn't left her with much choice.

She spends days in bed wallowing in self-pity and finding solace in her pillow.

'You can't carry on like this. Pull yourself together,' were her mother's orders, coming into her bedroom with a cup of tea and toast.

'I know and I will. I've got to get up today. I've got a photo shoot. Luckily it's my hands they're taking photos of and not my face.'

'Or your middle. You've put on weight.'

'Don't make me feel worse. I'm supposed to be losing weight not gaining it.'

She gets out of bed and stands in front of the mirror, smoothing her nighty over her belly.

'Did I do the right thing? You think I should have moved to Manchester to be with him don't you?'

'The decision was out of your hands. He wasn't ready for a serious relationship. At least that's the impression you gave me.'

Sandy sighs, wipes her eyes and opens her wardrobe to find something to wear.

'I know it's for the best, Mum, but it's hard.'

Her mum leaves her to dress. She puts on a pair of slacks but the zip won't reach the top. Her mum's right. She has put on weight, which is surprising given that she hasn't been eating properly. She's read somewhere that crying can help weight loss and when she's stressed it drops off. But not this time. Something feels different about her body but she can't say what it is. She ponders for a few moments; something is definitely wrong. She picks up her bra from the chair and gasps when she notices that her nipples have darkened and a line snakes up her belly that wasn't there before. She cups her breasts and they feel tender to the touch. It dawns on her.

Her period is late. She has a regular twenty-eight-day cycle and never been late before. Her heart slams in her chest and she sits on the edge of her bed, a wave of dizziness washing over her. An inner voice tells her to pull herself together. It was the first time. No woman gets pregnant the first time she has sex, which is why she wasn't worried at the time. She'd had a steaming bath soon afterwards. Her legs were like two lobsters when she got out.

Chasing the thought away she goes to the toilet willing her period to begin. There's a few spots of blood on the toilet paper. With relief she curses herself for being so reckless. She'd been carried away in the moment and next time she won't be so weak willed. She's learned her lesson. She's been lucky this time. It would have been an absolute disaster given that Jasper has disappeared up North. He would have been horrified.

13

RONA

'What time does the party start?' Rona asks her mother.

Rona is standing in the public phone box opposite her house. A queue is forming outside. It's only a matter of time before somebody bangs on the window if their conversation lasts longer than five minutes. She keeps in touch with her mother once a week at an agreed time but their conversations are short and to the point.

They are discussing Rona's nephew's eighth birthday party. There are lots of parties Rona has to attend as the doting auntie bearing gifts because her sisters Amy and Rachel have six children between them.

'Two o' clock. Is Bill working on Saturday?' Not waiting for Rona's reply she quickly adds, 'I expect he'll be busy.'

'I don't think he is working. He'll be able to come too.'

'He could drop along at the end, I suppose, if he takes his work boots off and doesn't smoke. The last time he was here it took me a week to get rid of the dreadful smell.'

Rona wants to scream at her mother. This is deliberate. She

doesn't want Bill in her house and makes no attempt to cover her disdain.

'I don't see him much, Mum. We're always working. If Amy and Rachel's husbands are going then Bill should be too.' She considers making a stand, by saying that she will only come if Bill is included, but doesn't want to rile her mother. Anything for an easy life.

'What a motley collection of people.' She gives a mocking laugh. 'It's such a pity love that you didn't...' but the pips go and Rona has run out of coins.

'Marry a lawyer, doctor or accountant,' Rona shouts at the phone. She slams it back on its cradle, then kicks the door. That's what she intended to say because as far as her mother is concerned she's married beneath her station. Bill is just a tradesman and therefore an embarrassment. It makes no difference that he is enterprising, a hard worker and a good man to Rona.

14

SANDY

The sickness returns. Sandy can't face food and the smells in the kitchen make her retch. The aroma of lamb and gravy and chopped mint that once stimulated her digestive juices makes her queasy. The only thing that helps is a glass of PLJ, Pure Lemon Juice which she keeps by her bed. The added bonus is that it also helps her slim.

'I think you might have a peptic ulcer,' her dad suggests when it has gone on for several weeks. He's suffered one and is aware of the symptoms.

Her mum stands at the stove stirring porridge. 'I think I've got a pretty good idea about what's been going on.' Her tone is accusatory and waving the wooden spoon, with porridge dripping onto the tiles she gives Sandy a cold stare, as if waiting for her to confess to having had sex outside wedlock.

'You're deliberately making yourself ill to lose weight.'

'No I'm not.'

'You're obsessed with modelling. Why can't you settle for an ordinary clerical job like your friends and find a decent man to marry?'

'There's plenty of time to get married. I'm only nineteen. I need to save up to go to Canada next year.'

'You can go there when you're older and married.'

'Just take the girl to the doctor. She's not well. This sickness has gone on for long enough.'

A wave of nausea engulfs Sandy and she rushes to the downstairs toilet. She kneels over the bowl. But it isn't food she throws up, or water on her empty stomach or even yellow bile. It's bright red blood. She gasps. Her parents come rushing in and her mum grabs toilet roll while her dad stands cursing. Her throat and stomach are burning. It is as if somebody has taken over her body.

'Forget the doctor. Go straight to the hospital. Something's very wrong,' he shouts, grabbing his jacket from the peg. 'I'm late for work. I'll come home at lunchtime to check how things are.'

The door slams and Sandy stands up, guided back to the kitchen by her mum. They sit at the table and her mum tells her to eat a biscuit to stop her from fainting. She looks as pale as the uneaten porridge in the pan.

The doctor feels Sandy's stomach and looks inside her throat.

'I don't want to make any guesses at this stage but I'll run some tests. Is there any chance you could be pregnant?'

'No.' She wants to tell him that she's had sex so technically yes she could be, but embarrassment burns inside her. She hesitates. 'At least I don't think so. I've just had my period, but it was lighter than normal.'

He frowns but doesn't give an opinion at this stage.

SEVERAL DAYS PASS. Some days are okay and other days Sandy vomits all day and can't eat a thing. She's on the brink of being admitted to hospital when the doctor calls.

'The tests have come back and you're pregnant.' He pauses to let it sink in. 'I'd like to get a second opinion about your sickness and how to manage it. You can drop along to the antenatal clinic at the hospital this afternoon.'

Sandy is speechless. Tears spring to her eyes. Her face colours and the room swims as she tries to digest the news. She puts the phone down with shaky hands. She's terrified and even more terrified of what her mum will say. Anxiety and dizziness wrap around her like a second skin.

Her mother is standing in the hallway. Sandy pushes past her into the lounge and collapses on the sofa sobbing.

'I knew it. You little whore.' Her mum claps her hand to her mouth, crumples in the chair opposite and gasps, her face a picture of horror, as if she's just received news of a close relative's death.

'When did it happen? You stupid little whore.'

She needs a hug and sympathy not this. 'Leave me alone.'

Sandy gets up and rushes to her room slamming the door behind her.

THE HOSPITAL IS AN IMPOSING red brick Edwardian sprawl on the edge of a Common in North London. Part of it has only just been rebuilt after being fire bombed during the war. As they enter there are nurses and sisters scurrying along the corridor, carrying clipboards and being briskly busy in their starched uniforms. Sandy and her mum join the throng, behind a group of doctors in crisp white coats and pin striped suits, with stethoscopes slung round their necks walking down the corridor in military precision. The smell of the corridor, detergent mixed with kitchen smells and fear make Sandy feel sicker.

When it is her turn Sandy and her mum are ushered into a small room. A sister, in a smart navy uniform stands behind a doctor, silently obedient with notes in hand ready to answer any questions.

'We want to run some more tests to be on the safe side and monitor you. Nurse will check your weight and take a sample in a moment. I understand you're not able to keep much down. We don't want you to end up being admitted into hospital.'

Confusion and unease twist in her gut. She's forgotten, momentarily that her mum is there, aware of her silence, the colour of her face merging with the whiteness of the wall behind her. In the company of professionals she is composed, a stern look on her face. Sandy can see her climbing on her moral high horse and dreads what is to come.

'You little tart.'

'I didn't mean to get into trouble.'

The doctor shuffles his papers and checks his watch. 'Go with nurse. She'll measure your height and weight and take a urine sample.'

'But what about my sickness? I can't cope.' Tears trickle down her face and the nurse passes her a tissue as if this is going to mop away the problem.

'You'll have to have it adopted,' her mum rattles on. 'Or track down that young man of yours and get married.'

'He's not mine Mum.'

'He got you into trouble. He can get you out of it by making an honest woman of you.' Her mum glares at her and fiddles with the clasp on her handbag, the usual sign that she is stressed.

'Let's not make any plans for the moment,' the doctor says in a calm voice. 'I have a remedy for your sickness. Let's sort that first.' He scribbles a prescription and tears it off to hand to Sandy.

'What is it?' Sandy's mum asks. 'There was nothing in my day. We had to drink ginger tea and eat dried toast and wait for it to pass.' She tuts, looking annoyed that her daughter is being offered a cure all pill when she had to grin and bear it.

'Distaval. It's new on the market. You're very lucky there's a cure for morning sickness because yours is extreme. It's called hyperemesis gravidarum. Did you know that Charlotte Bronte died of it? It's a serious condition during pregnancy.'

'Never heard of, Distaval did you say?' her mum asked.

'Otherwise known as thalidomide. That's the magic ingredient.' He smiles as though he is Santa in Harrods handing a box of Smarties to a child. 'It's a wonderful sedative but it's also used to get rid of morning sickness.'

'Well at least that's one thing taken care of but it doesn't get around the fact that my daughter is going to have a baby out of wedlock. What will men think of her? She's used goods.'

'I'm not here to pass judgement Mrs Lambert.'

'I know I've brought shame on you Mum. I'm sorry. Maybe I can get out of your way to save the neighbours talking and go and stay with Auntie Ellen in Scotland.'

'Dear God, you don't land yourself on someone else's doorstep. What you've done is unforgivable. You can't expect family to pick up the pieces for the sin you've committed.'

The doctor smiles at Sandy's mother sympathetically.

'Mrs Lambert, I can refer Sandy to a hotel in Brighton that takes in pregnant mothers. She'll be modestly housed in return for some domestic chores. But I'd say the best place for her is in bed at home where you can look after her and where she'll be most comfortable.'

'What type of chores?' Sandy asks. Her brain is a maelstrom of confusion and all she can visualise is getting fatter and ending up with stretch marks, a saggy belly and dry cracked hands. Sickness and dread ripple through her as she contemplates the end of her modelling career before it's begun. And with fear she wonders where her life is heading.

'Scrubbing floors, making beds, answering phone calls, if you're lucky. If you don't want Sandy at home it's your best bet but really Mrs Lambert Sandy is best staying at home.'

Her mum huffs. Sitting rigid, she keeps a stiff upper lip, exercising self -restraint. But beyond her expression Sandy knows that anger morphs with self -pity.

'That's out of the question. Please refer her. She can't stay at home and I don't know what her dad's going to say when he finds out.'

'I can also book a place for her in the mother-and-baby home which is run by a religious charity. She can go there six weeks before her due date - which we still need to establish – she'll have the baby and six weeks after the baby is born it can be adopted. There are plenty of couples looking for a healthy baby.' He makes it sound as though the baby is an item of furniture to be picked up by the rag-and-bone man, tossed onto a cart and taken away. 'You don't need to worry about that.'

It sounds simple, neat and conveniently packaged but this is her life being discussed as though she has no input. Sandy's insides feel as though they are folding in on themselves. The room fades in and out of focus, mostly out. She is lost.

She folds her legs, needs the toilet and wants to be alone. She feels tired, mentally and physically. She's lost track of time and looks at the clock on the wall. Wasn't she due at the studio soon? She can't remember. Her brain is a fugue. She gets up and rushes from the room, not wanting to hear about plans made on her behalf and without her consultation. She wishes it could all be over—she wishes it had never begun.

On the toilet she shivers as a chill seeps over her, deepened by tiredness, sickness and the damp musty air of the cubicle. A gentle pounding in her head increases to a throb and she blinks back tears. She tears off a piece of toilet paper and curses because it's hard and non-absorbent, like the paper her mum uses for baking. She dabs herself with it, hoping there will be blood, lots of it and that she's miscarried, but there is no blood and this baby, it seems is firmly entrenched inside her.

15

RONA

'I've got plenty to do around the house.'

Rona watches Bill as he pulls his socks on. She knows that he doesn't really have any jobs to get on with. They haven't seen much of each other all week and tomorrow she's working. Quality time is fleeting. She feels a stab of resentment towards her mother.

Bill's tone is cheerful. He canters on, listing the jobs that need doing but none of them are urgent and it's as if he's making the list up. It's obvious that he's masking his hurt, aware that he isn't invited to the party because he doesn't live up to her mother's high standards. She's sick of her mum's superior attitude. But Bill isn't the type to brood. It's typical of him to cover up his feelings in order to save Rona from feeling worse.

Rona cradles her warm mug of tea feeling blessed that Bill's parents have welcomed her into their family. Their home is relaxed and friendly and there are no airs and graces. She loves Bill's mother, sometimes more than her own, who is cold and snooty. Social class means nothing to Bill's folks. They are warm people who can see through a smart suit or a grubby pair of boots. The fact that Rona's father has been the director of a sock factory and has a large detached house with an apple orchard, while they are factory operatives and live in a two-up-two-down means nothing to them. Rona is thankful that she didn't listen to her mother ten years ago when she warned her not to marry Bill. 'You can do better,' she'd said. To avoid a family bust up Rona and Bill had married in St Ives with nobody present except for a witness pulled from the street. Her father was more accepting of Bill but he'd kept out of things - a lapdog knows better than to bite. He went along with what his wife thought and Rona wondered if he was scared of her. When he'd been ill Rona had stepped in, putting her career on hold to nurse her father because she was worried her mother would neglect him and leave him for hours while she went out galavanting and doing her own thing.

Like Bill, Rona prefers an easy life but something inside her snaps.

'But I want you to come.'

'It'll be awkward. I'm fine here, go and enjoy.'

'We need to rise above it. We can't go on like this.'

'Will Pete and Ed be there?' Pete and Ed are Rona's brother-in-laws, married to Amy and Rachel.

Ruth sighs. 'Yes.'

She doesn't need to press him further, knowing how much he dislikes arrogant Pete, bragging about his earnings in the city and where his career is destined and his endless name-dropping. And sneering Ed, who has the audacity to correct Bill's use of English and never in a subtle way. Rona remembers the look on Bill's face when Ed corrected him three times one afternoon for dropping his aitches, and the time when Pete and Ed had roared with laughter because Bill couldn't recall the name of the capital of Australia. The whole experience had been humiliating. Maybe it was best Bill stayed home.

· · ·

HER MOTHER'S house looks tired and in need of attention. After her husband's death, Celia went to pieces, unable to cope for months. In order to manage her grief she'd channelled all her energies into her grandchildren and neglected the house. The whitewashed exterior has peeled away, like burnt skin. The front garden is overgrown and swathes of fallen leaves haven't been cleared.

Her mother greets her with the expression reserved for door-to-door salesmen without even the hint of a smile. She looks to see if Bill is following on behind. Rona feels like a spare part, invited out of duty. Jamie, the birthday boy rushes to the door, skidding to a halt in front of Rona and jumping to grab his present from her hands.

'Thank you, Auntie Rona.' He snatches it and heads towards the kitchen shrieking to his friends as he tears at the wrapping. 'My auntie always buys super presents.'

Rona smiles as she follows her mother through to the kitchen, pleased that her nieces and nephews appreciate her, even though her sisters dismiss the presents she buys, without thanks or comments. They take her for granted. That's how it feels. After all, with no children of her own it isn't as if they must return the gesture. It's one way and expensive; not that she minds. She loves to make them happy.

Rona helps her mother lay the table for the party tea while the children play and the adults chat in the lounge.

'I need you to help me bake the cake for Louise's christening and do you think you could make the baby's christening robe too? You're much better at sewing than me.'

Amy has recently given birth to her fourth child. Her older sister is feeding Louise a bottle in the garden even though it's a chilly day. 'She's filling out.'

Rona feels a stab of sadness. It seems so unfair that Amy has four children and she has none.

'Tuesday?'

There's a clatter of plates and a clink of bowls as her mother lays the table. Rona is miles away, not listening.

She zones back in. 'I'm working and my sewing machine's in the repair shop.'

Her mother exudes the no-nonsense air of a gym teacher.

'Come over one evening then. I'll buy the fabric, you can use my sewing machine.' She's cornered Rona into getting her own way, as she always does.

The children rush in and sit down, devouring sandwiches, sausage rolls, jelly, ice cream and cake while the adults stand around the table chatting and attending to spilled drinks and making sure everybody has enough to eat.

After tea, the party moves to the lounge for games but the men stay in the garden to smoke. Rona chats to her sisters and holds baby Louise while the children pin the tail on the donkey, play musical bumps and sing ring-a-ring a roses.

'Rona, do you remember Sue, my best friend from school?' Amy asks, pulling her friend into the conversation.

'Wow, you've changed,' Rona beams. 'I wouldn't have recognised you. So which is your child?'

'The blonde one in the pink frilly dress, making a show of herself. She's called Lucy. I've got an older one too, Wendy, she's twelve. She's at home with her dad.' Sue rises from the settee, grabs her daughter and pulls her onto her lap.

'She's beautiful.'

'Strange isn't it that we're all grown up now, with kids of our own.'

'Rona doesn't have any children.'

'Oh.'

An awkward silence follows.

'My life had no meaning before I had kids,' Amy gushes.

'Really?' Rona wants to say. How awful, but she holds herself in check.

'Well you've got lots of nieces and nephews to keep you

busy. At least you can hand them back,' Sue laughs, but Rona can't laugh with her. The comment isn't funny.

Celia comes into the room with a parcel and asks the children to make a big circle for pass the parcel. She puts a record on and the parcel tumbles from one child to the next.

Rachel, looking done for and red-faced flops on the settee next to Amy, her legs flying in the air.

'Bet you're glad you don't have kids Rona.'

Rona doesn't know how to respond. Her heart slams in her chest and she fights the urge to cry. She forces a smile and tries to sound cheery. 'I'm tired just watching them.' It wasn't true but it was the type of thing people said at kids' parties.

'Think you're tired? Try having kids,' Rachel snaps.

I have a right to feel tired too, Rona wants to shoot back. I work all hours at the hospital. At least you don't have to work.

'How's the cat?' Amy asks, as if the cat is an acceptable alternative to a baby.

'She treats that cat as if it were a child,' Rachel tuts.

Rona can't stand to be there any longer. She's on the verge of getting up and storming out. She takes a deep breath and tries to steady her nerves.

'You're so lucky having four Rachel. We've been trying for a year and nothing's happening. I fell pregnant so easily with the other two.'

'I only have to look at Pete and I fall pregnant,' Amy giggles, adjusting Louise in her arms. A titter of laughter breaks out but Rona is too stunned by their tactlessness to join in.

'Four's a nightmare. I don't regret having Louise but it's hard work. Sometimes I don't get any sleep. And I've never been so broke.'

But I was, thinks Rona, broke, when I took several months off work to look after Dad. I didn't see either of you offering to help out. She says nothing.

All the grumbling makes Rona simmer with fury but she keeps her cool through gritted teeth.

Pass the parcel ends and there are noises of glee from the winner, a fat boy who has a lump of cake in one hand while he struggles to open the parcel with his other.

With the games over and the prizes claimed the children run to the garden and Celia breathes a sigh of relief, wipes her brow and pretends to collapse.

'You're lucky Rona that you don't have kids,' Celia says falling into an armchair.

'Yes I'd love to have your freedom,' Sue adds.

More hurtful words follow from her mother that are better left unspoken. She addresses Sue, as if her daughters aren't in the room.

'The thing is Sue I never wanted a big family. Two would have been fine, but Rona was an accident. We got carried away one night.'

She emits a piercing laugh but nobody joins in.

Rona forces a laugh, trying to lighten the conversation while tapping down emotions swirling in her stomach.

'Even if a baby is unplanned it's still very much loved,' Rona says in a wobbly voice in Louise's direction. Amy nods and Rachel agrees.

'No,' her mother snaps and Rona's heart slams in her chest, a wave of dizziness washing over her. 'You cried all night. You had colic, then earache. Amy and Rachel were dream babies by comparison. And you were the ugliest baby ever born with a mop of jet black hair and cradle cap.'

The last remark amuses her mother because more laughter follows.

'Of course, not everyone is cut out to be a mother,' she adds in a malicious tone, enjoying twisting the knife. 'These things happen for a reason.'

Rona inches to the edge of the settee, blood pulsing in her

head, her hand unsteady as she sets her tea cup down, liquid sloshing onto the saucer. She can't be there a moment longer. She feels so excluded and humiliated.

'I need to go.'

'So soon?'

Celia doesn't understand the hurt she's caused.

'Rona before you go would you mind babysitting next Saturday?' Amy asks.

Rona is cornered. She has no plans for Saturday but that isn't the point. Her time with Bill is precious and she wants to spend it with him, either in the pub or at home relaxing.

'Don't forget to come round Tuesday week,' Celia adds.

'I'm not sure what we're doing Saturday, Amy and I'll speak to you at the end of the week to let you know if I'm free, Mum.'

Rona longs to say more and be assertive but the words are shackled to her tongue. She's used to being cowed and putting others first and feels hemmed in by their persistence. It's easier to go along with what they want of her.

'Well let me know as soon as you can. I hope you can. We haven't been out for so long and without kids you can go out whenever you want.'

Rona wants to say to her you can always get a babysitter, but I can't borrow a baby of my own.

Outside on the driveway after saying goodbye the tears she has managed to suppress fall, making tracks down her face. The gravel crushes under her feet and she doesn't glance around, afraid that one of them will realise how upset she is. She wishes she could tell them the truth and share the secrets that normal sisters share. She wants to tell them that she longs for a baby and although they've been trying for years nothing has happened. They are her family. She has everything in common with them, and yet conversely nothing in common.

She gets off the bus, heads through the gate and into the house, reflecting on the afternoon.

Bill is in the kitchen making tea.

'Cup of tea love?' Ignoring him she goes into the hallway to hang up her coat, slumping on a chair in the kitchen, her hands holding her face as she mourns her non-existent child.

'I can see you've had a painful afternoon. Was it bad?' She feels a rush of love. He is her Bill. Loving, dependable and kind and she wants to cry all over again and melt into his arms, but she holds back, not wanting to burden him with her woes.

'Look at me.' He stands in front of her. When she doesn't respond he breaks the sentence into parts. 'Look. At. Me.'

She stands up, but it's an effort. He cradles her face in his hands and brushes his lips against hers. 'I love you.'

He has a thin scar running from the bottom of his nose to the top of his lip, puckering his mouth on one side but his smile is charming.

'I can't go on like this. Sometimes I wish I could just cut off from them.'

'You don't mean that.'

'Maybe not, but I get wound up and tearful when I see them.'

'Step away. You don't have to be at their beck and call.'

'It's hard to say no and they don't know how I feel so all they're doing is acting normally.'

'Why don't we move?'

'Move?' Rona looks incredulous. Bill has never wanted to move from the house he loves. It was built by his grandfather. Her spirits lift. Would he really move for her? A new environment might make it easier to conceive. She's heard of that happening. Although not intended as a cure for infertility, it would serve as a diversion. Change is the solution. He's right. They should move.

'We could rent this place out. Just for a year to see how things go. I've been offered a contract in North London. It's good money and the job comes with a house.'

'You didn't tell me.'

'I was going to say no, but, love, you need a break from everybody. It's tearing you apart, not just your family but mine too.'

'What would I tell them and what about my work?'

'We're in the middle of a baby boom. They're crying out for midwives all over the country.'

'I don't know anyone in London. Despite everything I'd miss them.'

'Think about it. We don't have to decide now. But stepping away from them for a while might help you. It's only for a year.'

'What if I ended up liking it down there? Could we stay?'

'One minute you don't like the idea, the next you do.'

'I'm just mulling things over that's all.' Rona feels brighter and positive. 'The more I think about it, the more exciting it sounds. There are loads of hospitals in London and mother and baby homes. I'm sure I could find something.'

16

SANDY

Outside the hospital the sun shines through the breaks in the cloud and Sandy's mum reminds her that the sun only shines on the righteous. It's an old wives' tale her grandma used to repeat when somebody was in trouble. She grabs her arm and hurries Sandy away from the building as if they have come out of a law court, rather than a hospital. They walk along a path lined with tall chestnut trees towards the bus stop and her mum orders her to stay quiet and not utter a word until they are well out of earshot. That suits Sandy. She doesn't want an interrogation about how she's ended up in the family way, or be accused of being a whore, again. It will come, she is sure of that.

Getting off the bus, they pass detached houses with neat lawns and a riot of colour and weed-free pathways. A small girl in polished red shoes skips along the pavement ahead of them and a Jenny Wren trills from a tree. The sky is blue above, yet storm clouds are gathering in Sandy's mind. Mothers are putting their babies outside to sleep in the fresh air, wrapped in crochet blankets, in coach built Silver Cross prams. Sandy avoids looking. She can't imagine attending to a baby all day, studying Dr Spock's *Common Sense Book of Baby Care* and preparing wholesome meals for a husband who devotes himself to his job rather than her. What a mind numbingly dull life that would be. Even if she could track Jasper down, she doesn't want that kind of life, at least not yet. This shouldn't have happened to her; she has dreams, ambition, places to go, glamorous, possibly even famous people to meet and money to make. The world is her oyster and she intends to grab and live it.

They turn the corner into their road and a mum is in the garden singing Lulla, Lulla Lullaby in a soft voice. Sandy's heart jolts. The woman waves. The melody is simple yet there is something about it that Sandy finds haunting and disturbing. A vision of the mother turning into a deranged woman out of frustration and lack of fulfilment flashes across Sandy's mind. She imagines her pushing the pram into a busy road and laughing as her child is mown down. Sandy's life is a car crash and there's not a thing she can do about it.

Her mum slams the door to the house behind them, marches into the kitchen and clatters her keys onto the table, ordering Sandy to sit down while she puts water on to boil. She sniffs the milk before pouring it into a jug.

'I don't want you to say a word to anyone about this. Do you understand?'

Sandy shivers at the table, hugging herself, despite it being a warm day. 'What about dad?'

'You leave him to me. I'll break it to him when I'm ready and can find the right words.'

'It was an accident Mum.' She takes the blister pack of pills the doctor has prescribed from her bag, pours a glass of water and swallows it. The nurse has estimated the pregnancy to be around twenty-four days, going by the last day of her period.

Her mum turns from the stove and tuts at her.

'What's wrong now? Don't you want me to get better?'

'Take them. You wake me up every morning throwing up. You know I don't sleep well.'

'I can't help it. Maybe you should take them. The doctor said it's for insomnia too.'

'Maybe I will.'

Sandy filters her mum's voice from her head while she rants on about bringing shame on the family and bringing an unwanted bastard into the world. The word sin is on replay and reverberates around her mind.

Building into a fury her mum slings the teapot full of scalding tea onto the table where it lands, spewing out hot amber liquid onto Sandy's arm. Sandy gets up and after putting her arm under a tap of cold water, tears trickle down her cheeks at the injustice of it. There's no apology from her mum, only daggered looks.

'Well what are you going to do?'

'Track down Jasper,' Sandy replies weakly because she knows it's what her mum wants to hear.

'Well that would be a start, it won't be difficult.'

Sandy has no intention of contacting him. He doesn't love her, it was plain to see that last evening when he made his big announcement and excluded her from his plans for the future. She is still bubbling with anger at the memory. Part of her knows that she's punishing herself by not trying to get in touch with him. A baby might change his mind and bring him round to the idea of being with her. But it wouldn't change the situation. She can't imagine herself having a baby or bringing it up. Just thinking about it makes her stomach churn and her head pound.

She has to find a way to get rid of it, before it grows any bigger and before it's too late. There's still time and there has to be a way. She's heard of it happening but because it's illegal she is hardly going to find an advert in the local paper or a card pinned up in the post office. There are people that can sort it out, even though it might involve parting with her hard-earned savings. Small price to pay for getting rid of this thing inside her.

She goes to bed early, feeling better after taking the Distaval and waking later to her parents screaming at each other. She knows that her mum has broken the news to her dad. She presses her ear to the wall to listen, piecing together fragmented sentences. Her dad is a man of principles and she hears that she's betrayed his trust and has hurt him deeply. The way he is ranting it's obvious he's disgusted with her.

'She's let us down. If she doesn't swallow her pride and marry the chap I wash my hands of her. She can get out and find somewhere else to live.'

Sandy hears panic in her mum's reply. 'She's promised me she'll track him down and if she doesn't, the doctor's booking her into a hotel for girls like her, down in Brighton. I don't want the neighbours finding out about this, any more than you do.'

Sandy is worried about her dad's reaction and is grateful that her mother has told him. He has the night to digest the news, sleep on it and hopefully be calmer in the morning. She lies awake when their voices descend to whispers. She plans the lie she will string in the morning, about contacting Jasper. She should do what they want and contact him, but her churning gut rules the day. She doesn't want to; it would signal the end of her liberty.

Her real plan is forming. She goes through everybody she knows. There has to be somebody who knows somebody who knows somebody. Her head screams, I've got to get this thing out of me and get my life back. I need my body back to how it was. This has to end, before it gets bigger. She thinks about the people she knows through work, the people she's met in the dance hall, the corner shop, bus stop and she thinks about the people she's met at school. It has been years since she left the secondary modern. She's forgotten most of the people in her class and only keeps in contact with a few girls but does bump into people from time to time at the Saturday dance.

The catchment area for the school was large and pupils came from different backgrounds and social class. There were wealthy pupils who lived in detached houses with big gardens and there were pupils from poor backgrounds living in hovels. It was easy to spot whether somebody was from a well to do home or whether they were poor. The well-off pupils were more likely to be in the top sets and their parents sent them for extra tuition and they spoke with a posh accent like the reporters on the news. The poor children were often under-weight with grubby appearances and swore in the playground. You didn't mess with them. Many of them were tough nuts and they'd threaten to beat you up. But some were the salt of the earth, kind and affectionate children who were nice to every-body and didn't see any point in working hard because they knew they'd be out to work as soon as they left school rather than staying on to do exams. These were her overriding memo-ries of school days and she wondered if things were any different several years on. The memories were dim images in an old sepia photo.

As she drifts in and out of sleep, the face of one girl looms in her mind. Kirsten. A whole raft of memories surround Kirsten. The collars on her school blouses were frayed, as if they'd been handed down many times. She had teeth like dirty pebbles and hair like fine copper wire and she spent lots of time with the nit nurse. Kirsten came from a family of twelve, which had always intrigued Sandy, she wondered how they survived and where they all slept. They lived on the poor side of town, in an area that Sandy's mum sneered about and warned her never to visit because she said it was dodgy. There were rumours flying when they were at school that Kirsten's dad had served time and that her mum went shop lifting in the Co-op because they were so hard up. She remembers school dinner times and the way Kirsten devoured her food. Most of the pupils, including Sandy were made to eat them, otherwise they'd miss their break time. Maybe Kirsten would know of somebody that could help. Sandy hasn't seen her for years and has no idea where she works, but she knows of somebody who will know. Ellen works in Chester's and Ellen is Kirsten's best friend.

Her dad leaves for work early the following morning and Sandy wonders whether it's so that he can avoid her. Her mum nags through breakfast about finding Jasper and Sandy can't wait to get out of the house, promising to find him. She heads for Chester's and finds Ellen at the biscuit counter weighing a mixture of Bourbons and custard creams for a customer.

Sandy waits until she's finished. It's early in the day and she isn't busy and when the customer leaves, Sandy asks if she can meet her during her lunch break. They meet in the Wimpy across the road and over coffee Ellen moans about her job, complaining about how the supervisor has scraped a cockroach from the top of a loaf of bread and served the loaf to an unsuspecting customer, and how she has to clean mouse poo from the biscuit shelves before the store opens.

'The place is filthy. One day someone will come down with food poisoning and we'll all get the blame.'

Sandy waits for a break in the conversation to ask about Kirsten. An address is scribbled on a napkin and she tells her the house is up near the brewery. Before Ellen has the chance to ask why Sandy wants her address some of Ellen's work colleagues come over to chat.

17

RONA

'You can't just up sticks.'

'Bill's been offered a fantastic opportunity.'

'You don't have to go too. Your family are here and your job.'

'It's only for a year. Bill's my husband. I go where he needs to go.'

Rona can hear her mother bristling at the end of the phone.

'Well I won't be able to trek all the way down there to see you. You know how much I hate travelling. And I'm moving house soon and thought I could count on you to help me.' Rona doesn't need reminding. She remembers the times her mother complained about going on holiday. It was always an issue in Celia's marriage, her father wanted to travel abroad, but Celia put the kibosh on his suggestions. 'And you know my knees play up and my ankles swell if I sit on a coach.'

She grumbles from one complaint to the next. Rona has heard it all before. It's as if her mother has forgotten the conversations they've had.

'I'm not asking you to visit, Mum. To be honest I'll be too busy working anyway.'

Rona has responded to an advert for a job at a mother and baby home which is part of a large hospital and with the help from glowing references she's been successful.

'And Amy and Rachel won't want to trek all that way. Not with all their kiddies in tow.'

'I'm not asking anybody to visit. We won't have a spare room.'

'Yes, quite. And you know what I'm like in hotels. I get a bad back when I sleep on a strange mattress.'

'We'll be back before you know it.'

'I'm wondering if...' Rona has run out of money and fumbles in her pocket for another coin before the phone dies.

'Can you hear me, Mum?'

'I was just saying, is Bill doing this deliberately, to take you away from your family? He's the wrong sort for you, I did warn you.'

'No, of course not.'

When the call ends Rona leaves the phone box, apologising to the people in the queue and crosses the road to her house. It has been a battle with her mother, lasting weeks and she's tired of banging home the same point. Celia doesn't like change, she resists it, determined to control any situations she doesn't like. Her sisters have taken the news well, by comparison, which surprises Rona as they'll be paying for babysitters in future. Rona smiles. It will do them good not to rely on their sister for favours.

Louise's christening was the last straw. Rona made the cake, the gown and the food only to watch a cousin become Godmother. Rona stays to clear the plates and glasses while everybody chats in the lounge. 'It would be so nice to be chosen to be a godmother, just once,' she says to her mother while rinsing plates under the tap. She contemplates telling her that she's been trying for three years for a baby and how hard it is. But her mother responds in a self-righteous haughty tone. 'You don't know the first thing about children Rona. You may have delivered hundreds of babies but you've never had one yourself. And you don't go to church.' That is beside the point. Celia doesn't go to church. In fact, she sneers at the teachings of the church, and to Rona's knowledge, her cousin doesn't go either. The harsh words snap the shutters closed and Rona parks the conversation on the draining board and goes upstairs to the toilet to stop herself from crying. As she pads up the carpeted stairs on stockinged feet she hears whispers coming from one of the bedrooms. She can't make out the words until she hovers outside the door to listen. Her sisters are talking about her. 'Have you seen her with that bloody cat? Anyone would think it's a baby the way she treats it.' 'She'd lay her life down for that cat.' 'It's not normal.' And 'God why would you want a cat? They use the sofa as a scratching post and snag your tights.' There's a titter of laughter and Rona retreats to the bathroom before she's discovered eavesdropping.

18

SANDY

Sandy takes the short bus journey to Kirsten's house and stands up when the chimney of the brewery comes into view. The grey sky merges with the drabness of the ramshackle Victorian houses. She follows the bus driver's instructions, turning into an alley where a group of small girls are playing weddings dressed in makeshift veils, a toothless old couple watching them from a gate. Rubbish swirls in the wind. She peers into yards where there are decrepit communal lavatories. The smell of overflowing cisterns hits her nostrils. A few houses are boarded up and corrugated sheets have been put up to stop intruders breaking in. At the end of the alley there's a piece of wasteland that Sandy assumes is due to bomb damage. Children in ragged clothing play on piles of building rubble and boys sword fight with pieces of old wood. They look like survivors of a besieged city and it's hard for her to believe that people live like this after the comfortable leafy area she's come from, a few miles away.

She picks her way over discarded rubbish and trodden newspapers, past a broken railing and onto the cobbled street where Kirsten lives, clutching her handbag filled with the money she's withdrawn from the bank in case she needs it today.

A family cross the road, their belongings piled onto a wooden cart. A gaggle of children run behind. Sandy guesses they've been thrown out of their home, by an unscrupulous landlord, to be replaced by higher paying tenants but they could just as easily be going about their normal daily business.

She knocks on the door and waits, her nerves dancing in her stomach.

The door inches open and a woman peers out.

'Who is it?'

'Mrs Skinner? I've come to see Kirsten. I'm an old school friend.'

'I thought the landlord had sent you.' She opens the door wide.

Her face is hollow, she has no teeth and her skin is like an alligators. Her legs are the size of sandbags and she looks older than Sandy's mother who has barely done a jot of work in her life. Her eyes are sunken into dark sockets and crow's feet and farm tracks weave across her face. The passage of time and drudgery of raising so many children has taken its toll. Sandy follows her along a dark corridor where cockroaches scuttle from view and they go into a room where a light bulb hangs from the ceiling. Sunlight pours through a crack in the window; the panes of glass are covered with discarded Weetabix boxes. A line of washing tied to exposed pipework hangs across the room and damp and mould cling to peeling wallpaper. Three boys dressed in raincoats sit on a tatty sofa. Kirsten is crouching beside an open fire, frying bread.

'Sand, what you doing here?'

'Ellen told me where you live.'

Kirsten stands up, wiping her hands on her apron. Aware that she hasn't seen Kirsten for several years, Sandy feels awkward and her confidence melts away. A chill snakes through her as she wonders how to begin. Unable to disguise the bubble of tears in her eyes, Sandy's face reddens and silent tears escape to run down her face.

Kirsten smiles as if she's read the emotions behind Sandy's wet eyes. It's a smile that Sandy remembers from school days when they were having fun in the playground.

'Come on let's go for a walk. Looks like you need a chat.'

Out on the street they walk in silence.

'I know I haven't kept in touch these past few years, but I need a really big favour.'

They stop. Anxiety threads its way across Sandy's face as she tumbles her confession. No detail is spared but when Kirsten asks about Jasper she lies and tells her that he's married and doesn't want to know. It is easier this way, but guilt prickles. She doesn't like lying but doesn't want anybody to persuade her to go looking for him. She wants to turn the clock back to how things were and pretend it never happened.

'And how can I help?'

'You always used to say your dad knew people and that if anybody needed something he could sort it.'

'My dad's left.'

Then the penny drops and Kirsten's mouth falls open.

'Your mum? Does she know of anybody?' Sandy asks, ignoring the horror on Kirsten's face.

'If you're thinking what I'm thinking, you can't. It's illegal. Women die.'

'It's my only option.'

'Have it adopted.'

'I don't want to give birth. I just want it to be over.'

'I suppose you came sniffing round here because we're poor. You think we're so desperate for money that we'll do anything. Well you're wrong. It's murder.'

'It's my body, I'll do what I like with it.'

They descend into the kind of shouting match they had at

school when they disagreed. It reminds Sandy of why they'd fallen out.

'Looks like you already have.'

'I made one stupid mistake.' Sandy is defeated, she's rolled the dice and lost.

'You're more likely to find somebody in your area, not here; a doctor or midwife struck off the register. Doctors live on the posh side of town. No criminal shits on their own patch. You need someone that knows what they're doing. It's unsafe otherwise. You might get an infection.'

'Look I'm willing to take the risk. Speak to your mum please,' Sandy pleads although she isn't sure who she's trying to convince. Her nerves are jangling and she knows there is truth to Kirsten's concerns.

Unease passes between them. They are back from the walk standing outside Kirsten's house.

'Alright, I'll ask her.'

They find her mother perched on a beer barrel in the backyard puffing on a cigarette as if sucking in a lungful of chemicals might somehow transform the constant toil and grind of her life. There's a sad accepting smile on her face as if she knows life isn't going to work out. Behind her, a tin bath hangs on the outside wall.

'Mam we need to talk to you. Best we go in the kitchen.'

Mrs Skinner eyes them suspiciously, tosses her cigarette away and grinds it with her broken shoe.

The kitchen is tiny, a square room no bigger than a cupboard. Pots and pans hang from a rack and plaster crumbles from the walls. Kirsten shuts the back door and lowers her voice. Sandy's head throbs as she waits for the mother's response.

'Do you know of anybody, Mam? Somebody that could sort her out? I've tried to talk her out of it but she won't listen.'

The frown deepens on Mrs Skinner's face. Sandy sees the hard life she's had beneath her eyes.

The question hangs in the air like a bad smell.

'There's a woman. She's been doing it for years.'

Kirsten grabs her arm. 'Mam.'

Sandy picks up the inference that she's considered asking for this woman's help, at some point in the past.

'Children are hard work. Look at me, for God's sake. We don't have a h'penny to rub together.'

'Which of us were you considering getting rid of, Mam?' Kirsten screams in her face.

Tears trickle down Mrs Skinner's face and she pulls an old tissue from her pocket. 'Her name's Gwen. Ask for her in The Three Tanners. It's on the corner.'

Kirsten's voice cracks and her face reddens. 'My God, Mam. I don't believe I'm hearing this. You're going to let one of my friends risk her life?'

Mrs Skinner's eyes blaze. 'You're beautiful. You've got a life ahead of you.' And turning to Kirsten she says, 'Why would she want to be burdened down by a kiddy?'

SANDY LEAVES them arguing and goes in search of The Three Tanners. A blast of beery air hits her as she opens the door and inside it's noisier than a turkey farm. Terror shimmies through her. The room falls silent and she ignores her pounding heart as eyes crawl over the well-turned out stranger, like a pack of sinister creatures. Nobody smiles, nobody greets her. The men playing snooker put down their cues. As she heads for the bar the silence is broken by a jeer, a smutty remark and then a cacophony of whistles. She ignores them.

'Do you know a lady called Gwen?

The chatter stops, as if a cold wind has blasted in. The jeers and cat calls are replaced by a cold stare.

'Number twenty, Turners Hill.' The barman points in the direction, knowing her shame.

Sandy hurries along, not daring to contemplate what the procedure will involve and whether the implements will be hygienic. Abortion is a word overheard but never talked about and not allowed in law. *This is something I need to do. I just want to be un-pregnant, despite the risks and it will be hell,* but her gut twists and pleads to turn around, go home and phone Jasper—the other option.

She passes a couple of children sitting on a wall swinging their legs like pendulums against the bricks. The house is in a row of red-brick up-and-downers; two rooms upstairs and two downstairs. Lace curtains twitch. She crosses the cobbles and slows her pace. She goes through a dark alley to a gate at the rear. A window is patched up with what looks like old corsets around the frame and next to it is a door with faded blue paint. She stops, her fisted hand in mid-air ready to knock. She can't do it. Conflicting emotions churn inside her. She can hear Jasper's voice at the end of the phone asking her to marry him and move to Manchester. She can hear her dad screaming at her mum that his daughter has brought shame on the family and neighbourhood. Nervous shivers take hold and her bold spirit melts. Fear rises like a high tide, ready to gush into something uncontrollable. She feels faint and collapses onto the damp bricks hugging her knees with competing arguments sword fighting in her head. The gate opens and a haggard woman as skinny as a stovepipe towers over her. Without speaking she offers a hand, helps her up and guides her into a dingy kitchen. It's steamy and overheated and smells of boiled greens.

Gwen glares at her. 'Who sent you?'

'A man in the pub.'

Gwen is jumpy and fiddles with the black straps of her shabby dress. 'Nobody's followed you here?'

'No.'

Gwen makes no secret of the body-scan to appraise Sandy's physical condition— and her summary of Sandy's financial status. She snaps into business mode.

'How much you got?'

'How much do you charge?'

'Fifty quid take it or leave it.'

'I don't have anywhere near that.' Fresh tears prick as she thinks about the Greyhound bus tour through Canada.

Gwen lowers her voice, her face cold. 'It's not an easy procedure and we're dodging the law. A qualified doctor performs the operation but you'll be blindfolded and taken by car to the location. Everything's sterilised. It's done properly. No crochet hooks, knitting needles, poisons or quinine. He knows what he's doing.'

'But the money.' Her voice trails off.

KIRSTEN'S WAITING for her up the road, leaning against a wall smoking a fag.

'Don't do it Sand. Please.'

'I haven't got enough money. Don't suppose you could lend me some?'

'If I had some money don't you think I'd be giving it to my mam for food? We're bloody broke,' Kirsten screams.

'I don't know what I'm going to do.'

'Have it adopted, track the father down, use a feather; look I don't know. Getting rid of it though. It's dangerous. It's not like syringing wax out of your ear.'

19

RONA

St. Agnes' Mother and Baby Home is run by a religious order and only takes unmarried mothers. It is next to a large teaching hospital. Straightforward births are delivered there but most of the time women are transferred to the hospital a few streets away, where a doctor is on hand to assist in the delivery. Rona works between the home and the hospital and she is often called out to deliver babies at home.

She's aware that there are lots of unmarried mothers who birth and raise their illegitimate children, but she's only come across this situation a few times in Blackpool. Most of the babies she's delivered are to married women. She understands the stigma and shame attached to extra-marital pregnancy and how such homes provide shelter for these mothers as they undergo their confinement and often the adoption of their newborn.

The mothers come to the home six weeks before their due date through to six weeks after the baby is born. They are about eighteen mothers living here at any time.

It's her third day and she has an appointment to meet with Dr Gerard who is responsible for the home. He wants to discuss the patients with her. He works between the home and the hospital. Dressed in her new uniform, she raps at his door.

'Come in.'

The doctor sits behind a mountain of paper and files. His white coat is crumpled. He looks overworked and a layer of stubble, a whiff of bad breath and tousled hair tells her that he's worked a long day and needs a break.

He doesn't shake her hand or smile and his manners are brusque as he indicates a chair for her to sit on. She knows that he isn't the caring doctor she is used to in Blackpool. She can't imagine what his bedside manner would be like. Mothers need caring, kind faces. He wouldn't be sympathetic.

'One moment Nurse. I need to make a call.'

He stubs out his cigarette in an ashtray as he picks up the Bakelite telephone and plays with the cord as he dials. It takes a while for the call to connect.

'More doctors smoke Camel than any other cigarette,' she reads on a poster as she waits and listens to the conversation. Another poster advertises some new pills from Germany. 'The complete sedative which is safe at night. Safe for infants, the elderly, mothers-to-be and patients under severe emotional stress.' Maybe she would get a prescription to help her sleep and take her mind off trying to get pregnant.

'We've had a couple of babies born with deformities, but I'm not unduly worried,' the doctor says into the mouthpiece. 'When I looked at the records of both mothers I found that they had a history of miscarriage before they were able to carry to full term. I concluded that they had a hereditary disease in the family although I'm not sure what it could have been.'

The doctor listens and says, 'Well keep in touch. I wouldn't tell anyone in your hospital your findings just yet, but it looks likely that the deformities in your region could be related to the atomic reactor being close by and the gas plants. It's beyond your control. Probably just a fluke. I don't think there's cause for worry at this stage. In any given cohort there will be babies born with handicaps.'

The doctor finishes the call. He looks exhausted, as if he is mulling over a dilemma. 'Sorry about that. I had to call a doctor friend in Australia. It's taken me most of the morning to get through. I saw you looking at the poster.'

'It's just what I could do with. Sometimes I can't sleep. It's difficult to unwind after a long shift.'

'Take some. I can give you a prescription. It's a marvellous drug and very safe. It's massive in Germany. Sales have rocketed over there.'

'What's the active ingredient in this wonder drug?'

'Thalidomide. It's safe for pregnant and nursing mothers too. Cures morning sickness and sleep problems. You can recommend it to your patients.'

'I try not to give sleeping pills or tranquillisers to mothers-to-be.'

'Why ever not?'

'I've always thought the only therapy that should be applied in pregnancy would be to deal with the threat to the mother or baby's life.'

'That's antiquated thinking. The modern way is to make gestation as manageable as possible. Thalidomide is perfectly safe. That's the great thing about it. It's been available in Germany for a long time and the company that produces it over here, the drinks company Distillers have tested its toxicity on rats for four weeks and there were no ill effects.'

'But what about if it passes through the mother's bloodstream? I'd rather be cautious. I don't recommend anything. Call me old fashioned.'

'Yes, you are.' He gives a sarcastic laugh. 'It can't pass through the placental membrane to reach the child in the womb.'

Rona doesn't like the doctor's tone. He's a know-all, but who is she? She's a lowly nurse. He has years of medical training and knows what he is talking about.

RONA SETTLES INTO A ROUTINE. She takes the bus to work most days or walks part of the way and then catches the bus. She would like to cycle but it isn't possible to keep her bike in the flat, with trudging it up the stairs when the lift has broken.

She loves the hustle and bustle of London and looks forward to free time with Bill ambling round the West End, drinking coffee in a cafe, browsing round Foyles bookshop and the large stores like Selfridges or Hamleys looking at toys she longs to buy. It is a city for the rich and poor. She loves the contrasts. From bankers and financiers in top hats and long coats striding along with tall umbrellas to men in caps and donkey jackets delivering coal in carts. Street performers play the violin at the entrance to the tube, with a hat on the ground to collect coins. Life is still strongly influenced by the war. Boys fight mock battles in the streets, wearing old army clothing and their fathers settle by the fire to regale stories of war, while their grandfathers remember further back in time to the Great War, when things were different and people thought it would be the war to end all wars.

The legacy of war is everywhere. There are bomb sites, un-repaired houses and temporary pre-fabs, but a new life is being carved. The city is changing and Rona loves watching the transformation. Everybody is working hard to make the city a better, more modern place to live in and there are good prospects.

Rona finds it hard to get to know Dr Gerard. He is stand-offish but she suspects it's because he works hard and is rushed off his feet. He doesn't engage in idle chat and pleasantries but the other staff are warm and friendly. She's surprised to see that he's married. She doesn't imagine him married. There isn't a look of contentment in his face that she's seen so often in other married men. Much of the time he's on edge. And when his wife arrives to bring him sandwiches in greaseproof paper one day she's startled.

A beautiful blonde lady dressed in a pink twin set with pearls around her neck stops Rona in the corridor. 'Excuse me Nurse. Is Doctor Gerard busy?'

'I can find out for you. May I ask your name?'

The lady chuckles and beams at Rona. 'I'm his wife.' She extends a hand and Rona shakes it. 'I'm Carol.'

If Rona had matched Doctor Gerard with anybody she wouldn't have matched him with Carol. She isn't the type of woman Rona sees him with. She is far too stylish and hardly a great match for a man who looks unkempt, has bad breath and works all hours. There's something superior about her that makes Rona feel intimidated. She smells of roses, has rouged lips and is heavily made up.

20

SANDY

The sickness has settled and Sandy doesn't need to take more Distaval. Popping a pill to get rid of morning sickness had been so easy, a miracle cure for a ghastly illness. If only she could take a tablet to induce an abortion, her problems would be over and she'd be on track with her life.

Her mum orbits the kitchen cupboards. She picks up her spoon to eat her cornflakes. Sandy hasn't returned to Gwen's house. There's no point. There has been no internal struggle, she simply doesn't have the money. She's considered throwing herself down the stairs, drinking a bottle of gin and taking a knitting needle to bed but she can't bring herself to do any of these things. It's too horrible and could leave her physically damaged and, for Sandy, keeping a perfect body means everything. It's a dilemma: internal scars or weight gain and stretch marks.

Her dad polishes his shoes on a newspaper with his back to her. He's given her the cold treatment since he found out and it's as if she doesn't exist. Breakfast is filled with his stock-market babble and pension forecasts and her mother nods to his every word. She feeds cutlery into a drawer from a tea towel.

'When are you heading off?' he asks Sandy's mum, sailing his black shoe through the air as he speaks.

'Where are you going?' Sandy asks.

'I'm taking you down to Brighton to that hotel. You'll work there until six weeks before it's due, then they'll send you to a mother-and-baby home. You'll stay there for another six weeks after it's born, then it'll be adopted.' She speaks in a matter-of-fact tone and doesn't ask for Sandy's thoughts. Her opinion is irrelevant. Her body has been hijacked by her parents who are filled with shame and disappointment and want their daughter spirited away. Sandy isn't in a position to protest.

'But, Dad, I can't scrub floors. I'll ruin my knees and my nails. I won't get another modelling contract,' she whines to her dad, addressing his shoes.

An ashen tone streaks his face, the shame taking its toll. 'If she won't go to the hotel for naughty girls in England she can apply to go to Australia.' Sandy's heart leaps at the thought of foreign travel, but sinks when he finishes his sentence. 'And marry a lonely sheep farmer willing to take on someone else's bastard.'

Sandy is used to getting her own way with her dad. But her pregnancy has changed everything. His attitude is dismissive and she wonders how long he's going to keep it up.

'She'll soon show, so I want her out of my house now and if she decides to keep the -' he nods at her belly - 'she's not to come home.'

'A decent, deserving couple will bring it up,' her mother snaps, as though this is her own personal tragedy.

21

RONA

Rona has long dreamt of living in a vertical city in a high-rise tower block, with a garden in the sky and large, open, communal grounds. They move into a rented flat in a twenty-floor block, which is a contrast to the Victorian semi in Blackpool. Stepping inside the flat for the first time she's overwhelmed by the modern feel. It's airy and spacious with bright white walls, large picture windows and a shallow balcony.

'This is super,' she gasps spinning round, glancing out over the sugar-coated rooftops, with arms in the air like an excited child on a sandy beach. There's no comparison to their dreary, dark terraced house in Blackpool. The flat is refined and has all the mod cons they need: a bathroom, a refrigerator and a washing machine tucked under the counter. On laundry day she wheels it out and hooks it up to the tap. She loves the novelty of it all.

'It smells different to home,' Bill says.

'This is home now. It must be the smell of central heating.'

'I preferred our coal fire.'

'But what a lovely place this is.' Rona spins round with her arms wide. 'Fitted carpets, a tin opener fixed to the wall, double glazing so the sound of the traffic doesn't disturb us and it keeps the heat in. I wouldn't go back to that semi in Blackpool if you paid me.'

Bill looks wounded. 'That was my granddad's house. It was good enough for him.'

'I suppose we've got to go back there, one day, but let's enjoy this for now.'

NEW RECIPES CREEP into their lives as they experiment with the ideas Rona cuts out of magazines. They swap Tuesday's toad in the hole for chicken curry and Friday's shepherd's pie for cold meats with a glass of German Blue Nun wine, the height of sophistication. And with all of this vibrancy and change of life-style transforming their mundane existence Rona believes that she will fall pregnant soon and without a pub just around the corner or a shed at the end of the garden to escape to, Bill spends more of his time with her.

RONA LOVES the flat but is often away on night duty either at the hospital or the nursing home. At the nursing home when it is quiet she sleeps in a box room at the top of the house from midnight until five o' clock when the babies need feeding and changing. The room is basic with bare floorboards. It has a bed with a thin uncomfortable mattress and a jug and pitcher with a bar of soap. If a woman goes into labour they knock on a hatch door, behind Rona's bed, which opens into the dormitory.

Rona finds it hard to sleep when she's away from home. She misses Bill's snoring and when it's the time of the month to conceive, anxiety steps up a gear as she realises it's a missed opportunity. Fear at never becoming a mother and frustration at not being able to control the circumstances collaborate to give her a thumping headache.

Sleep refuses to come. The glow of the moon shines through the thin curtains. She lies awake in fruitless pursuit of sleep, listening to the creaks and groans of the house. She sits up and slips on her dressing gown, eases slippers on and goes downstairs to make a cup of Ovaltine. At the bottom of the stairs she can see the glow of light coming from the night nursery where the new babies sleep in rows of metal cots. No longer needing a drink all she wants is to hold one of the babies and inhale the delicious scent of it.

She opens the door, hit by a smell of powder and warm milk. The night attendant is pacing up and down with a fractious baby in her arms tightly swaddled in a sheet.

'So beautiful and tiny.' Rona smiles and gives the baby a kiss on its forehead.

'It was born a few hours ago next door, in the hospital.'

'Boy or girl?'

The nurse hesitates, pity on her face. 'It's another one of those babies,' she says lowering her voice.

'What do you mean?'

'She's got no limbs. The poor mite.'

'Does the mother know?'

'She needs to recover before we can tell her. She's heavily sedated.'

'Oh gosh. It's going to be a dreadful shock. She'll blame herself, for sure. The parents always do, especially the mums.'

'It's not the mother's fault. Nobody knows what's causing these deformities. It could be something in the air, or in the water.'

'The doctor thinks that something in household use is to blame.'

'I expect the doctor will ask the mother lots of questions about her routine during the pregnancy, diet, a food she ate more than usual. We'll have to discuss the options with the parents. The best place for it is an institution. She's going to need a lot of specialised care.'

Rona is hit by a wave of anxiety, for the parents and baby. 'They might want to keep her.'

'They'd be mad if they do. No parent's going to want to be saddled with the burden.' She sniffs and puts the baby in its cot.

'Can I hold her?'

The nurse nods at the cot.

The baby stirs, opening her grey eyes and snuffles.

Rona unwraps the baby as if she's uncovering food that's gone off, unsure what to expect. Her heart slams in her chest as she claps a hand to her mouth. Tears prick her eyes. With no arms she has flipper appendages at the shoulder and has no legs but feet attached to the hip. Rona counts the baby's fingers. She has missing thumbs. The ground shifts under her feet and she leans on the cot bars to steady herself. 'She's a mess, poor soul.'

The nurse is folding blankets. 'Do you want to come into the kitchen for a cuppa?'

'There's something you can't help loving about her.' Rona smiles at the nurse. 'Yes a cuppa would be nice.'

'We'll leave it as long as we can before breaking the news to the parents.'

They sit by the Aga in the kitchen with a pot of tea brewing and hot buttered toast.

'Apparently, according to the midwife caring for the mother,' the nurse says, 'she felt different throughout the pregnancy to how she felt with her other pregnancies. The baby didn't move. She was offered an X-ray but turned it down.'

'She's got other children?' Rona is alarmed.

'This is her fifth baby.'

'She's going to struggle.'

'She won't be able to take her home. We've already established that. And besides, it wouldn't be fair on the siblings.'

'I don't see why she can't take her home.'

Rona gets the impression that she's said something absurd.

'Do you have children?'

'No. What's that got to do with it?'

'I can tell.'

'The parents will love her just as much as their other children.'

'These situations are never that simple. I know what the doctor will tell them.'

Rona puts her cup on the saucer, intrigued. 'What's that?'

'To forget about the damaged goods that can't be fixed, go away and try again for a healthy replacement. They'll soon get over it.'

'You make her sound like an old car. That's disgraceful.'

The nurse shrugs and pours herself another cup of tea. 'When there isn't enough money to go round—that's life love.'

RONA IS ASSIGNED to work on the ward with the mother of the deformed baby.

She's sitting up in bed having been under sedation for two days. 'Can I see my baby? Nobody will tell me anything,' she pleads.

Rona feels a pop of anger for the way the mother is being treated. She has a right to know what's going on but the doctor and his team are unskilled in handling difficult situations and lack the sensitivity to understand the mother's feelings.

Rona takes a deep breath, sits down beside her and musters the courage to break the news. When she's finished she pats her hand and waits for it to take it in. Her words are like arrows to the chest.

The mother has a blank expression on her face. 'I knew

something was wrong. There was a strained silence. Nobody would tell me anything. They rolled her in a towel and took her away.'

'I'm sorry. She needed to be checked and you needed to sleep.'

Her bottom lip quivers and her face is red. Rona thinks she's about to cry but she blows her nose. 'Bring her to me. What are you waiting for? I want to see my baby.'

'You'll probably want to discuss your options with the doctor?'

The mother frowned. 'Options?'

'Well, yes. What will happen next. There are places where...'

'My baby's coming home. She's not going to be thrown in some institution if that's what you're thinking. She belongs with her family and we'll manage well thank you very much.'

22

SANDY

Sandy listens to the snoring girls in adjacent beds in the damp dark basement. She reflects on the irony of her current situation that began in a hotel in Brighton similar to this one. A simple act of bedroom pleasure and the mistake of not taking any precautions turned into a disaster, destroyed her relationship with her parents, her career and her body. There's nothing she can do about it, except wait until it's over and the baby is adopted. Her mother has rattled on about adoption. 'It's best for baby and best for you,' was her mantra. Her mum made it clear that keeping the baby wasn't an option. 'Don't think you can bring it home,' and 'we're not going to support you,' and 'once it's adopted, I don't want to hear of it again.' She doesn't want to keep it anyway. Her mother didn't bother to say goodbye, her mood was sombre and she hadn't offered a reassuring arm around Sandy's shoulder. She was keen to get away from what her daughter had become.

A crack of light seeps through the only window in the room, illuminating a beetle scuttling into the darkness. Sandy would never have chosen to work in a hotel. The pay is rubbish, the work back breaking and the hours long. She's broken four nails and her hands, after plunging in buckets of hot bleachy water are cracked and aged. It wouldn't have been so bad if she'd been able to put away some money. But the girls worked at the hotel in return for food and lodgings and a small pay packet.

It's a busy time at the hotel as they approach Christmas. More guests arrive and all the rooms will be filled. It means tons of laundry and washing up. The pregnant girls aren't allowed in the dining room, reception area or communal places where they would be seen by the guests. They work in the basement area where it's hot and airless. They are only allowed out of the hotel on one afternoon a week and only if they are dressed in a big duffle coat, hiding their bump and their shame under layers of heavy wool. They also have to wear a scarf over their heads, to prevent recognition and the manager insists they wear a Woolworth's wedding ring during their employment.

'I WANT to see you on your hands and knees where you belong.'

Caught in the act Sandy puts the mop down. Mrs Buxton latches her chubby hands onto her hips as she shifts her weight from side to side impatiently. A satanic flash of her eyes cowers Sandy into the corner. Mrs Buxton is in charge and is loathed. She gets sadistic pleasure from making their work more difficult than it needs to be.

'How dare you use a mop? Your place is on the floor.'

Sandy examines her calloused hands and considers challenging her but thinks better of it. She picks up the scrubbing brush and kneels on the hard cold floor, the weight of the baby pressing against her internal organs. As soon as Mrs Buxton turns her back, marching up the back stairs to the ground floor Sandy raises her eyes to the girl cleaning the staircase and tuts. It's like a prison camp. They're forbidden from chatting but speak in whispers while they dress. Days pass in silence, only broken by the clank of the piping, the sound of the old-fashioned stove and the drips of water smacking a tune into the chipped Belfast sink where plates pile.

On Sundays the girls are marched to church to ask for God's forgiveness, hiding their shame under hats. They are lined up, penitent in the front row. 'So that God's message,' Mrs Buxton orders 'can be heard loud and clear.'

Sandy doesn't understand what the vicar is talking about. She smiles sweetly at him and tries to look sinless and interested in being a better human being but she finds the stained-glass windows more interesting, watching splinters of purple, scarlet and green form kaleidoscope patterns across the flagstones. It's easy to drift and imagine herself parading up the aisle in a skimpy bikini as the worshippers gaze on, marvelling at her slender legs and bosom.

The vicar's words rumble, like claps of thunder and Sandy watches beads of sweat make pathways across his furrowed brow and spittle froth at the corners of his mouth.

He looks at the girls in the front row, as if delivering a message specially for them. 'Did you know that wrongdoers will not inherit the kingdom of God? Do not be deceived: neither the sexually immoral nor idolaters, nor adulterers, nor men who have sex with men, nor thieves, nor the greedy, nor drunkards, nor slanderers, nor swindlers, will inherit the kingdom of God.'

His next words jab the finger of God firmly at her. 'Put to death, therefore, whatever belongs to your earthly nature: the sexual immorality, impurity, lust, evil desires and greed.'

Sandy stares at the gold cross on the altar and wonders whether the vicar is a sinner. Under the swathes of black robe, he can be anything he wants to be. He is young for a vicar and has a welcoming face and topaz eyes that glitter with the colours of the stain-glass. Sandy might have found him hard to resist if she was in a hotel bedroom with him. There is a distinct absence of Brylcreem, Old Spice and Palmolive soap. He smells the same as the church, with hints of tapestry, candles and old parchment. He has standards— vicar accredited standards — and won't let himself wander off course and away from the homely shepherd's pie dinners of his buxom wife. He'd never disgrace the Church by being found in a hotel bedroom with a floozy. Debauchery isn't on his menu.

In the churchyard, after Mass, the girls are allowed to wander between the grave stones while Mrs Buxton joins the other worshippers who are all worthy of tea and digestives and fruit cake—if there are any left over from the Saturday church fair.

The girls sit on a bench where they can't be seen chatting and stare at the Elsies, Adas and Harolds, long departed and remembered only by buttercups and weeds that grow across their names, lichen eating into who they used to be.

'What happens to dead babies? Where do they go?' one of the girls asks.

'Heaven like everyone else,' Sandy answers.

'I didn't mean that. How do they dispose of the baby?'

'They get burned in the incinerator.'

'That's horrible.'

'Same as bloodied rags and dirty incontinence pads. It's all environmental waste.' Sandy doesn't care what happens to dead babies. Does it matter? A dead baby will soon be forgotten. It isn't like a dead child or an older person who's lived a life.

'Don't they have a funeral and get buried?'

'No,' Sandy laughs and looks at the girl as if she's stupid.

'I've heard they get put into the coffin with a woman,' another girl adds.

'What woman?' asks Sandy.

'Any woman that happens to have died around the same time.'

How sad, for the living mother, with her baby six feet under, resting next to some old woman who has no connection to the family. Much better to get rid of it in a hospital incinerator; that way you can erase the memory clean and fast.

Fingers of sunlight cast shadows across the gravestones and sodden ground. Sandy thinks about nine months in the womb followed by a feast for maggots. It's a difficult thought to grapple with. And if God was real He wouldn't act in cruel ways, creating unwanted babies and ruining lives.

'The Lord your God is in your midst, a mighty one who will save.' They are the words on a gravestone. Sandy doesn't feel saved. She feels very alone. Where is God in her hour of need? Who is God?

23

RONA

The summer of 1960 is pleasant but not in the league of the never-ending exceptional sunshine and warmth of the previous year which brought better weather each day right through to October.

Clouds brush stroke across a deep blue sky as Rona waits for a Ford Anglia to pass. The sound of the Everly Brothers drifts from open windows. She darts across the road to the phone box for her weekly chat with her mum. She dreads this ritual, her mum singing her sister's praises and prattling about her grandchildren's antics and the milestones they've achieved. The conversations reinforce how inadequate she feels as her mother blasts praise on her sisters' maternal talents and their ability to juggle pie making and nappy washing, weeding the garden and darning their husbands' socks and always looking gay and fresh at the end of the day. She's sure her sisters could bake a cake, iron a shirt, breastfeed a child and suck their husband's cock all at the same time.

Rona senses criticism lurking behind every comment. 'I don't know how you can stand living in a flat. How's the cat supposed to go for a wee?' Where do you hang the washing?' Each rebuke is followed by an almighty tut. 'I couldn't do without a wirly in the garden.' And in her sanctimonious tone she asks, 'I hope you don't have black people living in your block of flats?' Rona doesn't mention the Caribbean music floating from the flat above, keeping them awake at night and the smell of spicy food wafting along the hallway. 'You mark my words, it'll all end in disaster. The darkies are taking over and don't think they can't put a curse on you through the floorboards.'

But the worst snipes were about their lack of children. 'You should be thinking about having a baby by now. You'll be over the hill soon and it'll be too late. You'll have to get a move on,' and 'if you don't hurry up and have a kiddy its cousins will be too old to play with it.' When Rona skirts around the jibes, making excuses and claiming to be more interested in her career than children she's accused of being selfish and self-centred. 'Old age will be a lonely place without children to look after you.'

Her words are like gunshot blasting through her brain and designed to hurt. Doesn't Rona already know all of this? They are thoughts that whirl in her mind every night as she lies awake. Her mother's rubbing salt into the wound and enjoys hurting her. Worn down she's about to confess that they have been trying for years but to no avail, but the words stick in her mouth like toffee. She doesn't want her sisters to know how hard the past few years have been. They wouldn't be sympathetic to her plight. They've never shown any sympathy to her misfortune. Rona remembers their laughter when the bullies tormented her at school. They'd treated it as a joke but it had been a nightmare for Rona. She'd dreaded going to school.

She looks at the sky and feels something shift in her brain, a wall of tolerance is breached.

'I'm pregnant,' she tells her mother.

It is silent at the other end. 'Really?' She can hear hesitation and disbelief in her mother's voice.

Rona can't retract it. The words are out. She'll look stupid and childish. 'Don't sound so surprised.'

'How far gone?' Celia asks in a flat voice. She's unmoved and her tone contains none of the elation from when her sisters made the same announcement.

'Three months.' Rona bites her lip to stop herself spilling more lies. *How am I going to get out of this one?*

'Was it planned?'

'Of course it was planned.'

'I just wondered... because of the flat.'

'What about the flat?'

'It's unsuitable.'

'There are lifts.'

'Oh.' She can hear Celia scrolling her mind for more negative remarks. 'Well that is a surprise,' she adds in the same tone, unable to fake excitement.

The conversation jumps to the weather and jolts awkwardly as Rona wonders how to bring it to a swift end so that she can get home. Eventually she ends the call, promising to ring her mother in a week and walks across the green and under an imposing cedar tree, in front of the flats.

The block stretches into the sky like a giant grey blob on the landscape, emphasising the frailty of the small prefabs that nestle beside it. Built after the war as temporary accommodation on bomb sites the prefabs are being pulled down to make way for more towers. Makeshift washing lines hang from some of the balconies and a man in a string vest is smoking, looking out over London. Music drifts from open windows and floats across the lawn into the mounting heat. She makes her way towards the concrete stairs, oblivious to the new graffiti scrib-

bled across the walls. She wrinkles her nose at the overpowering smell of urine in the hallway. The flats were pleasant
when they'd moved in but there are people who seem determined to turn it into a horrible place to live. The tears that
she'd held back swell in her throat as she thinks about Bill. She
will have to tell him about the lie and ask him what she
should do.

The lifts are out of order so she pants to the tenth floor, her
leg muscles stiffening with each step. Bill is in front of their
black-and-white TV watching Grandstand with a pint of ale
resting on the arm of his chair. The match is well into the
second half. 'Everything all right, love?'

'No, not really.'

He forces himself out of his chair. 'Want me to fetch you a
drink?'

Rona is more distracted than she usually is after the painful
chats with her mother. 'No, no. Well, actually... yes. Maybe I
will.'

'Gin, ale?'

'Gin please. Make it a double.'

'Don't follow me into the kitchen. You know I have to take
in the details of these spats between you and your mother
slowly, or I don't get them. You just sit-down, love, and take it
easy and shout if they score a goal.'

By the time he brings in her drink, she's switched off the
television. Bad luck on him. But he might catch the last few
minutes of the game if she calms down and doesn't cry. She
knows she's being selfish but doesn't feel in a nice mood.

'So,' he puts the glass into Rona's hand and wraps her
fingers round it, 'what has your mother said now?'

'It's not so much what she said as what I said.'

'Oh dear, that doesn't sound good.'

'I told her I was pregnant.'

'What?' Bill stares at her dumbfounded. 'But you're not. Why the hell did you lie?'

'She was off on one, crowing. Bloody Rachel and Amy. Aren't they amazing mothers?'

Rona's mouth twitches as she shrieks and her face is red and hot. 'Blah, blah, blah, I'm sick of it. I can't help it. I've had it up to here, Bill.'

'I can see that, but lying about something like that is bonkers. You're going to have to tell her you've had a miscarriage.'

'I can't do that. That would be the ultimate failure in my mother's eyes.'

'Or admit that you told a lie.'

'I can't do that either.' Rona's head is a tangled mess. Tears build behind her eyes. 'She'd want to know why. I'd have to tell her everything and listen for the smirk in her voice.'

'Is she really going to be that horrible?'

'You know what she's like. Anyway she's busy packing to move house. Her mind will be on other things by next week.'

Bill gets up to turn the TV on, his mind returning to the match. He's good at switching off when things get tricky with her mother.

'We'll talk about it later, when you've calmed down.' His eyes are fixed on the TV and she knows it's pointless discussing it. As far as he's concerned she's rejected his suggestions and that's the end of the matter. There isn't much more he can say. The problem is hers and she'll have to find a way of wriggling out of the mess.

The following week she doesn't bother to call her mother, hoping that if she leaves it a fortnight before talking, it will diffuse the situation. Rona is spiralling into her lie as she elaborates her story, rather than telling her that she's had a miscarriage since they last spoke. Week by week she tells her all the different symptoms. Being a midwife, she's clued up on pregnancy progression, taking her mother from vivid descriptions of morning sickness and back ache, to heartburn. As the weeks go on the lie becomes a fantasy. As she talks the lie morphs into reality and she feels as if she is pregnant. Without consciously planning a change in her diet she finds herself eating for two, taking comfort in glasses of milk to build her strength and eating too many homely puddings. She nurses a larger belly, standing in the phone box clutching the phone. She doesn't dream of becoming pregnant but lives in a bubble world where she pretends she is.

'You're going to have to tell her at some point,' Bill says over fish and chips.

'And what if I don't?'

'She'll find out.'

He takes her hand and squeezes it.

'We can always adopt and then she'd think it was ours.'

'You know what I think about adopting. I'm not bringing up another man's baby.'

Defiance crosses his face. She stabs a chip with added force.

She leaves him to finish his supper in silence. 'I'm going out for a walk,' she standing in the kitchen doorway.

'Are you alright, love? Look I'm sorry. I've failed you.'

'No, you can't help how you feel.' She smiles, but it's strained. This is about keeping up marital appearances, even though inside she's wriggling in pain. 'I still love you,' she adds, but the words feel hollow and meaningless, under these tough circumstances.

'Do you want me to join you? It's a nice evening.'

When Rona isn't working and the weather is good they take an evening stroll by the Grand Union Canal calling in to a pub for a quick pint.

'If you don't mind I'd rather be alone.' Her words ebb into a sad silence.

He dips his head to the evening paper spread across the

kitchen table. Why can't he say something to make everything alright? There is a solution and he is determined not to consider it. It's as if they are trapped in a deep mineshaft, neither of them knowing how to claw their way up. Her mouth gapes in silent frustration. She picks up a cotton scarf, ties it round her hair, and heads for the door.

She walks along the canal towpath and she shoves her hands in her cardigan pocket as she falls into a brisk stride. It's a quiet evening and the only discernible movement is the gentle breeze swishing through the trees. She stops to pick red campion, daisies and dog rose and she looks at yellow iris growing by the water's edge. She finds a bench and sits with her eyes closed, looking into the warm evening sun filtering through the trees. After another busy day on the ward this is bliss. Further along the path she hears children on the other side of the canal throwing stones into the water and laughing. They are throwing stones at the ducks and her instant reaction is to shout at them but her chest feels heavy and it seems too much of an effort to confront them. She gets up, the bench creaking and heads in their direction, scowling at them as she passes on the far side of the water.

She follows the path in the direction of the pub. There's a shape by the lock but drawing closer she realises it's a courting couple kissing. She misses a stinging nettle as it brushes against her foot and winces in pain. They part; he's playing with her hair. A pang of sadness tugs at her. This couple look as if they have everything ahead of them. There's something about the man that she recognises and she racks her mind trying to think who he is. It's somebody at the hospital, it has to be. She knows him and the recognition is like a punch in the gut. It's Doctor Gerard. The woman is one of the receptionists at the nursing home, a short woman with a thick waist and a large bottom. She's wearing tight slacks. He's stroking her bottom— obviously a bottom man. She has striking brown hair and it gleams in the evening light.

Her mother had an affair years ago and the hurting memories flood her mind. A wave of nausea crashes over her. There's no doubt in Rona's mind that Celia caused her father's death. There was an atmosphere between them and whispered arguing, doors slammed out of sheer frustration. Her father told Rona and her sisters what was going on but then he regretted it and reassured them that he still loved their mother and would stand by her. He put up with her behaviour because of the shame and embarrassment it would cause him and because of his position at work. But something in him died from that point on. He was always ill, and then he battled cancer. Rona vowed never to behave as she had, to be loyal and adhere to her marriage vows. Cheating from anybody sickens her to the bone and stokes feelings of anger.

She levels with them on the other side of the lock and decides that she won't skulk past in the hope that they won't see her. She wants to catch their attention and embarrass them. She clonks down a set of stone steps. She is beside the doctor on the narrow path. At first he smiles in recognition but it's a smile that slides from his face like butter from hot toast. He whispers in Marion's ear. Marion, who is nuzzling her lover's neck looks at Rona, her relaxed face cementing into a grimace.

'This looks like a cosy stroll. Where's Carol?'

'Oh, ah she's at home.'

'She knows you're here together?'

The doctor steps forward, taking Rona's arm and guides her away from Marion. A flush creeps up his neck and his discomfort is palpable. 'It's not how it looks.'

'I can see exactly how it looks. And what has she got that your wife hasn't?'

'Don't make things difficult, Rona. You've got your job to think of.'

'Are you threatening me? Because I could go to the manager and report you.'

'You wouldn't do that.'

'What you're doing is wrong Doctor. Just end it. You've got a wife who loves you,' she hisses and yanks her arm away from his tight grip, lurching away in a hurry, her heart racing.

24

SANDY

It's nearly New Year, 1961. America will break relations with Cuba in three days time, spiralling the world into shock with fears of a nuclear war and the end of the world. The biggest party of the year will soon be underway, but not for Sandy... not this year, to her bitter disappointment. Sandy gets off the train at London Victoria and dissolves into a spill of other passengers heading for the tube and concourse where buses depart. The wind moans and rattles the windows of the bus and snowflakes dance the route to the home for unmarried mothers where she will have her baby. The snow globed bus travels through a festival of lights and happy people scattering from shops, with bags and smiles and memories of Christmas spent with loved ones.

The shops dribble into the premises of accountants, solicitors and architects with their Georgian fronts and brass plates, then fade into housing. The bus comes to a halt on a tree-lined avenue.

'They say it's haunted,' the driver chuckles as she clambers off, to stand outside high walls and in front of an imposing pair of wrought-iron gates. 'Used to be a lunatic asylum.'

The bus pulls away. The building overlooks a park and a war memorial. She buttons her coat against the cold and pushes the creaky gate. She can taste soot in the air mingled with snow. She heads along a path to a set of steps leading to wooden doors, pinned back, despite the elements, so that visitors can wander in. Spying Sandy through a window Matron emerges from office chores. She's a tall woman and her mean eyes carve into Sandy, sweeping over her like a lighthouse on a cliff top. She wears a stiff grey dress made of rough fabric, a starched white apron, crowned with a frilled meringue hat over grey hair.

'You must be Sandy. Come into my office. There's paperwork to sign so that when the time comes you're ready to hand over your baby for adoption. And do you have your maternity allowance?'

Signing away her unborn baby feels like a lead weight lifted from her shoulders. The matron marches ahead, pointing to various rooms en-route to the ward where Sandy will spend the next weeks. They pass the delivery suite where she will have the unwanted part of her insides ripped out. The place smells of untold stories and secrets, burned milk and scraped plates. The ripe scent of shame hides behind the fragrance of pine emanating from an austere Christmas tree in the day room.

Matron stops outside a room where chimneys of chromium commodes and a clatter of aluminium utensils gleam. A visitor passes by and smiles at Sandy in sympathy, bearing the customary bag of fruit and a knitted matinee coat.

'You will be expected to help with the day-to-day running of the home. Washing equipment, floors and helping out with laundry duties.'

Sandy groans at the thought of more laundry and scrubbing floors on knees with the pressure of the baby pressing against her ribs and bladder. All she wants to do is rest and preserve her energy.

Matron passes Sandy to the care of Nurse Rona who takes her into a side room to check the foetal heart rate, take urine and blood tests and check her blood pressure. The smell of disinfectant fills her nostrils. Rona, a tower of efficiency hides behind a clipboard of questions, her glasses resting on the bridge of her nose as she asks questions and ticks boxes.

'Do you have any questions?' Rona asks as she scrubs her hands with her back to Sandy.

It occurs to Sandy that she knows nothing about giving birth. She doesn't know what to expect. She's muddled along, through morning sickness, heartburn, craving foods she doesn't eat, feeling the baby flutter in her belly and getting more tired by the day. But she has no idea about labour pains and how they will be controlled and how long the labour will be. How will I even know that I'm in labour?

She detects a hint of accusation in the nurse's tone and in the way her smile is directed outward but not at Sandy.

'No.' She has no questions. None that she can ask. She put her trust in a man, for five minutes of pleasure. How dare this nurse sneer down at me? Doesn't she realise that every day I wake, reminded of my stupid mistake? I'm paying the price and if I could turn back the clock, I would. Sandy notices that she wears a wedding ring and reading between the lines imagines she lives by a high moral code; it's written in her demeanour.

25

RONA

Rona shifts in her chair, a dull ache in her lower back from the wooden slats. What was it about waiting rooms? She knows how her expectant mothers feel, she's tense and anxious. This is the third visit to the doctor in as many weeks. She was okay about the appointment before she got here but butterflies the size of blackbirds are crashing around in her tummy.

Bill wants her to cancel the appointment. 'You're not pregnant. They've done the test.' But he's wrong, the test is wrong, it has to be. She has all the symptoms and hallmarks of pregnancy are branded all over her: sore nipples, swollen breasts, nausea and her periods have stopped. It is obvious. Sometimes tests are wrong. God knows they've been trying long enough. And the weight. She's put on so much weight. Didn't that tell them something? Pushing unsteady fingers through her messy curls, she exhales through pursed lips. How much longer? I have to get back to work. They need me. We're short-staffed.

'Mrs Murphy? You can come through now.' She follows Doctor Edwards into his consulting room. He closes the door behind them. She perches on the edge of another uncomfortable chair, fighting to keep her hands steady. She grasps them firmly around her handbag and tries to keep still.

'Have you got the results?' She already knows the result. Her baby is due in February. She worked it out, plotted it in her diary. She knows the exact day that she conceived. She remembers it. Most of the time their lovemaking blurs into a haze, but not on this occasion. It felt special because this time it was baby making. They'd made love in the lounge on Bill's chair, *The Grove Family* chirruping from the TV in the corner. It was the best sex they'd had in ages and the following day — the same day she'd lied to her mother— her breasts felt tender.

The doctor leans across the desk and clasps his hands. Panic sears through Rona. She'll ask for a third test and another until the result is positive.

The doctor oozes sympathy. 'We have, and I'm sorry but it's still showing as negative. You aren't pregnant.'

His words hit like a punch. Her mind tells her to accept it. But her heart counters. 'It has to be wrong. Call it mother's instinct, or whatever you like but I know that I am pregnant. My periods have stopped, my breasts are sore, I feel sick, I've put on weight.' A rigid band of pain moves across her temple. She closes her eyes. *Every woman she knows can have babies. Why can't I?*

'A third test would still come back negative. I'm sorry Mrs Murphy, I really am.'

Rona isn't listening. Denial is her solace. She'll prove him wrong when the baby's born. He might be a doctor, but I'm a woman and I know my body. The doctor is still talking. It's one of those things, nobody's fault. Rona can tell it's what he says to every woman in this situation It's better if it isn't somebody's fault —not her's. She cries and the doctor pushes a box of tissues towards her.

'Maybe you're just very tired and overworked. I do understand. We both work in the NHS. The body can do all sorts of strange things when it's stressed.'

Her work is hard, but it always has been. Rona's long days are spent on overcrowded wards, pinning terry nappies, making bottles and sterilising bedpans. Her life is a succession of emergencies, successes and tragedies, a never-ending chain of actions that make the difference between life and death and it does bring stress.

'Have you considered taking some time off to rest? Or getting an easier job? I see that Chester's are advertising.'

'I can't do that. We need the money. And the mothers need me. I can't let them down.' Her passion for midwifery burns as bright as the day she started. She isn't about to chuck it in to work in Chesters.

The doctor sighs. She isn't making his job easy.

'Have you considered adoption?'

'Bill won't adopt. He doesn't want to bring up another man's child.'

Rona stares at the doctor and then at her distended abdomen. Okay, she's eaten too many cakes, but she is eating for two.

'Sometimes you have to accept God's plan.'

What is he saying? There will be no baby for her and Bill because that is God's plan? No pram pushing in the park, no school run, no happy family or everything she's ever wanted. And worst of all, her mother proved right—that she is useless and has married the wrong man? What a cruel God he is, if God exists at all.

Rona leaves the surgery. The sky is a scrubbed pigeon and it looks as though the heavens will open at any moment. She pulls her umbrella from her bag and wants to collapse on a bench and howl. But with a storm threatening, the first drop of rain hits her cheek and with head bowed she scampers down the steps and tumbles into the closest shop, Boots the Chemist.

She isn't sure how she ends up in the baby aisle at the milk powders and bottles. Her mind is miles away and her feet are glued to the floor, unaware of the woman standing beside her jabbering on.

She catches the tail end of what the woman is saying. 'All they do is feed, feed, feed, all day long. It's costing me a fortune.'

Rona turns. The woman is jigging a pram, calming her restless baby. She isn't sure if the woman is talking to her or any passer-by that will listen.

Rona can't think what to say. She's only fed other peoples' babies. She doesn't know what it's like to be responsible for another human being twenty-four hours a day.

'Oh yes, I guess they do,' Rona replies. On a good day she would have told the woman that she's a midwife and knows all about babies and how tiring motherhood is. She would have told her not to waste her money and given her the well-rehearsed patter about breast being best and to follow all the tips in *Dr Spock's Common Sense Book of Baby and Child Care*. But Rona isn't in the mood for helpful advice.

The woman smiles at Rona's belly. 'When's yours due?'

It's one of those awkward moments and normally Rona would feel insulted by the comment and answer 'I'm not, I'm just fat, thanks,' and watch the woman back out of the shop shame-faced. As icebreakers go it's a high risk one. Rona stares at her belly. She's wearing a high-waisted, pleated skirt, that's tight around the waist and without her stomach-gripping pants, everything is sagging. She's never had a washboard stomach but she can understand why others might assume she is pregnant.

'February.' She bites her lip, gearing to the next stage of her lie, as if it's a project in progress.

'Will you breast feed? I tried breast feeding but I ended up sore. He was latched on all day.'

'Bottle.' Rona doesn't know why she's said this. Given the choice she'd breast feed. She reaches up and takes a tin of Cow & Gate from the shelf. 'If it's good enough for royal babies it's good enough for mine.' She pats her belly and feeling bolder by the minute grabs a bottle and teat from the shelf below the powders.

'You know you can get a free sample of that don't you.' The mother nods at the tin.

'Thank you, yes, I'll fill out the coupon.'

Feeling a fraud Rona makes her way to the till, smoothing her skirt over her belly. Just because the doctor says I'm not pregnant, she thinks to herself, doesn't mean I'm not.

26

SANDY

Sandy's feet are ice blocks under the starchy sheet. She misses her hot water bottle, her dressing gown and a cup of sweet tea brought up by her mother every morning. The forty odd girls in the home are expected to get up at seven and carry out morning chores unless they are in their period of confinement.

Sandy has been in the home for two weeks and has sunk into depression, it's a lull in her life akin to convalescence and she can't psych herself to do much. To begin with she was restless and anxious for her parents to visit. She wanted to see familiar faces and restore a connection with the outside world. Other than her parents and Kirsten nobody knows about her condition and she wants it kept that way. Kirsten has been sworn to secrecy. She's told her close friends that she's travelling, to account for the time away. She's written to her parents, begging for them to visit and to bring Marmite and bananas, but she hasn't received a reply or a phone call. They have frozen her out of their lives as some of the other families have done. There are very few visitors, except for the occasional trickle on a Sunday afternoon.

She swivels out of the rickety iron bed, her feet connecting with the cold lino and sits for a few minutes admiring the stately garden with its two lakes, imposing cedar trees and lawn edged with dark and heavy rhododendrons. The view is one of the only pleasures of being in the home, but in January it's drab and monochromatic. Beyond the cedars, spindly tree limbs form tangled masses against a harsh sky. The other five girls in her room are dressing in silence, taking it in turns to wash in the sink.

It's Saturday and after the morning chores, they can go out for the afternoon or play bridge in the day room. Visitors are allowed on Saturday and Sunday afternoons. During the week they are expected to spend time in the day room knitting for their babies and if they don't know how they have to learn. Sandy hates knitting. Neither her mother nor her grandmother taught her. She doesn't have the patience. It's tedious and a pointless waste of time knitting clothes for a baby that is going to be adopted. They are expected to buy a brown box from the local newsagent out of their own money, decorate it with pretty paper and crafts and fill it with knitted garments as well as some terry nappies as a gift to the adopting parents.

'You'd better hurry up and learn to knit.' Sandy is struggling to cast on. The nun who teaches knitting is tutting at her efforts. Sandy blushes.

'Your mother is waiting in the visitors' room.'

Sandy doesn't know whether to be pleased or worried. She wasn't expecting her mother. She goes to the visitor's room and finds her mother at the window. She gives Sandy a watery smile and a brief perfunctory kiss on the cheek. A whiff of hot nylon stockings and heavy foundation conjures memories of home. Her mother removes her hat and unbuttons her coat, revealing a dress like a bus seat cover, it's the same type of ugly thing she wears every day of the year. Now that she's here Sandy isn't sure that she wants to see her and wishes she'd written first rather than arrive out of the blue. She sits as far from Sandy as she can, as if she is a disease.

The nun brings tea and biscuits.

'I can't stop long. I've got to ...' She pauses and it's clear that she's trying to think of an excuse not to stay.

'How's Dad?'

'He's fine. He's building a dressing table for our bedroom. He's been doing a lot of carpentry lately.' She smiles into her tea.

'Does he talk about me?'

'He says you're not to bring it...' and she nods towards Sandy's bump with distaste, 'home. You must do the responsible thing.' She sniffs. Sandy's mother is deeply ashamed of her and nothing is going to change that.

'I don't intend to. I can't wait until it's adopted then I can get my life back.'

Her mother stiffens. 'That's not very motherly. How did you become so callous?'

Sandy sighs. She can't win whatever she says, so she changes the subject.

'How long did it take you to get here?'

'It was a dreadful journey. The bus was late and there were too many stops.' She huffs and tells Sandy what she would have been doing on a Saturday afternoon rather than having to traipse 'halfway across London' for what she calls 'no good reason.'

They sit in silence drinking tea and fumbling for words.

Sandy is relieved when she says it's time to go. The atmosphere is suffocating. She opens her handbag, takes out a five-pound note and hands it to Sandy.

'That's all I've got. Buy yourself something nice and don't tell your dad.' She snaps her bag shut and walks to the door. Their shoes squeak on the lino in sync and her mother comes to a halt outside a room.

'Is that Mrs Jeffreys? And her daughter.'

'Who's Mrs Jeffreys?'

'The secretary of the Women's Institute and the winner of the prize turnip competition, three years in a row.' There is a glaze of triumph in her voice. Sandy watches a smirk dance on her mother's lips. 'Looks like her daughter's in the family way too. She kept that dirty secret quiet, after telling me how well her daughter was doing at teachers' college.'

'Come on Mum.'

Her mum scuttles down the path, as if she can't wait to get away. Sandy was wrong to think that a visit from her parents would be good and wished she hadn't bothered to write.

SANDY LIES in the dark listening to the crying. It comes from the bed in the corner. Lisa cries every night, clutching a teddy. She's only fourteen, a timid girl who walks with her face to the floor as if all life has been sucked out of her. None of the women know her circumstances, but there are rumours that her father has stolen her childhood. Her mother visited a few times, always with a stern, hard face as if she is ready to reprimand Lisa.

The oldest mother is Jennifer, she's forty-five and she pads over to Lisa's bed and slips under the covers to comfort her. She does this every night when she hears Lisa crying and takes responsibility for her like a mother. Jennifer is the mother hen, the matriarch, a wise woman. She's matter-of-fact but cuddly too and knows everything there is to know about pregnancy and childbirth because she's been through the ordeal twelve times. She has a keep-calm-and-carry-on approach, that served the nation well during the war; it's an approach that helps the women to focus on the difficult days ahead rather than wallowing in their self-pity.

'There, there, it's alright,' Jennifer's soothing whispers work on them all. An ethereal calm blankets the room before the whispering starts.

'I wish a knight on a white horse would come down to save baby and me,' Molly says into the darkness.

'Keep knitting,' Jennifer replies. 'That's the only thing you can do for baby. You can't provide what your child needs, but there is a couple out there who can.'

Sandy feels herself tensing with irritation at the crass remark. She refuses to knit. She has no connection with the baby growing inside her.

'Knitting? To hell with that. They can clothe the baby themselves. Nurse Rona and the others are wrong to encourage knitting. It's plain cruel to encourage something that's going to strengthen the mother and baby bond.'

Molly wants to keep her baby and her situation is unfair. Her boyfriend jilted her when he found out she was pregnant. Love couldn't survive their class divide. He comes from a wealthy family with strict moral standards and they were opposed to their son marrying down and threatened to disinherit him if he married Molly. They'd never liked her, especially when they found out her father was a foreman in a factory and hadn't encouraged the relationship. She was shocked when he didn't stand by her. She thought he'd rise above his status-obsessed parents and declare that he loved her and would put Molly first.

'It'll be hard whatever we do,' Jennifer says.

Jennifer has answers for everybody's situation, but a quickie with the milkman wasn't her finest hour, even by her own admission. Her husband has stuck by her though and visits every day with flowers or fruit—it's all front to show marital solidarity. But he isn't prepared to raise the child as his own, especially when he's already brought up twelve of his own.

Maggie stirs in the bed next to Sandy. Her baby is due any

day and she's suffering from back ache and heartburn. All five women in the ward are due in the next two weeks.

Maggie is cheerful for three in the morning, laughing her situation away with jokes, but she locks her sadness away in a box. 'There's nothing we can do to put the genie back in the bottle,' she chuckles. 'Next time I'll keep my legs shut.'

'I don't know how you can laugh about it,' Linda mutters from her bed. 'I shouldn't have done what I did, but giving my baby away is going to be the most painful thing I've ever done in my life.'

Lucy confesses her circumstances to the others. She had been looking after her sister's children while her sister was in hospital, when she ended up in bed with her brother-in-law. He blamed her for teasing him for weeks with her low-cut dresses and red lipstick. He told his wife that she'd led him astray. And he'd slated Lucy telling her she had wanted it more than he did. 'You were gagging for it.' But Lucy says he forced himself on her.

Sandy doesn't like the sentimental clap trap the women spout. Linda is the worst.

'You don't know how you're going to feel about the baby. You might feel differently once it's born.'

'You haven't got a clue. Once you look into baby's eyes you won't want to let it go. It's irrelevant that it wasn't planned. None of us wanted a baby. Most of the women that come here are innocent teenagers. We're not criminals. We're victims of men's predatory moves and broken promises and that's nothing new and it will never change. While there are men and women on this planet it will keep happening. You think it'll be easy to go back to your old life, knowing that your baby is out there? You won't ever forget it and you'll spend the rest of your life wondering and asking, "what if?"'

'With all of my babies I felt the same and just because I've got to hand this one over it's not going to be any different,'

Jennifer confesses. 'Except that it is different. It will be torture. It's going against nature. Babies are supposed to stay with their mothers. It's going to be humiliating, gut wrenching even and I've no idea how I'll cope. I remember the feeling and knowing that the pain was worthwhile. I remember the clean nightie, a wash and brush up and a cup of tea. It was the feeling of achievement. I'd been through something special and yet it was the most natural process in the world.'

'I wanted to get rid of it,' Sandy says with conviction, 'and if somebody came along with a magic wand, I'd still choose to get rid. You're not going to make me feel guilty because I don't have any feelings for it. I can't help how I feel and when it's born, I won't feel any different.'

Sandy huffs and turns over. Conversations like this only happen at night when everybody lies awake fretting into the noises of the house. In the daytime they talk about irrelevant things to the constant clicking of knitting needles around the small fireplace giving out a cheery glow against the strained atmosphere. Nobody discusses the details of what will happen during childbirth, but in the middle of the night somebody will ask Jennifer a question because she's the only one who's been through it before.

It bothers Sandy that she feels indifferent towards the baby growing inside her when the other women feel so much love, but she isn't going to tell them. She's witnessed their screams when couples come to pick up their babies and the anguish they'll carry with them for years. Is she callous just because she's consumed with thoughts of how the pregnancy has destroyed her future? Will it hit her like a tornado, when she hears the first cries of the baby? And if she doesn't feel anything at all will it come home to roost years later?

27

RONA

'I can't end it. We work together. It would be too awkward.'
'I feel uncomfortable, knowing what's going on. It isn't right,' Rona says.

'Well maybe you should find a new job.'

This would suit him and give him an easy way out of the sticky mess he's got himself in, but she isn't going to give him the satisfaction and besides, they need the money.

'And make it easy for you?'

'Don't you dare breathe a word.'

He isn't going to intimidate her. He's worried about his position at the hospital and everything he's worked for.

'We clearly don't get on,' he says.

She's astounded. He's clever at twisting things round. 'What we have is a working relationship, Doctor Gerard,' she says, keeping her cool.

'And all I'm doing is getting on with my work.'

'Well get on with it then,' she snaps.

They are in Doctor Gerard's office. Rona has knocked on his door to ask him something and finds Marion there. They've been up to something and are dishevelled. Marion has adjusted her blouse, her face pink and the doctor moves to his desk.

He hands Rona some leaflets from Distillers, advertising thalidomide and asks her to pass them round her patients. 'The liquid version will be out soon. It's particularly suitable for children to quieten them down. Parents in Germany are giving it to their babies in the cinema to keep them quiet while the parents watch a film.'

'You'll be giving that to witnesses of your sordid affair then.'

Rona knows that she's risking her job by confronting him about the affair, but she doesn't care. He's her boss and he can fire her at any moment, but what he is doing makes her blood boil and she can't stand back and watch, having to greet Carol with a welcoming smile when she pops by, as if all is well. It goes against the grain of how she operates and what she stands for.

28

SANDY

Sandy wakes with a dull pain in the bottom of her back and assumes it's constipation. She turns, facing the window, trying to get comfortable, and watches a sliver of pre-dawn sky fade from ink black to slate grey. As the pain worsens she listens to the rhythmic breathing around her and contemplates calling for the nurse for some laxatives. She moves her leg, puts her foot on the floor, followed by the other and sits up. The pain is radiating from her pelvis to the tops of her legs. Several girls are awake, propped up on one elbow. In the grey light their faces look ghostlike.

Sandy tries to stand up. She's never had constipation this bad before. She can't move and waits, wondering whether to ask one of the girls to fetch the nurse. She feels her bowels groan and manages to get to the toilet in time. Padding back to her bed water trickles down her legs and forms a pool on the floor.

'Your waters have broken love. Best call for the nurse.' Jennifer is sitting up watching her. 'Don't be scared. It's the first sign that baby's on its way.' Sandy is more than scared. She's shivering. Terrified, she realises she hasn't a clue what to expect.

The nurse checks the foetal heartbeat and confirms that labour has begun. Half an hour later, after a heavy blood-stained show, Sandy is on her way to the hospital. The hours disappear in a blur as contractions come in waves, crashing over her body. Her legs are hoisted into stirrups and the doctor frames the space between her legs. Instructions come at her from all directions. A nurse, a doctor and then a second nurse and doctor. Why are there several of them? 'Just relax,' 'try to stay calm,' 'keep pushing.' Their voices cut through the bubble surrounding her. She's woozy, blood whooshing through her ears as she tries to stay calm. It will soon be over. She vomits into a waiting bowl.

Silence unfolds across the room. Sandy waits for the first cry, but it doesn't come. The labour pains ebb away, replaced by a searing sharp sting, as though a razor blade has slashed her. She grips the midwife's hand but the hand is cold and limp, her face white. Time seems to stand still. Everybody's faces are frozen and Sandy feels as if she's floating above the scene in a dream. More nurses come in, they stare, mumble and leave the room. A feeling of panic coils around her like a noose. She tries to speak, but her voice doesn't sound as if it belongs to her. Her words float loose. A sense of unease crawls through her veins like a toxin and then tiredness blurs the horror on their faces and peaceful sleep carries her away.

When she comes round a nurse is stitching her. Her mind is foggy. At first she doesn't know where she is as her mind scrolls through scenes in her life. And then it hits. She's had a baby. It isn't in the room. Shouldn't she be feeding it? Looking after it? Her voice is weak and as dry as sandpaper. She opens her mouth to speak but the words are swallowed up. She hears the rattle of a bin, a whoosh of water, the rustle of paper and then the door clicks shut. She drifts into troubled sleep, waking hours later when footsteps approach her bed. Her eyes are heavy and an effort to open.

'Where's the baby? Is it a boy or girl?'

The nurse stands at her bedside. There's something unnerving about the way she's peering at Sandy through eyes filled with sympathy and compassion.

'Is it dead?'

'It might be better for the poor mite if it was dear.'

Hours later she wakes with a ravaging thirst. The room is empty. She drifts through sleep until she finds the energy to pull the cord to ask for food and drink. She doesn't want to ask for the baby.

'Is it a girl or boy?'

'The doctor will tell you.' The nurse blushes and hurries away.

What's happening?

The midwife comes in to check her blood pressure and stitches.

'Is it a boy or girl? Can I see it?'

The midwife has secrecy buried in her expression.

'Doctor will come and see you in a bit. You need to rest.'

Something pops in Sandy's head. 'Why can't you just tell me what I've had?'

'Doctor will be in to discuss things with you.'

It is as if she's speaking from a well-rehearsed script. She turns to wash her hands in a robotic manner and tucks Sandy's sheets in. Alarm courses through her. Something is wrong.

'I'm only asking what it is? Is that so bloody difficult to answer? I know it's going to be adopted. You don't need to shield me. This has been planned for months. If you don't tell me I'm going to spend the rest of my life wondering. You can't do this. I've a right to know. I demand to know.'

The midwife says nothing. She checks her watch, takes Sandy's pulse and notes the result.

'Just tell me,' she screams.

Her outburst takes the midwife by surprise, but it prompts her into action. She hurries to the door. 'I'll fetch the doctor. He'll explain.'

'Explain what?' Sandy screeches into the empty room, anger and despair bubbling inside.

It's ages before the midwife returns with the doctor. They stand solemnly at the end of the bed.

'You've had a boy.'

Sandy stares at the midwife, dumbfounded. 'Why couldn't she have said?'

'What are you going to call it?'

Sandy is more confused than ever. 'I've no idea. I've not thought about names. What's going on?'

'I'm afraid it's bad news. I'm very sorry but...'

Just say it, Sandy's head screams.

'Your baby has no arms.'

The words hit her like a truck. Her throat constricts and she retches. She folds over, unable to take in what he's saying. There's no room inside her head for anything other than those two words—no arms.

'What? No...no.... this can't be happening. No, please.'

'I'm very sorry, this must be a terrible shock for you.'

His words stumble over each other in a haze and all she catches are the words 'the baby isn't going to live.' The room seems to collapse around her, narrowing into nothing but the rushing of blood in her ears.

'Do you want me to call your parents?'

'No.'

They are the last people she wants to see.

'You might want to have him baptised.'

Why the hell would I want that, she screams inside? Her brain kicks in with a jumble of questions but it's as if somebody else is asking them. She feels detached from her body.

'No arms. Why? What did I do wrong? What if I have another baby in a few years time? Will it happen again?'

'I can't say. The chances are that this is just a one off. A freak of nature. There have been other babies born recently with no arms, some with no limbs at all. We don't know why.'

'What's going to happen if it doesn't die?' Tears spring to her eyes, not for the baby but for herself. 'Nobody's going to adopt a crippled baby.' Sandy spits the words, aware of how dreadful and calculating she sounds but the question has to be asked. This is the last thing she needs, to be lumbered with a crippled child. Whatever would her parents say to that?

'Will I have to keep it?' she asks, dreading the answer.

She feels a sense of rage, that fate, or God, could be so cruel to her, to punish her for what she's done. This baby was unplanned and unwanted. She's to blame. She sinned. She'd let herself and her parents down and hasn't made any effort to get in touch with Jasper. But thank God she didn't get in touch with him. That is the only blessing in all of this. They could be married now and about to bring the baby up together, both of their lives changed forever by the awful burden they face. A leaden weight sinks to the pit of her stomach as she thinks about that dreadful scenario. She just wants to get dressed to escape and forget that this has happened and erase it from her memory.

'That would be very foolish.'

Relief washes over her. 'I couldn't cope on my own with a normal baby, let alone a crippled one.'

'Don't worry, you won't be taking the baby home. Let us take care of things. Nature will take its course. And if he does survive the next few weeks there are places where we can send him. Rona can you bring a consent form for Sandy to sign.'

'Have you thought about a name?' the doctor asks.

Why is he obsessed with naming the baby? It doesn't make

any difference to her what it's called. They can give it whatever name they like.

'You choose something,' she replies, irritated. She doesn't want to give him an identity. She wants to sever the link. She doesn't want to see the monster she's created and hopes they won't suggest it. Thankfully they don't. She's done the hard work, the painful bit and now he is their problem to deal with. Sandy is wheeled onto a ward where mothers are nursing their newborn babies.

When the nurse leaves she stumbles into the bathroom and throws up. When she's emptied her stomach, she leans on the side of the bath and pulls herself upright. She studies her pale features in the mirror. Who is this woman staring back at me? She's never looked less like herself.

The following morning, a few women ask what she's had and she tells them she's had a boy. She can't believe they don't know what happened. All the babies are brought in except for her baby and it's as if she's being punished further by being put in the general ward rather than in a side room. She's the only unmarried mother on this ward. They realise something is wrong but don't ask. She feels self-conscious and excluded, especially when visiting brings doting husbands laden with gifts. They fill the ward with the smell of flowers.

She passes the day mostly asleep, filtering their happy chatter. When darkness falls and the day slips into night, the babies are taken to the nursery so that the mothers can sleep. The ward is silent and that's when Sandy's mind comes alive with images of her son. She tries to wash them away, focusing on going home, but they crystallise. She can hear his cry. Piece by piece he becomes a person with his own smile and laugh. His eyes are blue and they cut into her like a pair of blades. His hair is blond and curly. She wants to touch him and smell him. He has hands that come out of his shoulders like flippers. And as the image comes into focus this is when she knows that she loves him beyond all doubt and doesn't want to give him up. She'll fight to keep him. The need burns like electricity. He is hers and he needs her, despite the fact that she has nothing to give. Her heart emits a dull thud. Is it too late? The doctors and nurses have been around the ward carrying out day-to-day routines but they avoid telling her what's happening.

Dawn breaks and Sandy calls the first nurse she sees, but the nurse is brusque and evasive. Sandy is told that the doctor will 'soon be doing his rounds.' She should address any questions to him. 'Bedpans are my domain love, questions are his; he has a certificate that says so.'

'I want to see my baby before he dies to give him my love. I just want to see him. Maybe he won't die, if I keep him warm in my arms,' she pleads, trying to keep the desperation out of her voice.

'You can't see him.' The doctor's answer, when it comes, is cold.

'You think I'm incapable and just a child.' Her voice cracks. She throws back the covers, hot with fury.

'You'd be foolish to saddle yourself with an invalid.'

'He's my baby, I don't care what's wrong with him. I love him.'

She doesn't know what she's saying. She feels delirious. She lets loose, a torrent of unchecked words said in the heat of the moment. She doesn't want to be a mother, not now and maybe never, but this baby is here now and he needs her—something has kicked in that came from nowhere. The doctor's brow beads with sweat and he's keeping something from her. His chin wobbles as he speaks. There's something about his demeanour that makes him come across as unprofessional and inexperienced and Sandy can't muster any respect for him.

A rigid band of pain moves across her temple when she realises he's come with more bad news. Before the words are out, she's guessed. This is cruel and unfair. She has so many questions but he isn't answering any of them.

'We've dealt with it,' is all he says.

It is as if her baby is a nasty smell in a lavatory, not a human being and she's left wondering whether he's been buried or incinerated and why aren't they giving her the chance to see him? She doesn't have the mental strength or resolve to ask as shock jolts through her. The doctor is in a hurry. He hasn't got the patience to waste time answering questions when there are more important patients to see to. He turns on his heels as if he can't wait to leave. There's a swish of his white coat, the squeak of his shoes on the lino and he flies through the swing doors, leaving her to deal with her grief.

Sandy wakes during the night thinking about everything. There's something that he didn't tell her and she doesn't feel comfortable. The doctor left her feeling as though her heart has been ripped from her chest, but she knows deep down it's for the best. She has to move on and will put it behind her. Keep strong, she tells herself, pretend it hasn't happened and erase it from your memory. But that's a hard thing to do because she never so much as touched the child she gave birth to, and the stretch marks aren't going to disappear in a hurry. They are like a badge of honour, or a dog marking its territory with the cock of the leg on a lamppost. They say to the world, 'I am a mother.' And the memories will be etched across her mind forever.

Instinct makes her feel intense regret that she never got to hold him and say goodbye. The unfair part of it was that this poor, deformed baby had to face his first hours of life alone. He was a small, vulnerable, broken baby, that's all he was and she was everything he had, but he never got to know it.

29

RONA

I t's a jaw-dropping moment as Rona and Doctor Gerard deliver the baby. Quiet calm descends and Rona feels as if she's floating, looking down on the scene unfolding. This isn't real. It's a horror film. Time stands still as Rona tries to maintain a semblance of professionalism but is unable to help for the first time in her career. She can only stand by as the doctor cuts the cord, sedates Sandy and stitches her.

'We'll keep her sedated for as long as we can.'

Rona knows that Sandy is unmarried and has no partner. Her plan is to have her baby adopted; she needs to be told what's happened. It doesn't feel right to keep her sedated unnecessarily. But she doesn't want to break the news. Concern lays low in her belly as she struggles to take it in. Nurses drift in and out of the room, hands clapped to mouths they whisper and frown with shocked faces, all coming to see the macabre spectacle. She snaps out of her trance. She has a job to do and heads for the sink, filling a bowl of warm water to clean the baby.

'Maybe we should call the mother's parents to be with her.'

The doctor ignores her.

'When you've finished go and put him in the cold room,' he orders in a brusque tone, drained of any emotion.

Anger roots in the pit of her stomach.

'He'll die there. I'll do no such thing. He's a baby, not a side of lamb.'

'He's deformed. He won't live. It's kinder this way.'

'He's got no arms, but he's still a human being. He'll freeze as fast as any other baby. What you're suggesting is murder and I'll have no part in it.'

'How many deformed babies have you delivered?' His acidic words hang in the air between them. 'Just do as you're told.'

Rona longs to defy him but is struck by how afraid she feels. His words and his cold stare press down on her. There's no air in the room and her face is clammy. She doesn't like the insensitive doctor. There's a nasty streak to his character, amplified by situations that he can't handle. He doesn't cope well when he feels his control slipping.

He washes his hands at the sink while Rona dabs the birth debris from the baby's body. He has forked hands—with two fingers that look like a pair of scissors coming out of his shoulders— other than that he's a perfect child. She can't see anything else wrong with him.

'Poor little mite.'

'This is no time to be soft. You've got to be tough in this job. We're dealing with life and death.'

Rona dabs at his hands. She's flooded with a tide of love and protectiveness towards this helpless mite.

Sandy is wheeled into a side ward, leaving Doctor Gerard and Rona alone in the delivery room. She weighs the baby and wraps him in a towel. She studies his soft hands and compares them to her own wrinkled mitts that are sun-dried and dappled with liver spots. Everybody's hands tell a story. They are a memory palace containing a mansion of deeds and are the powerhouse of the body, the work horse and she can't imagine what life would be like without them. How on earth would this child manage? He's a feisty soul, his lungs are strong as he wriggles and cries on the worktop. He isn't about to give up, that's plain enough and yet how will he cope, day to day as he gets older? Her hands served her well, they've made her a living and cared for others. They've painted her face in the mornings and replaced eye bags and cheek blotches with colour. They are doing hands: holding, chopping, sewing, cutting, making, mending and cooking. Rona closes her eyes, joins her hands together in prayer, passing the problem to God to solve. Her mind is filled with questions. What has caused this to happen? She has no idea.

Doctor Gerard seems to know what she's thinking.

'It's a one off. A sad but very rare genetic malfunction.'

The cause of his deformity is irrelevant to Rona, but she's certain of one thing.

'God has a purpose for him. I know it.'

'Don't get attached. He's not your problem. He's nobody's problem. Put him in the cold room, then speak to the mother's parents.'

'You sound like Frankinstein when he created the monster.'

'That's what it is, a monster and it'll cause havoc for anybody lumbered with it, not to mention costing the tax payer thousands in care.'

'That's a callous thing to say. We need humility. He's an innocent baby. Look at him. He's strong. He wants to live. We need to help him grow strong.'

'It's got no arms, that makes it enough of a burden but what you haven't considered is that there's probably other things wrong with it as well. It might have brain damage and might not be able to see or hear. Its internal organs could be damaged.' He gives a morose shake of his head. Rona can tell that he thinks she's stupid for caring.

She feels a wave of defeat. He's the doctor and he's probably right. Through tears she carries the baby into the cold room and puts him, naked on the stone windowsill as instructed. She's condemning him to death and tries not to dwell on it. It's horrific. She's a midwife and is supposed to give and support life— not take it away. This isn't right and God will punish her and send her to hell.

She walks into the visitors' room like a robot, to speak with Sandy's parents who are waiting. They are talking and look relaxed. Milky tea has been poured from a flask into red plastic cups on the table next to a row of magazines. A picnic basket of empty wrappers and browning apple cores sit on the floor.

Sandy's father rises from his armchair, alarm on his face. Her mother is stiff and prim, her beige wool coat buttoned to the collar and she looks as though she's only here under sufferance.

'Sandy's had the baby but I'm afraid there's been a problem.'

Rona isn't sure how she finds the words to explain what has happened but she's glad when the talking is over and she waits for their reaction. You can never tell how people are going to react to shocking news. There's a strained silence as they absorb the news and retreat into emotional lockdown where it's safe.

'Has Sandy seen him?' her father asks.

'She's heavily sedated.'

'Is he going to die?'

'We're expecting him to pass away peacefully. We'll take care of things.' Rona hates lying, it goes against her nature. She's always been an honest person. A ghastly thought enters her mind. Taking care of things means leaving him to starve to death. How long would it take? And how barbaric it is. She wouldn't treat an animal this way. She doesn't want to be the one to check on the baby overnight. A wintry chill ripples through her as she stifles the urge to vomit.

Sandy's father turns white, then a shade of grey.

'I think I'm going to be sick,' he mutters with his hand to his mouth.

Rona opens the door and points the way to the toilet.

Alone in the room with Sandy's mother, her demeanour unnerves her. Her hands are clasped on her lap and she says nothing. Rona thinks it strange that she isn't asking how her daughter is, but the fact that they are there must mean that they care.

'And what if he does live? What then?'

'There are places where we can send babies like him, or he can be adopted as planned.'

'Right. Well we'd better get off home. We've been here for hours.' Her face is like stone, without a hint of a smile or warmth. Rona feels uncomfortable.

'It was a relatively straightforward birth, if that's any consolation. She had a few stitches.'

'Right.' She checks the time.

'Do telephone if you'd like to talk to us, won't you?'

'I don't think that will be necessary. It's over. The past nine months have been hell for us and hugely stressful on my husband, you have no idea.' It's as if she is blaming Rona. 'I don't know what we'll do with Sandy. I suppose she'll have to come home.' She sighs and takes a hankie out of her bag. She blows her nose and heads for the door. Rona has been dismissed and without a thank you or a goodbye she leaves, trailing the scent of Chanel perfume.

Alone in the room blood whooshes in Rona's ears as she struggles to stay calm but she's racked with fear and a deadening feeling. She wants to go home too. She needs air and Bill's arms. She's been on night-duty but another member of staff is sick leaving her in charge, it's another double shift with day following night.

Doctor Gerard clocks off at midnight and will return at four in the morning. He's expecting the baby to pass away by the time he returns, and tells her once it's over he will arrange for a funeral director to organise the burial.

'Check the other departments, Nurse, and see if there have been any female deaths in the last twenty-four hours. A tandem burial will be the most cost effective and least distressing way to go. We need to have it cleared up quickly.'

Rona doesn't leave the room. It's her break and she curls in the armchair and falls asleep. Nobody will come looking for her. An hour passes and there's a knock at the door. It's Alice. Her eyes spring open, her mind returning to consciousness. My God, I delivered a deformed baby are her first thoughts. It's getting late, past midnight. There's no clarity or insight at this hour, only the endless churning and turning of thoughts, the recriminations and the what ifs.

'Rona, sorry to disturb you but have you seen Doctor Gerard? I want to give him these files.'

'Alice.' Rona unfurls her legs and rubs her eyes. 'You get off, I'll give them to him. Is he in his office?'

'No and not on the ward either. I think you'll be lucky, fingers crossed. Nobody's in labour. No problems reported.' She smiles, raising two crossed fingers in the air.

'I take it you heard about my delivery earlier on?'

'Yes, another one. I've just checked on him.'

'How is he?'

'He's a got a strong pair of lungs on him.'

'He's probably very hungry by now. Did you feed him?'

'Doctor Gerard said not to,' Rona says. 'Nil by mouth.

'It's hard this way but I guess it's for the best. We'll have to wait and see what happens. Good luck.' She gives Rona an encouraging smile and leaves the room.

Rona does the ward round, checking all is well and as she moves from room to room she can't find Doctor Gerard. And then she remembers; he clocked off at midnight.

She pauses outside the cold room, her shaking hand on the handle. He's instructed her not to go in and to treat it as a neonatal death. Life is cheap and if it isn't perfect, it's easily disposed of. It's about the survival of the fittest. Life, she reflects is so much easier for animals. She remembers her Grandma Gladys flushing kittens down the toilet as soon as they were born. It was something you did and nobody gave it too much thought. Nobody wanted them and there were too many. She remembers her Auntie Betty's cat having a sore leg and being put to sleep with chloroform. It was so cut and dried where animals were concerned. But imperfect babies? What is society supposed to do with them?

She slips into the cold room and the baby is howling on the window sill. The air is damp and she shivers against the chill. Her heart lurches as she picks him up and holds him to her chest, wrapping her cardigan around his naked body, rubbing him and blowing air onto his face to get him warm. He feels so cold. 'My baby,' she cries, 'my sweet, beautiful little boy, stay with me, don't go.' Rona thinks about the fragility of life and how it can turn on a sixpence; that was an old expression. She isn't going to let him slip away. If she leaves him, he will surely die. To hell with Gerard. She can't let that happen.

With him in her arms she goes to the milking room. With the baby under the crook of her arm she prepares a bottle of milk and sits down in a rocking chair to feed him. He drinks the full three ounces before stopping. She pats the dribbles around his mouth and puts him over her shoulder, rubbing his back to wind him.

'Shush, shush, little Toby.' She gets up and paces up and down, her own life crowded out by the need to keep this boy alive, at whatever cost. She hadn't intended to give him a name but everybody should have one and Toby suits him. She kisses his head. 'Toby. Nobody else is going to name you, so for the time being you're my little Toby.'

She hears something. Whispers and a giggle. She strains to listen. Everything is quiet, apart from the ticking clock and a distant cough from the ward. This is the quietest the place has been in the time she's worked here.

The noise comes from the opposite direction. She opens the door leading to the baby room and tiptoes along the varnished wooden floor to the next door, the rubber on her soles squeaking. It's a broom cupboard but the whispers are coming from inside.

She makes out the faint sound of Doctor Gerard's mumbled voice and a woman's murmur. She's sure it's Marion. They are brazen, flaunting their sordid affair but Rona is brazen too. She's called him to account on a couple of occasions and he's denied having an affair despite being caught out and he's furious with her for insinuating anything untoward.

She hyperventilates, breathing in gulps as she clutches the sleeping baby to her chest and with her other hand tugs at the door. Marion, who's been leaning against the door inside the cupboard tumbles onto the wooden floor. She's half-dressed red faced and bare legged, with her boobs bulging from her unbuttoned shirt. Her skirt is on the floor around her ankles. She scrambles to her feet like a calf taking its first steps.

On wobbly legs and confronted by Rona, she dusts herself down, smooths her hair and tries to cover herself behind Gerard.

'You're trash. I've a good mind to report you.'

The smell of body fluids mingles with Jeyes Fluid.

There is a moment of dithery throat clearing as he rushes to dress. 'Get on with your duties, Nurse,' he snaps.

'We can't leave this baby to die.'

'It's too late to organise an adoption.'

'I'll wait in your office while you dress.'

He pushes the papers around his desk, composing himself and clawing back his authority over her. The baby in her arms gives her strength. Nobody can beat her. If this special scrap can fight, then so can she. Nothing matters except this precious baby. Saving his life means everything to her.

'Why is it too late to organise an adoption?'

'Because I've already told the mother he's dead.'

Rona stares at him, open-mouthed. She can't believe a doctor of so many years experience would do such a thing. 'Why on earth did you do that when it's not true?'

'I thought he would die.' He pauses. 'I've delivered three crippled babies in so many months, all with similar deformities and two of them didn't live. I wasn't expecting this one to make it and we don't know what else might be wrong with him, or that he will. I made the decision that it would be kinder to tell the mother he'd died.'

'Kinder? Whatever happened to the truth?'

He leans back and sweeps his hands through greasy hair. He is tired and strained and probably hasn't slept in days. Rona bristles. It's as likely his guilt keeping him awake at night as his work. She quells the annoyance stabbing in her head.

'What would you suggest I do?'

'Just tell the truth for God's sake. Admit you made a mistake.'

'I can't do that.'

'Well let me take the baby.' Her sentence is a strangled croak. She hasn't planned it but now that she's said it, it makes sense. 'I'll take him home with me. I'll make it all go away. You'll never have to worry about the situation again.'

The suggestion takes him by surprise. Her words hover over them, thick and pensive. 'You want to take him, what and bring him up as your own? In that state?'

'He needs love. Who else does he have? His mother doesn't want him. She's not married. She can't support him even if she wanted to.'

He covers his face with his hands and leans back in his

chair. Rona strokes the baby's head, her heart hammering in her chest. The doctor sighs, uncovers his face, his eyes anchored to her.

'I could slip away tonight and never come back. Nobody need know.'

'Don't be ridiculous.'

'I could report you to management for what I saw this evening. You'd lose your job.'

'Are you blackmailing me? I wouldn't do that if I were you.'

'Do you want to take that risk? I've never been more serious about something. I'll do what it takes to keep this baby.'

'You don't have a birth certificate.'

'You could write one.'

'And lie?'

'You're good at that.'

'Unless…' He sounds as though he's on the brink of a decision. But whatever he's about to say dies on his lips.

'What were you going to say?'

'I could produce a death certificate for the authorities.' A thread of steel slips into his tone. 'The rest is up to you to work out. I will have nothing more to do with it. This conversation did not happen and, as far as I'm concerned, the child expired naturally and as expected a few hours after birth.'

They let the silence give them time to absorb it, each contemplating their side of the plan hatching.

'Look, Rona, you have no idea what you'd be taking on. Let nature take its course. Please. This scheme of yours is madness.'

He moves towards her, a sickly smile on his face, his arms open to take the baby from her. Her grip tightens. 'Let me save you from the worst decision you'll ever make.'

'Didn't you deliver a baby without limbs several months ago? You didn't take the same attitude then, so what's changed? Or did you? Did you murder that child too?'

'Of course not. The circumstances were totally different.'
The parents were married and financially secure for one thing.'

'We can't play judge and jury.'

'Just stop, Rona and think about what life would be like for
him. Think about all the things he won't be able to do.' He
picks up a pen from his desk and points it at her. 'For God's
sake, woman, he won't even be able to pick up a pen.'

'Negative, negative, negative. When he's older he can be
seen at Roehampton Hospital where they're experimenting
with prosthetic limbs. It's not all doom and gloom. And he'll
learn to compensate by using his legs. You're writing him off
without giving him a chance.'

'You're thinking from an emotional perspective rather than
a sensible one. Give me the baby. I'll arrange for him to be sent
to an institution. There's somewhere in Sussex, called Chailey.
I've heard good things about it.'

'He needs loving parents, not to be thrown into an institution, out of sight and out of mind.'

'They can provide the specialised care he needs.'

'And what about love, Doctor? Who will provide him with
that?' She lets the thought settle. 'I don't trust you. You'll put
him back in the cold room with the window open so that he
catches his death.'

With no reaction from the doctor, Rona tries a different
tack. 'Cover for me and your secret will be safe.'

'You'll have to move out of London. Get as far away as possible. Are you prepared to do that?'

'Yes. I was going to hand my notice in anyway. We only
planned to be in London for a year, for my husband's work.
We're moving back to Blackpool.'

'When did you last see your GP?'

'Six months ago.'

'What for?'

'A pregnancy test. It came back negative.'

He squeezes his chin, in thought.

Rona is conscious of the time. The night nurse will be heading downstairs to feed the babies. Anxiety laps inside her.

'Sometimes pregnancy hormones are too weak to pick up a positive result. It's rare, but possible.'

'And if I didn't know I was pregnant and with no other symptoms it's feasible I didn't know until it was too late.'

'Rare, but it does happen.'

He smiles for the first time and Rona feels optimistic. She's won him over. They can pull this off. The plan can work. She just has to stick to her story.

'But you would have called an ambulance.'

'I'm a midwife. I know what to do. My waters broke. I gave my husband instructions. He delivered the baby.' Rona is building a picture in her head. She will have to live with this version of events for the rest of her life. She can see Bill, panting and pushing along with her during labour. She must believe her story and stick by it, otherwise how is anybody else going to?

'Your husband,' he gasps. 'What the hell's he going to say? You can't go home with a baby, especially this baby. This is ludicrous. Give him to me. Now.'

'My husband will say exactly what I tell him to. He'll be fine. He wants a baby as much as I do. The secret will be safe.'

'He might be, but what about your friends? Family?'

'I don't know anybody in London and I haven't seen any family or friends for nearly a year.'

'They all know you weren't pregnant.'

'Actually my family think I am.'

'You're insane.'

There's a noise in the corridor and a door opens. It's now or never. Her heart bangs in her chest. She isn't sure if he'll make a grab for the baby or push her through the back door. Time stands still, with Toby's future held in the balance. This could go either way but during their conversation Gerard has referred to the baby as him rather than it; he's seeing him as a human being.

'Go now, if you're going. And may you never live to regret this night.' He opens the door and ushers her out of the tradesman's entrance that leads into an outside yard.

Inches apart she can smell his milky tea breath as he unlatches the door. 'Good luck. I don't want this to backfire on me. I don't want to see you again.'

'Don't worry. I loved this baby the minute I saw him. I won't let him down.'

30

RONA

Clutching the baby Rona elbows the door open into the corridor, wrinkling her nose at the overpowering smell of urine in the communal hallway. She loves the views over the city and thought that she'd get to know lots of people. But it hasn't happened and she loathes the place. Menace and danger crouch in the hallways. There are shady characters lurking after dark. The lift rarely works. The cat can't go out. Noise and smell travel from one flat to the next. It's anything but peaceful. And whatever she does inside the flat to make it cosy and homely it doesn't feel like home. She longs to return to their Victorian terrace in Blackpool. She didn't appreciate the good things about the house until she'd left and went to live in the tower block. The chats with neighbours on the doorstep, the garden, the pub and shop on the corner, she misses them all. The house needs some work, but she's hopeful that they can make it perfect for bringing up their son.

She blinks in the harsh electric light. A gang of Teddy boys huddle in the far corner of the hallway. They are often here, staying up all night and usually looking for trouble.

Rona hopes that this morning they'll let her pass without

comment. She's just walked two miles from work with the baby in her arms and she's frozen to the bone. But as soon as they see her, they elbow each other and sneer.

'You had a baby, love? Didn't notice you was up the duff. You hid that well. 'Ow's about a flash o' yer tits? Bet their big and full of milk.'

Milk. The baby's next feed. The Cow & Gate tin is tucked at the back of a cupboard in the spare room. Things happen for a reason. Rona ignores the youth's comments, but their voices follow her up the staircase, echoing off the concrete walls. She doesn't bother to try the lift. It hasn't worked for weeks and there's no reason to believe it will today.

Inside the flat, she heads for the kitchen to put the kettle on, closing the kitchen door behind her, in case Bill wakes. Rona's hands and feet are numb with cold. She sits at the table, cradling the baby and wonders what on earth Bill is going to say. The easiest bit is over. The baby is safe, she's found a way to convince the doctor, but Bill is the biggest hurdle and she knows that she doesn't stand a chance against his intransigence when it comes to raising another man's child. Tears swell in her throat as Bill's face floats through her mind. When he'd married her he'd promised her the world and she'd trusted him to stick by her, whatever issues they faced. But for the first time in their marriage she's afraid and uncertain. A crack has opened in their marriage. It's a gaping seam and she doesn't know whether it's fixable. She's stopped talking about babies, realising how destructive the conversation was.

Rona creeps into the spare room and fumbles in the cupboard for the milk and bottle. She pauses outside their bedroom. Bill is snoring like a pneumatic drill. She wants the baby fed and settled before confronting him. She has an hour before he gets up for work. He starts at seven.

With the baby fed and winded she puts him in the laundry basket, padded with soft towels. At six she hears the alarm go off and several minutes later his feet on the lino on his way to the bathroom. There's a whoosh of water as the toilet flushes and then boiler cranks to life. Her heart pounds in her chest knowing that he'll soon be dressed and in the kitchen expecting to start a normal day. Today is not normal. Today is the most extraordinary day they have ever faced. He'll be late for work and may skip the day altogether. This is going to be the most difficult conversation of her life and she isn't looking forward to it. What if he shouts at her and demands that she take the baby back? He may force her to make a choice—her husband or her son. Her son— she plays with the word. She will leave. No choice to be made. This has to remain a secret. Please God don't let him try to make me take him back, don't let my marriage be over. I need him now more than I ever have. And whether he knows it or not, he needs us. She prays as she sits at the table, willing God to make things right. Everything hinges on Bill.

Bill coughs his way into the kitchen smelling of Old Spice. He doesn't notice the sleeping baby in the laundry basket. It gives Rona a moment to collect herself. Fear and anxiety race through her body. She can feel the blood drain from her face. She's planned what she's going to say but the words are lost to her. She has never been so scared in her life.

'Love, what are you doing in here? Why didn't you come to bed?'

'I haven't been in long.'

'Hard shift?' he asks with his back to her, pulling out drawers and preparing a bowl of cornflakes.

'We were short-staffed.' This isn't true. She says it without focusing on the conversation, her mind elsewhere.

He boils a kettle of water on the stove, makes her a tea but still doesn't notice the basket. The baby sleeps through the chatter and tinkle of cups and bowls.

'A doll.' Bill smiles casually at the basket, as if dolls are a regular purchase. He holds a teabag on a spoon, his hand hovering over the bin. Rona is silent. 'For one of the nieces?'

The baby moves and cries.

Bill steps back startled. The teabag splats to the floor. 'It's a baby. What's it doing here?'

'Shouldn't you be going to work soon?' She takes a sip of water from the glass on the table, her lips trembling.

'Whose baby is it?'

'Do you want me to make sandwiches? I can do.' Her stomach flutters with nerves and she feels the urge to go to the toilet but can't leave Toby there alone with Bill's questions floating above them.

'What's going on?'

'This is our son, Bill, he's a gift from God.'

He opens and closes his mouth, tries to formulate words—and fails.

'The mother gave birth a couple of days ago.'

'What's it doing here? I don't understand.'

She rubs her palm with two fingers. It's what she does when she is covering something up.

'Oh no, please don't tell me you've...'

'...Stolen him? What do you take me for?'

'He needs his mother, Rona. I'm worried about you. You're not well.'

'I'm not ill. He needs two loving parents—us, Bill.'

Bill reaches for her hands, his face full of concern. 'I won't go to work today. I'm taking you to the doctor. But first we need to get him back to his mother.'

Rona pulls his hands away and gets up. She opens every cupboard as if she's forgotten where the bowls are kept, banging them shut, working herself into a state. She pours too many cornflakes in a bowl and when she slops the milk it sloshes over the counter. She stops, trying to quell the tears rising inside her. Bill wraps his arms around her and guides her back to the chair.

The baby whimpers. She has to remain calm. There's a lot to discuss but the fact that Bill thinks she's insane isn't going to help.

'You need to listen to me Bill and listen carefully before you jump to all sorts of conclusions.'

The story tumbles out of her, every detail from Sandy's feelings towards the baby to the doctor's lie and Rona's agony at being instructed to put the baby in the cold room to wait for him to die. She waits for Bill to respond but he's flabbergasted and can't take it in. She picks the baby up, uncovering the towel so that he can see Toby.

The colour drains from Bill's face and he turns grey. 'I feel sick.' He gives a morose shake of his head and flees to the bathroom. Rona hears him throwing up and the toilet flushing. He returns to the kitchen and sits down. There's tension between them as she bites her lip, terrified of what he's going to say and afraid that he'll call the police or social services.

'What do you want to do with it?'

'Bill, he's not an it. He's a baby.'

The comment puts a huge gulf between them.

'You know what I want,' Rona says, her voice raised and insistent. 'I want to keep him. If we don't keep him he'll live in an institution.'

'You don't know what's wrong with it.'

'We can see what's wrong with him. It's not the end of the world.'

'Those are the visible things. There could be anything wrong with it. Have you considered that?'

'Just have faith, please, for me. Remember what God said in James, chapter one. If any of you lacks wisdom, let him ask of God, who gives to all generously and without reproach, and it will be given to him. But he must ask in faith without any doubting.'

'This is all wrong. This whole baby thing has got way out of hand.'

'You never wanted to adopt,' she shouts, wishing she hasn't reminded him. She sounds like a broken record and knows it's unfair of her. He has a right to how he feels.

'I want it to happen the old-fashioned way or not at all.'

Rona steps over to his chair and hugs him but he tenses with the contact. 'So do I, and as much as I love you very much it's not going to happen. You have no idea how hard these past years have been.'

He looks at her. 'And you think I haven't suffered too?'

As she kisses his cheek, she feels a rush of faith. He loves her. He'll come round, he has to, he's not going to risk losing her, surely?

'Adoption isn't a lesser choice. It's related to childlessness and that stigmatises it. We're all so hung up on tradition, passing down our blood and traditions and family names and that we must have our own biological children, but it doesn't matter.'

'It matters to me. Stop dismissing how I feel.'

'I just want you to look at things in a different way. Stop being so stubborn. Adoption is about giving a child a meaningful life.' She pauses and smiles at the baby, who's asleep again in the basket. 'It's about the child, not about us Bill. It's not about fulfilling our need, it's about restoring his right to a loving and secure family.'

Her words stand solid, suspending the moment. He sighs and in a split second she feels a tenderness towards Bill. She's chiselled into his black-and-white way of seeing things.

'I don't want to be stopped in the grocery store and asked what's wrong with his arms?'

'People wouldn't be so rude.'

'Wanna bet?'

'I'll protect him from the outside world. We'll protect him. We're good people. Doesn't he deserve a chance in life?'

Bill pushes her away and buries his face in his hands. 'Daisy wasn't given a chance,' he mutters.

'Who's Daisy?'

When he doesn't answer she asks again.

'I've never told you. None of the family talk about her. It's as if she never existed.'

Rona listens and doesn't interrupt, shocked that he's kept a family secret from her.

'I had a sister, born when I was ten. She died when she was five months. They said she had something wrong with her. After she died, they gave up talking about her. They erased her from our family history, but she's still here. I haven't forgotten her.' He bangs his chest. 'It was weird. It still feels weird all this time later.'

'I'm sorry.' She strokes his head.

'Throughout the whole time we were trying for a baby I kept asking myself how I'd feel if we had a baby and it died. I don't think I'd be able to cope.'

'This baby's a little fighter. The doctor didn't think he'd live but he's strong, he's not giving up.'

Bill smiles, unguarded for the first time. 'He is sort of sweet.'

'I think this is fate. He's meant to be with us, Bill, I know it.' She lifts the baby from the basket. She pulls her chair to his and sitting down puts a hand on his back and rubs it.

Bill forces a smile. 'He can stay.'

'Thank you, thank you.' She hugs him with tears streaming down her face.

'Just for today. We're going to have to work out what to do.'

'Bill, please, let him stay.' Her hopes are raised, then dashed.

'You make it all sound so simple. You've kidnapped a baby.'

Angry at the comment, she gets up and heads for the kettle, suppressing the urge to explode. This isn't kidnap. Surely, he can see that? She has the best intentions. She's rescued a baby that had been condemned to die. Nobody wants him, not even his mother and he wouldn't have been a great candidate for adoption. His future lies in their hands. Collecting herself together, she tries to explain this to Bill.

He sighs. She stops talking. She's done enough explaining and isn't getting them anywhere. The ball's in his court. She can't make him do something he isn't happy with, but she doesn't feel very rational about the situation. She can't give up. She'll win him over in the end, because she always does.

Bill throws every negative factor and fear into the conversation: the possibility of a visit from the police or social services and a ton of negativity towards crippled children. Rona wonders if parenting isn't for him. Even without a handicap, children are hard work. She's prepared for it, but is he?

She rubs his arm. 'Let's get out of London and go home.'

'I've got three weeks left on this contract.'

She can see the exasperation in his eyes but she isn't giving up. 'Tell them your parents are ill, tell them you've got a family crisis. It happens all the time. Life doesn't go to plan.' The baby is back in the basket sleeping. She grips her cup, as if it's a life raft.

'Don't corner me, love.'

'I'm sorry. I'm trying to help.'

'You can't think that we can arrive in Blackpool with a baby in tow. The whole family are going to be suspicious. They'll know something's not right.'

'My mother thinks I'm pregnant.'

Rona waits for the bombshell to hit. He stares at her. 'What? You've kept that lie going?'

'I just didn't correct her.'

'You've planned this all along?'

He looks disgusted.

'No of course I haven't. Stop painting me as wicked.'

He gets up and pushes his chair in.

'Where are you going?'

'Work. I'm late.'

'I thought you'd decided not to go in today.'

'I can't leave the lads in the lurch. It'll give me time to think. It's a complete mess.'

'It's not a mess, it's a miracle.' She was talking to a closed door.

31

SANDY

Sandy returns home to her parents and for weeks the atmosphere is strained. Her father barely speaks to her, as if waiting for her to move out and make a life for herself. The baby is never mentioned by either of her parents. She doesn't even hear them whisper behind her back. They've erased him from their memory and Sandy knows that she has to do the same, and forget that he ever happened and learn from her mistakes.

She considers herself lucky. Her baby died. There was nothing she could have done. It was out of her control. She was spared the agony and trauma of having a beautiful healthy baby prised from her arms by a stranger. She had seen that happen to so many women over the time at the home and it was heartbreaking to see. She'd heard a story about a woman who'd suffered a breakdown and spent six months in an asylum, being told there was no baby, no adoption and that the whole thing was in her mind. The more the woman had protested the more ill she became— and in the end they'd given her pills to shut her up.

But Sandy's circumstances were different. Nobody wanted a crippled baby, even if he'd lived. He would have been an outcast to be laughed at, jeered at and bullied with a lifetime of struggle ahead. Despite these thoughts, there would always be a niggling doubt at the back of Sandy's mind; did he really die? She hadn't seen him so she didn't know for sure. There had been no closure. She tries not to dwell on it but occasionally her mind drifts back to the birth and the days that followed and she's always left feeling perplexed.

Sandy's figure returns to its normal shape which means that her life is back on track. With a trim figure she can get modelling work and then her lucky break comes. She secures a contract in New York.

In the summer of 1961 Sandy flies for the first time in her life. It's a terrifying experience. Nobody in her family has ever been on a plane. She doesn't know what to expect. She thinks she is going to die and end up as a headline in *The Times*. Her mum is worried and keeps reminding her to lock her suitcase—and her bedroom, 'because it's a big city love and people get murdered in big cities,' she warns.

When the air hostess opens the aeroplane door, Sandy is met by a slap of heat that takes her breath away. It's humid and clammy. She takes her cardigan off and it's like walking into a giant oven. She piles her cases onto a trolley and manoeuvres around the airport maze to the taxi rank.

'The Ritz-Carlton please.'

She's never stayed in a hotel before, let alone such a glamorous one. She walks through the lobby as if her whole life depends on how she moves. The elegant furniture and the sweet music give her the shivers. Men are looking at her and she marches to the reception desk and announces herself. The staff command bellboys and clerks. She signs her name and sweeps into the lift with the bellboy. The room looks as grand as a presidential suite and there is a gigantic arrangement of flowers and a basket of fruit. She will be staying for two weeks and after the photo shoot she'll be touring on a Greyhound bus to Canada— her dream fulfilled.

32

JASPER

J asper immerses himself in his work. His brief is to travel around Manchester capturing homelessness and the horrors of deprivation faced by millions of families. The newspaper is led by a social campaigner who wants to reveal true-life conditions in the city with the aim of sparking social change, and the assignment appeals to Jasper because he wants to look beyond the official version of events and report the real stories of his time. He wants to show how the poor live and is passionate about fighting for the underdog. He takes pictures of Salford's slums with half-naked children playing in the rubble, a five-year old with his head peering into a drain - and a family of six sharing a bed are among his most acclaimed shots.

He makes friends with a man living in the same digs and they go to dances on a Saturday evening. He dates a few women but can't settle into a relationship with any of them because he isn't over Sandy. In the precious few semi-conscious seconds between sleep and wakefulness each morning, he dreams of her smile and the graceful way she walks. It is a moment of pleasure before his remind him that she rejected him and isn't answering his letters. He's convinced that her rejection goes back to the time they'd made love. Sleeping with her so soon ruined the relationship. He'd been caught in the moment, desperate for sex. She hadn't taken him seriously after that. He'd let her down by putting lust first and moving away. She didn't trust him and how could he blame her?

In January 1961 he secured a new post, working on a column for a distinguished medical journal in London. It's the first time he's returned to the big smoke since moving to Manchester. As the train pulls into London Euston, he's made up his mind; he will call round to Sandy's house and even though he knows she doesn't want him he has to make his peace. It will probably be a waste of time. He'll have the door slammed in his face, but he'll be able to give closure to the yearning for her that he still feels.

It's a crisp day, the sky a brilliant blue and a far cry from the grey skies and damp chill that blankets Manchester. He steps off the bus around the corner from where Sandy lives and strides along her street thinking about how lucky he is to have such a fantastic job waiting for him, in London. There is only one thing missing in his life. If he can convince her to give him another chance, he's certain they can make a happy life for themselves. He's saved up and can take her to Canada for a holiday. He approaches the house, his heart banging in his chest. It's now or never, his only chance to make amends.

He's struck by a sudden thought. He rubs his forehead. What if she's met somebody else? The thought hasn't occurred to him until now, although he knows it should have done. It would explain her silence and make sense. A beautiful girl like Sandy won't be single forever. She'll be snapped up. What on earth has he been thinking and what gave him the right to imagine that she'd welcome him? He's being ridiculous. He left her, putting his career first. She has every reason not to give him a moment's thought.

He stands at the gate. With his confidence seeping away, he

knows it's a mistake to push the gate and head up to the door and knock. He turns and takes a few steps. Something brushes against his leg. It's the neighbour's cat purring at him. She remembers him. He bends down and a stroke of her soft black fur makes him change his mind. He hasn't come all this way to give in. He'll act like a man, make his peace with her, wish her well in her new relationship and maybe stay for a cup of tea—for old times' sake.

The gate clatters, he beetles up the path, gives a hard rap at the door and waits for an answer. If she's out he isn't sure that he'll find the resolve to come back later. It's now or never. The door opens and there's a tinkle as the catch on the chain falls. Sandy's mother is dressed in a blue housecoat with curlers in her hair and she's scowling at him. Some things never change, it's like coming home.

'What do you want? I thought you were the Avon lady.'

'I was hoping to see Sandy. I know it's been a while. I did write to her several times.'

'She doesn't want to speak to you.'

'Can't we let her decide that?'

'Goodbye.'

The door slams. Nasty woman, Jasper thinks. It's like trying to get past a Rottweiler. Short of waiting for hours on the corner of Sandy's street for her to appear, he can't think of what else to do. He needs to accept that she's moved on, but he wants to talk to her.

IN LATE FEBRUARY JASPER, is asked to interview a German pharmaceutical company, Chemie Grunenthal regarding the side effects being reported in a number of medical journals about one of its drugs, thalidomide, which is available in Britain under the brand name Distaval. The adverse reports have gone unnoticed in the lay press but are appearing in medical journals. Medicine interests Jasper and he speaks German. His boss is a former doctor and reads one of the reports. It's only a small piece and if he hadn't been interested it would not have caught his eye. He sees the potential for a great story.

The report, written by a Scottish doctor reads: 'I have observed four cases of peripheral neuritis in patients who have taken thalidomide.'

Another report, written by a German doctor reads: 'I would like to draw your attention to an illness that I first came across in 1959. It's a picture of peripheral neuritis after prolonged use of the widely used sedative thalidomide. I have diagnosed fourteen cases in my practice. The illness begins with a numbness in the toes that spreads to the balls of the feet, then to the ankles and the calves but not beyond the knee. Months later, the numbness begins in the tips of the fingers and to date there is not a single recovery after the drug has been stopped.'

Jasper is aware of how successful a drug thalidomide is to Chemie Grunenthal. Sales have climbed and the drug is available in forty-six countries, with sales nearly matching those of aspirin. But as time goes by, the reports about adverse effects of the drug grow louder and stronger. There are examples of vomiting, nausea and hair loss. Jasper's magazine sends him to Germany to interview the company. They are reluctant to be interviewed. Jasper, with his keen sense of justice doesn't like their attitude. The interview proves to be a waste of time. They are closing ranks and categorically deny a problem with their drug. They are dismissive of the reports. One of the board members tells him, 'It's a completely harmless drug.' 'As safe as water.' 'It's been in use for several years with amazing results.' And the 'possible connection with polyneuritis is a remote one.' He is asked to take some new promotional literature back to distribute to doctors' surgeries in Britain. His anger mounts.

Returning from Germany, his attention turns to America, where, after a late start, preparations are under way to market thalidomide on a scale that will dwarf that of the rest of the world. The Germans are eager to exploit their wonder drug throughout the world and although competition in America will be fierce because many different types of sleeping pill are already available there, the profits will be huge. But the stumbling block is in securing an American licence and this is proving difficult. Several American drug companies turn it down but eventually Richardson-Merrell signs an agreement with Grunenthal to market and manufacture it in America. They plan to market the drug for a host of conditions from anxiety, alcoholism, anorexia, asthma, cancer, cardiovascular disease, premature ejaculation, nervous exhaustion, tuberculosis and more. Thalidomide is an elixir to cure the ills of mankind but beyond what the Germans have told them, like Distillers in Britain, Richardson-Merrell knows little about the drug and performs no tests on it to establish its safety. All they do is distribute samples to doctors across America.

Jasper is told that it's a safe drug and safe for everybody including pregnant women. During his interviews he wonders if the drug can pass through the placental barrier. Some experts say it can and some that it can't. This is the subject to write his article on. He isn't the only one to be wary about the drug. Doctors are voicing their concerns and in the United States, Dr Kelsey, head of the Food Drugs Agency, is dragging her feet on the drug's application. It's her job to evaluate data on new drugs before they are licensed for sale and distribution in America and she feels that the data on thalidomide is inadequate to warrant FDA licensing and until their testing of the drug meets her criteria, she refuses to approve thalidomide for use in the United States.

Jasper telephones Dr Kelsey's office to ask for an interview. The situation in the United States is intriguing. Thalidomide has been so successful across Europe, surely America would wave it through, so why haven't they? It's being hailed as the greatest pharmaceutical breakthrough of the century and perfectly safe. He has some leave to take and some money saved and decides to fly to New York and interview her in person.

He steps off the plane into the bright sunlight of a warm New York June day, his jacket slung across his shoulder. He loads his luggage onto a trolley and heads for the taxi rank where he's driven to his first hotel. He's scheduled a meeting with Dr Kelsey in the lounge the following day. The hotel is expensive but convenient. He doesn't intend to stay there for more than two nights though and will spend the rest of his week in a budget hotel, several miles away from Manhattan.

'THE STUDY they submitted is not the data I requested.'

The waitress pours their coffee as they settle into the discussion. Jasper thinks Dr Kelsey isn't an unattractive woman but she isn't attractive either. She has no womanly curves, and a thin face with high cheek bones and short, scraped back hair.

He smiles across at her. 'I don't imagine you'll be Miss Popular. These drugs companies don't like delays.'

'And if they push me too far I won't be happy.'

'It's hardly an experimental drug. It's been on the market in other countries for three years. More coffee, Mrs Kelsey?'

Mrs Kelsey bites into a biscuit. The atmosphere buckles into an awkward silence before she speaks. 'Are you aware that there have been numerous cases of polyneuritis? I'm not going to rush this drug through. They need to provide sufficient data to prove it's safe.'

'What did they say to you when you expressed your concerns?'

'They had the audacity to tell me that I was being unreasonable.'

'That's terrible.' Jasper scribbles notes as she speaks.

'They said that nerve damage is rare and reversible as soon as the patient stops taking the pills and that millions are benefiting from thalidomide. But I know that in England, according to reports in your medical journal, that damage is permanent in twenty percent of cases. They know about this research but tried to fob me off by saying they would put warning labels on the bottles.' She huffs. 'As if that would be enough.'

'What data do you want them to come up with?'

'Studies that show thalidomide will not harm the foetus in a pregnant woman.'

'To my knowledge pregnant women have been taking the drug for several years,' Jasper counters.

'There's always a need to study the effects on a foetus. There's a strong possibility that the drug could damage foetal tissue which is delicate, especially in the early stages of pregnancy.'

'Would you licence the drug if they can provide studies on the foetus?'

'Yes. If the data is conclusive.'

'But if they don't already have the data it's going to take a while to get it.'

'And I don't trust their methods, quite frankly.' Defiance flashes across her face. 'How do I know they won't pay for an expert to publish a few articles in medical journals with misleading results? It happens all the time in the pharmaceutical industry. They know I want data so my bet is they'll find a way of coming up with something.'

'I've had lengthy conversations with several doctors across the world who believe that thalidomide is causing birth defects.'

'I have heard such theories myself. There have been clusters of birth defects. But I've heard different theories. One piece of research says it's due to a new detergent, another says it's radioactivity in the air, or that it's due to a virus. Who are we to believe?'

'But the thing these women have in common is that they all took thalidomide in the first trimester of their pregnancy.'

They fall silent. Somebody catches Jasper's eye and he nearly drops his cup. Her back is to him and she's standing at reception. Her flowing blonde hair is familiar.

'And I understand that Grunenthal are printing brochures entitled "Thalidomide is a safe drug" to be distributed across Europe to allay these fears,' Mrs Kelsey scoffs.

After the meeting Jasper walks through to the reception, scanning the area, from the settees outside the elevators to the hallway. There's a notice indicating the way to the ladies' powder room so he goes in that direction. As he reaches the door, he hovers outside, aware that he's suspiciously loitering outside the ladies' powder room. He finds a settee, perches on the edge and picks up a copy of the *New York Times*. A small column on the front page reports Doctor Kelsey's latest move to delay the licensing of thalidomide. He hopes to spot the girl he saw to confirm, if nothing else, that it isn't Sandy. God damn that woman. Why is she still on my mind, after all this time? he thinks to himself. It isn't healthy to be stuck in this state. He has to move on.

33

BILL

I t's midday and Bill has a raging appetite after a morning of bricklaying. He usually brings cheese-and-pickle sandwiches and a Kit Kat with him but Rona was too busy fussing over the baby she'd stolen, to think about his lunch. He looks forward to knocking off time at five o' clock. Sometimes he calls in for a beer in the pub before heading home, but today the beer and Rona's pie and mash are marred by the burden that sits heavy on his shoulders. The baby. Slapping mortar on bricks, like icing on a cake has given him time to think but it will take him a million years to get his head around what was going through her mind when she decided to snatch a baby. She's lost the plot. She doesn't appreciate how hard it is for him. When a couple can't conceive, it seems that the woman is the one to get the sympathy while the man's feelings are totally ignored, as if he doesn't count. Bill feels like a spectator, standing strong and never showing any emotion. Rona and everybody else are wrong. It has affected him, deeply.

Bill doesn't like surprises and Rona has just given him one hell of a surprise. How does she imagine they can afford to bring this baby up? Especially when they don't have much put by.

Bill sits on a pile of rubble and waits for his workmates to come back from the boozer. He isn't in the mood for a laugh over a lunchtime half. As soon as he's finished the chips he bought from the chippy, he'll return to work. He deals with stress best by carrying on and working.

'Alright mate? You look a bit down in the dumps.'

Ed, the site manager has joined him. It doesn't happen very often but Bill doesn't mind. He's a nice chap, in his sixties and at times he's more like a mate than a boss.

Bill forces a smile, aware that his problems are scribbled across his face.

Ed hands him a pork pie. 'Will this help?'

'It'll take more than a pie mate.'

Ed chuckles. 'What's up? Tell your old boss.'

Bill isn't used to talking about his problems, let alone to a man, and especially not to his boss but he's sick of holding it in and there's something about Ed's sympathetic manner that lures him in. He takes a deep breath. 'It's Rona.'

'Every problem in the whole universe stems from a woman,' Ed laughs taking a bite of pie.

'We've been trying for a baby, but nothing's happened and now she wants to adopt.'

'And you don't, I take it?'

Bill snaps his Kit Kat in two. 'Correct.'

'We adopted both our boys. There are many routes to parenthood, you know, it doesn't have to stem from a roll in the sack— but love is love.'

'Really? How could you love someone else's kids, though?'

'Parenthood is one hell of a lot more than biology.'

'I admire you for it Ed; just not sure I could do it. It doesn't feel right. How did your sons turn out?'

'They've both done me proud. It hasn't been easy, I can tell you that for nothing.'

'What if the child turns out to have something wrong with it? What then?'

'If your own child was born disabled you wouldn't give it up. So, tell me the difference.'

Bill can't think of a reply. It's a valid point. He admires Ed. He has courage and guts, but is he as strong as Ed? He isn't sure.

'If you love your wife, you'll give her the chance to make you a father—you'll be a great father.'

'There are no guarantees. I might be a crap dad.'

'Have you thought about walking away from the marriage? That way you won't have to bear the pain that you've failed her.'

'No,' Bill replies emphatically. There's no way he'd consider that. He's sticking by his marriage vows in sickness and kidnapped babies.

'Well what if she gets so frustrated and depressed over your insistence that you don't want to adopt that she ends up having an affair, just to get pregnant?'

'Rona wouldn't do that. She's a good woman.'

Ed's points are starting to rock his boat. Frustration mounts and he feels the beginnings of a headache coming on.

'You sure about that? People do things out of desperation.'

And didn't he just know it? Bill stares at him. 'Yes, of course. I trust her implicitly.'

'A real father is the one who gets up in the night. Biological fathers don't do any of the dad things better than adoptive fathers. In fact, a whole lot of biological fathers do worse. You'll be fine, you really will.'

A silence unfolds across the rubble and neither men seem keen to disturb it. Ed checks the time. 'We'd better get back to work.'

Bill picks up a rock and crumbles it in his hand, scattering the mess around him and in a splinter of time everything locks into place. The uneasy feeling in the pit of his stomach has cleared. The sun nudges through the clouds giving his epiphany moment a divine edge. He knows what to do, but he'll wait until the end of the day to make sure he isn't going to change his mind.

Ed gets up, brushes the dust from his trousers and puts the lid on his Tupperware box.

'Ed.' Bill puts a hand on his boss's shoulder and squeezes it. 'Thanks mate.'

'Anytime.'

BILL PUTS his tools down shortly after five and with his decision made he goes in search of Ed. He's catching up with paperwork in the site office. Bill knocks before he enters.

'Can I have a quick word?'

'What's up? How much did you get done this afternoon?'

I've finished the other wall.'

'Good work, you're one of my best brickies.'

The compliment takes Bill by surprise. He doesn't consider himself to be any better than the average worker. Guilt washes over him as he prepares to tell Ed that he needs to leave.

'Glad to hear it, but I'm really sorry. I need to go back to Blackpool. A family problem has cropped up.'

'Why didn't you mention it earlier?'

Bill isn't worried about finding a new job. He has his reputation in Blackpool and can easily gather work and re-start his business. Jobs are plentiful. The newspapers are jam packed with vacancies and he can walk out of here and be back in work by Monday. He isn't worried about accommodation, either, because until the tenants can vacate the Blackpool home he

knows of a friend with an empty pre-fab close to the sea where
they can stay for a few weeks.

'I've had a lot on my mind.'

'Can you give me a couple of days to find a replacement?'

'Not really. I need to get up there over the weekend. Listen,
I'm really sorry to let you down.'

34

SANDY

Brave, giddy and innocent Sandy gets ready for her first photo shoot in Manhattan; she's posing as a professional model but feeling as though it's her first day at nursery school.

The lift pings and she steps into the lobby where her American agent is waiting. He's smoking and he holds his cigarette at arm's length while he scans her appearance. She feels like a prize pig in a market.

'First things first darling,' he says, linking his arm in hers and guiding her to the entrance. 'You need to learn all there is to know about make-up.'

Sandy's confidence takes a nose dive. What an insult. She considers herself to be an expert at applying make-up.

'For five bucks we can get you sorted and you're going to need some false eyelashes.'

He shakes his head and after all the effort to get ready Sandy feels underdressed and shabby. In England she has worked without false eyelashes and the way he is looking at her, anybody would think she was in rags. Agents notice everything. The salon is the closest thing to a private club for models and actresses and is run by two Italian men. The walls of reception are crowded with autographed pictures of everybody who was ever anybody in the world of fashion and modelling. Personal notes are scrawled over the signatures, such as 'To Carlos, you gave me such beautiful eyes.' Beautiful faces surround her and Sandy wonders if there's a place on the wall for her. She has to pinch herself to believe she's in New York where it all happens and every chance she can succeed and reach the pinnacles of the modelling world.

After a short lesson in how to apply makeup they pick out lashes and trim them and then they show her, step by step, how to put them on. 'Draw on your eyeliner first very thin. Curl your natural lashes out, then brush them with mascara so that they blend in from below.' When they are finished Sandy is unable to believe the transformation. Whatever would mother, a simple woman from Wigan think of me? She blinks and feels ready to take on the meat inspectors but she's terrified that once she takes off this amazing face, she will never be able to put it back on again. Come the next morning she'll have to get up an hour early to put on her new face. The lashes transform her and she can't wait for her friends' reaction when she returns to England, if they are still attached.

Sandy doesn't sleep a wink; her mind buzzes with thoughts of all the places in New York she wants to visit. She thinks of the people she wants to send postcards to but she doesn't have any, so she makes lists and tries to remember. She writes down everything she's had for dinner and how much she's seen already. The highlight is coffee in an American diner, or as they call it 'a cup of Joe.' The coffee is strong and smooth and so much nicer than the Camp coffee in a bottle she is used to at home. For Sandy the diner is the quintessential American experience. Posters of Elvis and Marilyn beam from the walls, smiling waitresses in little black skirts and frilly white aprons whizz around on black and white tiles.

She loves the chrome-flashed experience and even though she isn't going to ruin her figure, it is enough to sip coffee while watching the waitresses serve huge wedges of cherry pie and cream, tall strawberry shakes and stacks of fluffy pancakes dripping in syrup. What a long way England has to come, to match this incredible dining experience. The only time her family eat out is to picnic in a damp field or eat a pot of cockles at Southend-on-Sea and that's in the bus shelter if it's raining. A special treat is fish and chips wrapped in the *Daily Herald*. Nothing compares to this wonderful New York experience.

After the second day's shoot, Sandy climbs the steps of the hotel and walks towards the lift, avoiding eye contact with admirers milling around reception. They are like flies to a cow's bottom.

She's been standing all day and her feet ache. She can't wait to crash on the bed and close her eyes before running a bath. She presses the button and waits for the lift to drop and the doors to open. Several men cram in behind her. She presses the floor number and one of them leans over to press another button. A familiar combination of male smells tickles her nostrils as the lift whirrs, edging upward. With her eyes to the ground she doesn't pay attention to the men, who are chatting about business.

As the doors open one of them turns to speak to her. Their eyes connect. Her heart jolts in her chest.

'Sandy.'

He has his finger on the button to hold the door open.

My God, Jasper what are you doing here?'

'I could say the same to you. I thought I saw you in the lobby yesterday. I thought I was imagining it.'

She feels her face pink and prickles of heat rise on her back.

Jasper steps out of the lift, his finger still on the button and Sandy follows.

'I'll join you fellas for breakfast, tomorrow morning, alright?'

The three men in the lift give him a knowing smile and Jasper is embarrassed. 'Just an old friend,' he calls after them.

When the lift doors shut Sandy can't believe that he's here, in New York and staying in the same hotel. Of all the coincidences that could happen in life.

'Is that what I am?' she asks, awkwardness settling over her, she's alone with the man who broke her heart. 'An old friend? Great.'

'No, of course not. You were...' He struggles to find the right words.

'It's great to see you, Jasper, it really is,' she gushes, putting a hand on his shoulder with determination to smooth away the lingering awkwardness.

They stand in the stuffy hallway, with an urgency to bring each other up to speed on what they're doing in New York at the same time and in the same hotel, how incredible is that? Their questions trip over each other until the conversation slows to a calmer pace.

'Why didn't you reply to my letters?' he asks. 'It would have been nice to get a reply even if you'd told me to take a running jump.'

'Letters?' Sandy is confused.

'Yes. I sent you about ten, in all.' His voice breaks through her thoughts. 'Do you think your mother could have...?'

'Destroyed them? It wouldn't surprise me.'

His voice is gravelly. 'Why would she do that? I don't understand.'

'Probably thought she was trying to protect me.' But Sandy doesn't think it's that at all. It's exactly the type of thing her controlling mother would do, out of spite, revenge for getting pregnant out of wedlock. She feels the first stirrings of hate towards her mother. 'I can't think of any other reason.' Her voice splinters as she tries to remain calm. The last thing she wants is for Jasper to read her thoughts.

'It doesn't matter,' he says cheerfully. 'Listen, you're probably shattered but what about a quick drink before we turn in. It's still early—and this is New York.'

It's later than she thought and she has to get up early the following morning and needs to catch up on vital sleep before the next shoot. 'You can buy me a Martini, but I can't be long.'

The quick drink turns into several as she listens, yawning through tiredness rather than boredom, as he explains his latest project to her—it's a series of interviews about the drug thalidomide.

'I came over here to interview the Federal Drugs Agency to find out why they weren't approving a drug that has been hugely successful in Europe.'

Sandy stifles a yawn as she struggles to keep up. The waiter's weaving between tables and she snaps her fingers at him and orders a strong coffee.

'What's the name of the drug again?'

'Thalidomide.'

'I've heard of that.'

Sandy frowns. The name rings a bell. 'I've heard of that.'

'It's marketed under the name of Distaval in England.'

Realising that this is the drug she'd taken for morning sickness she inhales a sharp intake of breath at the wrong time and chokes. The choking stops her from hearing what he's saying next but she catches the words 'side effects.'

She puts her cup on the saucer and stares at him. 'What did you say? Side effects of taking the drug?'

'No pharmaceutical industry in the world carries out any kind of testing to ensure the safety for the unborn child of a drug given during pregnancy. There are deformed babies being born all over and some doctors are asking questions about whether thalidomide could be responsible. At this stage it's all uncertain. My thought is that there needs to be a system, applicable internationally, for detecting previously unknown or poorly understood adverse effects of medicines. The system is haphazard and negligent. Before marketing a drug, firms here and in Britain don't have to prove the safety of their drugs, or provide substantial evidence of effectiveness for the product's intended use. They dish out the drugs as samples and that's enough to protect the company. A system of proper trials needs to be implemented. That's what I'm interested in and the people who want to make that happen. Drug companies should provide evidence of adequate and well-controlled studies.'

Sandy feels faint. 'They didn't test the drug before it went on the market?'

'They experimented on rats and no matter how high the dose the rats were given it had no toxic symptoms. There are a few laws in Germany governing drug regulation but it's not tight enough by a long shot. Through my work I want to change that.'

'How, though?'

'Interviews, publicity, uncovering the truth. The truth is out there, somewhere. You've just got to find it. That's what journalists do, we uncover the truth. It's like being a cop.'

Sandy stifles a yawn. He's gone on long enough. It's been lovely to see him and have a drink but it's time for bed.

'Are you tired?' He puts a hand on her arm.

She doesn't want to be rude. 'Yes, but carry on, tell me what you're doing here in New York. I'll be fine for ten more minutes.'

'Doctor Kelsey of the Food and Drugs Agency is interested in the effect of drugs on the foetus. She conducted studies on rabbits in 1943 which found that the developing foetus can't break down drugs as efficiently as an adult can. The foetus is at greater risk than the pregnant woman from damage by a toxic drug. There are so many questions but few answers. The greatest danger to the foetus is in the first three months of pregnancy. Many parts of Europe are very backward. In southern Spain, a deformed baby is blamed on the sins of the mother and hidden away.'

She goes still and looks towards the wall.

'You look pale.'

'I should go up. I'm very tired.'

'Can I see you again?'

'Is there much point?' She sounds blunt and modifies her tone. 'What I mean is we've moved on Jasper.'

'But I like your company. I never forgot about you. Please? Dinner? Tomorrow evening.'

'Let me sleep on it. Maybe.'

As Sandy walks back to her room she realises that she still has feelings for him and this panics her. She thought she was over him. He's let her down but she had no idea that he still loved and wanted her and had made an effort to stay in touch. Her damn mother. At times she hates her. She remembers her words on replay months ago. You've brought disgrace upon yourself and shame on your family. What you've done is a wicked thing, unforgivable. Whatever her mother felt, she didn't have the right to throw his letters away and deny her the chance to get back with him. It was cruel and calculated. Given the way she'd wanted Sandy to contact Jasper and tell him about the pregnancy so that he could put things right and marry her, her mother's rationale is strange. It doesn't make sense. She can't wait to challenge her when she returns. As Sandy turns the key in her room door, her mind is made up. She'll show her mother. She'll get back with Jasper and rekindle their feelings, just to spite her.

35

RONA

etween feeds and nappy changes Rona rushes around the flat, opening wardrobes and packing cases, like a woman possessed. All she can think about is getting away from London, making sure the baby is safe and escaping trouble. She doesn't know where she's going or whether Bill will come with her. Toby is her responsibility and even if Bill isn't going to stick by her, she can't let the baby down. It's too late. If she took him back to the nursing home she'd be in a lot of trouble. She can't risk that.

At the back of her mind she knows that she's on her own. Bill isn't as strong as she is. He can't look beyond the baby's disability. What the hell has she done? The stress of trying for a baby was so overwhelming that her feelings drove her to a state of insanity.

With the flat half-packed she sits down, with the sleeping baby in her arms as she watches the sun sinking in the sky. Bill will be home soon and angry that she hasn't done what he'd asked her. She's worried that he'll take Toby back. He'll try to wrench Toby from her arms. This is like the judgement of King Solomon in Israel, when he ordered the baby to be cut in half.

She isn't going to let him take Toby away. He's hers and belongs to her now.

She switches the radio on shortly after five. They are discussing the Soviet unmanned space probe. Rona isn't interested in space missions. She finds it very boring. She hears the key turn in the lock. Bill's home. Her breath comes in loud rasps. She makes a dash for the baby, asleep on the settee, a fist of panic squeezing her insides.

'I'm home,' he says coming into the lounge without cheer or expectation. He stands by the settee.

'What's going on Rona?' The boxes and bags along the hall speak for her.

'I need to get away from here. It's too risky to stay. People will get suspicious and ask questions.'

'When are we leaving?' he asks calmly, as if this is an everyday event. He throws his keys on the coffee table. She can't believe what she's hearing. Her heart bangs in her chest and bile rises in her throat. Were they going to pull this off? He's prepared to risk everything, to give it a go, even though this is the most difficult and challenging thing to ever happen to him. She realises how much he loves her—one day he'll love Toby with just that kind of fierceness.

'What are you saying Bill?'

'I've made a few phone calls.'

'You've told someone?'

'Of course not.'

'Bill I've been so scared. I love him. I need him. He needs us.'

'I've arranged for a van to pick us up on Saturday. It's only a couple of days to wait. And I've sorted us somewhere to live.'

She stands up, a beaming smile on her face and kisses him on the lips. 'I love you so much. Why did you change your mind?'

'Don't pretend this is going to be easy. What we're doing is wrong.' He stops, his frown deepening, lips pursed as if gearing up for the next stage of his speech. 'Have you even given this much thought beyond being emotional?'

'What do you mean?'

'Rona, come on, honey, wake up to the reality. He could die. There could be more things wrong with him. He might need operations. How's he going to cope with life? There won't be clapping, or banging, or waving or riding bicycles or swimming. He's a cripple.'

'Don't you think I know all that? I'm not stupid.'

'Alright, calm down.'

'I've got my faith Bill. Sometimes bad things happen that put us directly on the path to good things. He'll have love. Love is all he needs.'

Bill puts his arm on Rona's shoulder and says nothing for a moment. Then he says, 'Think how it will be for him. Not being able to do those things.'

'Sometimes you have to stop thinking so much and let your heart direct you,' she whispers.

'Let me hold him.'

Rona is startled. It's the first time he's shown an interest in Toby. She passes the baby to Bill and he sits down and unwraps the blanket exposing his stunted arms. His eyes well up as he stares at the flipper-like hands coming out of Toby's shoulders.

'How's he going to feed himself or hold a pen to write his name, what about all the normal things we take for granted?'

'I'll tell you how Bill, we'll throw obstacles in his way. And we'll watch him struggle. And we won't help. And it'll break our hearts. But we'll give him what every other child has and we'll ask him to do what other children do. And we'll watch his pain without interfering until he works out a way. And then we'll love him until our arms ache. It's God's plan.'

'God's plan?' Bill stares at her. 'If God exists then he's not a loving God, he's evil.'

'You don't mean that.'

'I'm scared Rona, I'm really scared. What was so wrong with just with the two of us? We were happy enough.'

'I know we were. But it wasn't enough. Life feels complete now we've got him.'

'We'll have to register him with a doctor as soon as we get to Blackpool and think up a story. God Rona, I hate lying. It's not in my nature. I hate this whole thing. It doesn't sit easy.'

'Nor mine, but the more I practice what I'm going to say, the more it becomes reality.'

'Which is?'

'You're forgetting that I'm a midwife. I'll spin a plausible story. I had terrible pains. I didn't know I was pregnant. I gave birth in the kitchen unexpectedly and I knew what to do. And you're forgetting that my mum and sisters think I'm pregnant.' She looks down at her visiting bag containing all the implements needed for a home birth.

Bill stares at her, his eyes big and terrified. 'My God you planned to steal a baby from the beginning. Huh, you might have got a normal one.'

He steps closer to her, a glaze of horror across his face.

'No,' she screams. Her face pinks in shame. 'What do you take me for?'

'Oh, come on, Rona you planned to steal him.'

The accusation cuts through her like a knife. He doesn't trust her, after years of being together. She could never do that. He has it all wrong. This is a different situation. The baby is handicapped, nobody wanted him, he was left to die.

'I rescued him. Remember that before you go twisting the facts. He was left to die.'

Bill sits down, covers his face with his hands and cries. This is the last thing Rona needs. She needs him to be strong and act like a man. How can they get through this if he's already buckling?

He wipes his eyes and sniffs. This isn't like him. The stress is getting to him and for a moment she feels guilty. She caused this. He didn't ask for it to happen but she's putting him in an impossible situation.

'They'll wonder why you didn't take him to the doctor to have him checked.'

'Well I will do.' She looks incredulous. 'In a few days, when we get back to Blackpool.' She sounds self-assured but underneath her nerves are jangling.

'You could say you were scared and worried that a doctor might take him away and put him in an institution.'

'That worries me anyway. He's not going anywhere. He stays with us.'

'Yes but, Rona, he needs specialised care.'

'And he'll get it.' Her hands fly into the air in despair. 'But he doesn't need to live in an institution, miles away. We'd never see him. He needs a bedroom with aeroplane wallpaper and a teddy bear called Boris. He needs a front door to shut the world out sometimes and he needs a treehouse to climb in.'

'You're nuts, a treehouse? I'm not even going to humour you. I don't think you're understanding the enormity of all this. You've no idea what caused the deformity. What if we're at risk?'

Rona got up to straighten cushions, something she always did when she was wound up. Hearing this she tosses a cushion at him. 'At risk. This isn't something we're going to catch. Maybe if he has children when he's older they might inherit the deformity, I don't know. I don't have all of the answers Bill, but don't worry, you aren't going to wake up tomorrow morning with flippers and a nasty little rash.'

'Well hallelujah, at least you've admitted that. It's not just today, or even next month that we have to worry about, it's the long-term repercussions for the rest of our lives—or the rest of his life, whichever may be longer.'

'Are you with me?' Her face was hard. 'Because if you're not...' Her voice trails off.

'Yes, of course I am. I just feel helpless for the first time in my life.'

She stands in front of him and takes his hand. 'You'll make a great dad. I know you will. This is going to work. Have faith.'

'I wish I had your confidence love.'

THE FOLLOWING day Bill is quiet and preoccupied. It isn't like him and Rona hopes that by giving him space and time to think things over, he will come round to the idea of bringing up a special baby. She's aware that it's a tall order but there's no turning back. He's got to get used to the idea. Toby isn't going anywhere. He's staying right here, with her.

Bill goes to the pub at lunchtime, giving her a peck on the cheek and a cursory glance in Toby's direction. He says he'll be gone a while and as the door closes behind him, she thinks he'll never come back. There's something about the distance in his manner making her worry that he'll throw himself off the canal bridge. He can't swim and would drown. When he doesn't return home fears mount and she thinks about ringing the pub.

Just before dinnertime she hears his key in the lock and relief washes over her. She rushes into the hall to greet him. She wants to fling her arms around him but can't bring herself to because she's alarmed. Instead of asking him if he's alright she tells him that dinner is nearly ready in a semblance of making things normal. Her heart lurches when he doesn't smile or respond. He's ashen, visibly unwell and there are hollows under his eyes. Without a word, he slumps into his armchair. She can smell beer breath and the pungent aroma of stale cigarettes on his clothes.

· · ·

TOBY IS asleep in the washing basket by her side of the bed. As soon as they are settled back in Blackpool, Rona is going to use some of their savings to buy a cot and everything else he needs, but there's no rush, he's tiny and fits in the basket. Bill turns to sleep, moving further away from her than normal, his arm around his pillow. Fingers of sleep push towards her and soon she's out for the count. Something wakes her. She isn't sure how long she's slept. Sleep abandons her in seconds and the worry of Bill sneaks into her mind under the cover of darkness, unpicking the threads of their previously comfortable relationship. Turning over to check on Toby she's thrown into panic. Bill, who should be silhouetted under the bed covers is gone. Toby is gone too. Her heart jolts in her chest. She pulls back the covers, dazed and muddled-headed. There's a scratching noise coming from the lounge and she strains to listen. In the darkness she can see Bill crouched over the settee.

Something inside her somersaults and she lurches forward, catching Bill in the splint of time as he moves to smother Toby with a pillow. A scream pierces the silence as she pushes him, grabbing Toby and holding him against her pounding chest. Bill stumbles to the floor. In the shadows his body convulses in painful heaving sobs. Rona flops onto the settee, crying and shivering with fear.

'You were going to kill him,' she screeches.

'I'm sorry.'

He's huddled into a foetal position and Rona thinks how wretched and weak he looks. This isn't the man she married. Does she even want to be with him anymore?

'What were you thinking?'

'I don't know, alright?' He puts one hand on the edge of the settee and pulls himself up, his head bowed.

'Why should we be the ones to carry the guilt?'

'Guilt?'

'He's not my child but I'll be expected to feel guilty for the way he is. I'll have to absorb people's horror and disgust when I take him out in public. I'll spend my life apologising for what he is and seeing pity wherever we go. It's bad enough being the only ones without kids, that racks me with guilt. I felt like an odd ball then, but this. For God's sake Rona, wake up.'

Bill wipes his tears away and builds into another frenzy. She can see the anger in his body mounting. She doesn't know what he's capable of and she doesn't trust him anymore.

'Are you with me on this because it's not changing a thing? I'm bringing him up on my own if I have to.'

'Don't do this to me.' He stares at her, pleading. 'Don't make me choose, please.' He reaches out and yanks her nightie, holding a fistful of cotton.

'Let go. Just calm down.' She pushes his hand away and paces the room.

'You need to get a grip, Bill.'

'Alright. Stop going on at me. You've thrown me into this. You gave me no choice. You may as well have held a gun to my head.'

'Don't be dramatic. The neighbours will hear and wonder what's going on.'

'Sod the neighbours. We'll be out of here in a few days time.'

'Come and sit down.' She pats the settee beside her. 'Let's pray together.'

He hesitates, then sits, his face calmer. They hold hands as Rona whispers the Lord's Prayer. When she's finished they sit in silence watching Toby sleep. Bill rubs her back and sighs, then gets up and goes into the kitchen to make tea. Her nerves dance in her stomach, not knowing what will happen next but all the time he is here, even though he's unstable, has to be a positive thing. She'll have to keep an eye on him and watch over Toby with extra care. Bill will come round, she knows he will.

36

SANDY

Sandy wakes thinking about the things Jasper has talked about. She'd been tired and tipsy but the conversation was piecing itself together. He's in New York to interview somebody high up in government who is stopping a drug going on the market in the U.S. He said it's a drug known as thalidomide. It's the drug she took for morning sickness, a brilliant pill that had zapped her sickness in one hit. She has to know more about his research without revealing her pregnancy. He must never know.

She washes and styles her hair, makes her face up and polishes her nails before leaving her suite. She thinks about the day ahead. The lift doors ping open and Jasper's there, as if he planned it. He beams at her, says good morning and ushers her into the lift.

'What a coincidence. Join me for breakfast?' It doesn't feel like a coincidence but she doesn't mind. She's glad. Maybe he'll suggest that evening out.

'I won't thank you. I'm watching my weight.'

'You can't starve yourself, honey. How about dinner instead

and a trip to the top of the Empire State building? You still eat dinner, I take it?

'I'd love that.' Excitement makes her tingle and she beams at him in delight.

THEY MEET in the foyer at seven and Jasper hails a yellow cab.

'You look beautiful,' he says when they are driving towards the skyscraper on Fifth Avenue. She wears a soft blue Audrey-Hepburn style dress with a sash tied around her waist. Sandy has the same elegant style and elfin beauty as Hepburn and can carry it off. People hurry along the sidewalks and Sandy marvels at the forest of tall buildings and spectacular show of lights lining their route. She loves New York and its cacophony of culture and wants to take it all in energy and time permitting.

They emerge onto Fifth Avenue, step out of the cab and Sandy gasps at the tall building in the night sky, a stairway to heaven awaiting her. Four beacons of light shine at the foot of the tower as a symbol of welcome and freedom to visitors.

'It's amazing to think that in 1776 this was the site of an unsuccessful revolutionary battle.'

He's a well-read man, it's one of the things that makes her want him. Intelligence is an aphrodisiac. He's a great catch.

'You're gazing a quarter of a mile into the sky,' he says. They stand at the side of the road with the lights of Manhattan like twinkling diamonds. Her heart lurches as he makes sure they're safe to cross. Until now, she didn't know how much she wants him and what a mistake she made letting him go.

'First let's have dinner then we can take the elevator to the viewing point.'

They go into a restaurant on the corner of the street where meat is turning on skewers in the window. It isn't busy. The

walls are covered in wood and the lighting is soft. They're
ushered to a window seat and handed menus.

'It's great to see you again Sandy. I didn't think I would.' He
touches her hand and smiles.

'A lot's happened I guess.'

'Sounds as if something pretty big happened to you.' He's
frowning. She hopes he isn't going to press her.

'Oh just life, you know, work mainly.'

'Mainly? What are you not saying? Did you meet anyone
after me?'

'No. I've been busy trying to get contracts and this came
along with the chance to travel for a couple of weeks in Canada.
I jumped at it.'

'Well good for you.'

Sandy waits until their meals are on the table before she
asks him about his work.

'I think I've heard of the drug you were talking about last
night. A friend of mine took it during pregnancy for morning
sickness.'

'The German manufactures, Grunenthal maintain that it's a
suitable drug for pregnant women. But when a Finnish doctor
asked them a series of significant questions, their ignorance
was astounding. They don't even know whether thalidomide
passes through the placenta to the growing child. They think
it's unlikely that the drug would be harmful even if it did. He
asked them which organs thalidomide is broken down in and
they said probably the liver. Probably, unlikely and not known,
are words they use when questioned but there's no categorical
certainty. It's all speculation.'

'I'm surprised they give pregnant mothers anything. It's
better not to, to be on the safe side.'

'Well I think many doctors don't like to, as a rule but they've
been weakened by the positive literature that Grunenthal has
distributed claiming it's safe. Let's face it, you or I have no idea

the level of misery a woman with morning sickness suffers. It's like the common cold, it's something that we face as part of normal existence, it isn't going to kill us and it's an irritant for a little while. But wouldn't it be great if you could take an innocuous pill to alleviate the symptoms and get on with your daily routine? Nobody knows for sure. It's an interesting subject and I'm enjoying my work. But the fact remains, this drug has never been tested on pregnant animals let alone pregnant women.'

'Maybe it didn't need to be tested.'

'This story will shock you. It's just a rumour, but even rumours stem from something. I'm well connected in the medical world, so I hear things. Apparently back in 1956 the wife of a Grunenthal employee was given samples of the drug and gave birth to a daughter with no ears. The story's been hushed. The parents were told to keep it a secret. All Grunenthal has done since is dampen fears about this drug while at the same time pumping out literature across Europe telling doctors and patients it's one of the safest drugs ever to be invented.'

'Well if it's a secret how do you know about it?'

Jasper taps his nose. 'Connections darling, that's all I'm saying.'

'Should you be telling me then?'

Jasper waves his hand at her, smiles and takes a sip of his drink.

Sandy's greed is germinating an idea. 'Just supposing Grunenthal turns out to be wrong and the drug is causing deformities, as you suggest that it might be? What then?'

'Well, obviously it would be withdrawn from the market.'

'Yes, but would mothers be able to claim compensation?'

'That would be a long way down the road. At the moment this is just speculation.'

'But possible?'

'I guess. If it comes to it, they should be held to account.'

Sandy puts her wine glass to her lips. Pound signs ping in her head. If her deformed baby turns out to be a victim of this drug, just think what she could do with the money? Visions of travel and nice clothes float in her mind—why shouldn't she gain from it, after all—she suffered.

THEY HEAD to America's cultural icon, designed in its distinctive art deco style.

They peer through the perspex across the twinkling city in its full glory.

'Years ago, you could peer over the wall. They had to put this barrier up to stop people from jumping over.'

Sandy can't imagine jumping from a tall building. If she wanted to take her life she'd take an overdose. It's easier. The only time she's ever been depressed was during her pregnancy, with nobody to open up to and a mother who'd shunted her off to Brighton with everything kept a deadly secret. She wonders how things would have turned out if she'd contacted Jasper and told him about the baby. At the time she was too set on getting rid of the baby; if she couldn't abort it, then she'd farm it out to an infertile couple and get on with her life. Jasper slips his hand into hers. She has a fizz of longing for him, but mixed in with that is a feeling of regret. If the baby was healthy they could have made a go of things but not with the disability. She shudders to think what might have been, saddled with bringing up a deformed baby and how it would have ruined her life.

They chat as they watch the night lights.

'Imagine if the lights went out, plunging the whole of the city into darkness. It would result in anarchy.'

'Do you remember the war? My dad was a warden, going round at night and making sure there were no chinks of light coming through peoples' curtains and now look; a city bathed in light with no fear of being bombed.'

The air is chilly and they go back for a drink in the hotel. Her mind keeps returning to the thought of compensation. If a storm brews over this drug, in a couple of years, she could visit the doctor and see where she stands. She'd tell him that her life was a mess after losing her much-loved child. Having a deformed baby was suffering enough, but the nightmares, and inability to move on—well, that was ongoing trauma and deserving of a lot of compassion. And with the baby dead any money due was rightfully hers.

They drink too much and Sandy sways as she walks, with Jasper steadying her with an arm around her waist. He hovers outside her room, while she fumbles in her bag for the key, a cheeky glint in his eye as he waits to be invited in.

She feels the pull of attraction as his lips move towards her. They kiss in the corridor. She doesn't want to open the door and risk them tumbling in, with regret hanging over her the following morning. She's been there once and drunk or not, she isn't going to repeat the experience and end up pregnant again.

His fingers trail up the inside of her thighs as they kiss.

She's torn between a desperate urge to sweep him into her room so that he can devour her and a nervousness that makes her push him away as she snaps back to reality.

'Do you want me?'

'It's getting late. I've got to look my best for tomorrow's shoot.'

'Tease.'

It's on the tip of her tongue to tell him they don't want to make the same mistake again. If they're going to get back together, how on earth can she keep the secret from him? It's bound to come out, secrets and lies always do and she isn't very good at holding her tongue.

'Okay, I'll see you in the morning my love.'

She closes her door on him reluctant to let him go, but determined to stick to her guns and not relent.

37

RONA

Rona and Bill stay in a pre-fab near Fylde for eight months before returning to their house in Blackpool and move back just in time for Christmas. Things are easier with Bill although he rarely holds Toby and there's a distance between him and the baby. Rona worries that people will pick up on it, but she reasons that many fathers would have difficulty bonding with a disabled child.

Her mother and sisters have distanced themselves and she's knows it's because they don't know how to react to Toby's disability. She's tired of her mother's disgust. She's never held Toby and recoiled if Rona tried to pass him to her, as if he has a disease. She stopped visiting and he gets none of the attention she lavishes on her other grandchildren. Her suggestions to put the baby in institutional care are based on her fear. All she cares about are other peoples' reactions and what people think. 'Do you really want him to be stared at when he gets older?' she keeps asking Rona. 'He needs to be in a special place, with his own kind. And how on earth do you expect to cope?' She has no faith in her daughter and the fact that Rona loves Toby means nothing to her.

When she'd seen him for the first time she clapped her hand to her mouth and shrank away in horror. It was an extreme reaction that Rona has never seen from people in the street. She'd rushed from the room and her sisters said nothing, gathering their coats and using important business as an excuse to get away. It was obvious that they didn't want their children around Toby. The following week, after making a dozen excuses, her mother came for coffee. Rona thought she was going to apologise and make amends, maybe with a gift for the baby or an offer of help. But worse followed. Rona was shocked when her mother accused her of not heeding her warnings about marrying Bill. 'I told you Bill was no good, but you wouldn't listen. He's to blame. It's obvious that the baby has inherited something dreadful from his family.'

THERE'S a knock at the door. Rona isn't expecting anybody. She's decorating the Christmas tree and hanging an angel on the top. She steps down from the chair, worried that it could be her mother. She can only think that it could be her mother, but she's surprised to open it to the doctor.

'I was just passing on my rounds and thought I'd call in to see how you are getting on. Is now a convenient time?'

She invites him in.

He puts his bag on the settee and mumbles something about the weather.

'Coffee? I was just putting the tree up. It'll be his first Christmas.

'Not for me thanks. The tree is beautiful.'

'What can I do for you, Doctor? I haven't missed any appointments, have I?'

Rona has been for several hospital appointments to have Toby checked and she was told that he might have to have an operation on his shoulders when he's older. For the moment, things are going well and there are no health concerns other than how he will manage as he grows. She'll meet problems as they arise and deal with them.

'I wanted to ask you something. Have you read the news stories about the drug thalidomide? It's being taken off the market because of concerns about it causing birth defects.'

'I did see something.' Rona picks the paper up and finds the small article entitled, 'Sleeping pill is withdrawn, abnormal birth reports.'

'We're warning pregnant women to stop taking it and to hand their packets of Distaval into their nearest pharmacy. Midwives are knocking from door to door gathering in packets.'

Rona is certain that Toby's mother had taken the drug. She remembers her saying how much better she'd felt, after taking a couple of the pills. Rona remembers thinking how incredible it must be.

'I know we discussed possible causes of Toby's handicap when you registered with us. But his stunted arms look very like the arms of the other babies that have been linked to Distaval. I can't see any reference to it in your medical records, which is odd. Were you prescribed it?'

Rona is scared. He's taken her by surprise calling round and she isn't prepared. She needs to keep a low profile. She isn't sure how to answer and hesitates, frowning while she thinks to buy her time.

'I did,' she says carefully. 'But the doctor didn't prescribe it. A friend gave it to me. I'd been feeling sick and she said it helped her.'

'Okay, well I'll make a note on your file. I'm thinking way ahead, and this is purely speculative at this stage but you may or may not qualify for compensation, if the pharmaceutical company award it, given that you took unprescribed medication. But that's a long way down the line. It's early days.'

Rona isn't interested in compensation. She's managing fine. She wants a quiet life.

'You're a midwife so you'll understand how these things work. It will go to the Supreme Court and my guess is that the manufacturers will defend themselves by claiming that they observed the testing standards.'

'I'd like to examine Toby again if I may.' Ruth stifles a sigh. How many times have various doctors examined him? She hopes it isn't going to be like this for the rest of his life. He's not a freak to be poked and prodded.

'The name given to his condition is phocomelia— it means seal-limbed. I want to discuss my plan of action for Toby. When he is eighteen months old, I want him to go to St. Mary's Hospital, Roehampton to be fitted with prosthetic arms.'

Rona is horrified. 'Is that really necessary Doctor?'

'The makers are trying to make the replacement appendages work like real limbs. They might not be as bad as you think.'

Rona tries to imagine a pair of cumbersome implements attached to his flipper- like arms. She isn't happy.

'They don't sound as if they'll be very comfortable. He'll spend all day trying to work them.'

The doctor ignores her concerns. 'I think you'll find that as he gets older he'll want to appear as normal as possible in order to fit into society.'

Rona is determined to stick to her guns. Toby's her baby and she will make the judgement about what is best for him.

'Why does he need to look normal? They'll only give him an outward appearance of normality.'

'You don't want him laughed at or treated differently.'

'But he is different.' She feels a prick of anger. 'We can stick as many doll's arms on him as you like but we're never going to make him normal.'

'We just want to help him so that he can do all the things that other children can do. That's what this is about, giving him something to pick up things with.'

'A pair of arms will slow him down. He'll find a way of doing what other children do. I know he will.'

'Modern engineering ingenuity can give him some of the functions that thalidomide has stolen from him.'

Rona isn't convinced. 'He'll learn to hold a pen with his mouth.'

'You may find the school won't take him unless he's got arms fitted. I doubt they'll be able to provide him with one-to-one help. I have to warn you not to expect him to have as much intelligence as other children.'

'I'll go into the school and help him myself if it comes to it. And I don't believe there's anything wrong with him. So far he's achieving all of his milestones.'

'The school might not take him without artificial limbs. You need to bear that in mind.'

Rona is irritated. She doesn't want to think about Toby's future. It's too early. She wants to enjoy his first Christmas and take each stage as it comes. She doesn't want his life to be planned or put limitations on him - if she has pre-conceived low expectations for him—what can he aspire to? If issues arise she'll take it in her stride and deal with it.

When the doctor leaves Rona thinks about what he's said. She sits down with a cup of tea. If Distaval has caused so many deformities it's shocking and something will have to be done. Having worked in the National Health Service she imagines how the doctors who have prescribed the drug must be feeling. She feels the weight of the mother's burden, the guilt they must feel is immense. The health professionals would be advised by their professional bodies to say nothing and admit nothing to avoid incriminating themselves. There had been a couple of

occasions when Rona obtained a prescription for Distaval for women suffering from sleeplessness and morning sickness. She shudders to think that she might have caused a deformity. She feels sick and bile rises in her throat. She thinks of all of the mothers who've taken the tablet, in good faith, who are racked with guilt.

38

SANDY

S andy gets home in the late autumn of 1961, having taken a tour to the Canadian west coast. She visited Banff and Vancouver on a Greyhound coach. With her love for Jasper rekindled and his recent move back to London she's looking forward to spending time with him and seeing where it takes them. She has every hope that things will work this time. She needs to confront her mother about the letters. But home again with her parents, she doesn't feel confident and strong enough to do it. Something inside her collapses and she feels small and weak-willed. It's a shame because she's gained confidence at work, coming on in leaps and bounds and has discovered an energy she didn't know she had. Her parents created an atmosphere a long time ago, that's intimidating and puts her on edge. She has to tap down the emotions swirling in her stomach and not let them get to her.

She is dating Jasper regularly but is careful not to let him pick her up. They meet at the end of the street and he drops her on the corner. She tells them she's going out with work colleagues and girlfriends because it's easier. They don't like her socialising with anybody and don't make things easy for her. Her mother watches by the window and her father shows his disapproval with a rustle of the paper and a draw on his pipe.

One Saturday afternoon Sandy meets Jasper. They're going for a walk in Regent's Park and then to a cafe for tea and cake. They saunter around the flower beds, laughing and comfortable in each other's company. They pass poplar trees standing like brooms by the water's edge and clank along the crisscrossed iron bridge while swans glide towards the Regency terraces.

In the middle of the bridge, Jasper drops to his knee. Shock courses through her as she realises what is about to happen.

'I love you more every day, Sandy,' he takes a small box out of his trouser pocket and opens it. A beautiful diamond glitters under the fading light. Sandy gasps and claps her hand to her mouth.

'Will you marry me, Sandy?'

'Yes,' she says without hesitation.

They laugh as he slips the traditional solitaire onto her ring finger.

As they walk towards the tube, her elation turns to horror when she remembers her dirty secret. Would he still want her if he knew the truth? She doesn't want to tell him. It might spoil things. He'd wonder why she hadn't contacted him and had never said anything. He had a right to know, both at the time and subsequently. Even though it was his child and he can take half of the blame, she feels ashamed. He might feel differently about her knowing what she'd done, particularly when he finds out that she planned to give the baby away. And what would he think if he found out that it had died? He would want to have known, she was sure of that. As they chat, her mind is in overdrive working out what to do. She can keep it a secret and pretend that it never happened, erasing it from her mind. Or she can come clean. Better to be honest; she can't marry him with secrets in the cellar. It would only come out later, these things always do. She knows how it will come spilling out. Her mother will say something and then step back to gloat in the fallout. This whole mess is out of her control.

'I love this time of year when you can kick leaves across the grass.'

'Me too,' she replies, a glaze of anxiety mixed with happiness working its way around her stomach. 'And the smell of bonfires.'

She can't do it. Not yet. She isn't certain how he'll respond and can't risk it. She needs to work out the perfect time and place to tell him.

He stops walking and turns to face her.

'Let's get married soon. Let's go to Gretna Green and do it in secret. I don't want a big wedding, we don't need the fuss.'

It isn't how Sandy imagines her wedding day. She wants church bells, a big cake, bridesmaids and lots of friends. In normal circumstances she would have been hugely disappointed and cheated by his suggestion and would have protested and got her own way. But she had to admit this way makes sense. Her parents won't be there to ruin the day.

Waltzing down her garden path after saying goodbye to Jasper Sandy is ready to confront her mother.

'Have you seen the paper today?'

'I haven't got time to read the paper, Mum. What's happened, then?'

A pungent smell of boiled onion wafts around the tiny kitchen. The paper is spread across the table, where cutlery and napkins for dinner should be.

'What am I supposed to be looking at?'

Her mother stabs her finger at an article in the top corner of the page.

Sandy reads the headline. 'Hunt for stocks of thalidomide.'

'That's the drug you took, for morning sickness.'

Sandy pulls out a chair, folds the paper and reads the article aloud.

'Health workers have been active since last week retrieving supplies of thalidomide. Thalidomide, which is marketed under various names (Distaval in the UK) was first licensed in the UK in 1958 and withdrawn at the end of last year following concerns that it caused birth defects. People with tablets or syrup containing the drug are asked to return them to their family doctor.'

'Have you got any?' Her mother is still ashamed that her daughter was pregnant. She stirs the gravy as if she doesn't want the discussion but feels that she ought to.

'I don't think so.'

Sandy has the packet in her drawer but after a discussion with Jasper she has decided to keep it as evidence, in case there is serious money to be made from a compensation claim.

'It...'

'Him. It was a little boy Mum.'

Her mother is ruffled and carries on busying herself around the kitchen.

'His lack of arms may have been caused by the drug. If you've got any leftover you must hand them in. We don't want them getting into the hands on another pregnant woman by mistake. That would be really tragic. Especially if they were married.'

Sandy can't believe what she's hearing and is her mother really that dumb? She folds the paper. 'And what difference would marriage make for goodness sake?' She's kept her feelings under wraps for too long and they bubble over. 'A crippled baby was born. He died. Isn't that tragic enough for you?' she snaps.

Behind Sandy the lounge door closes. She hears the creak of the armchair as her dad throws himself into it, the volume of the TV increases, making it known that he's drowning out the conversation.

'In your case it was a blessing. But for a married couple it would be a tragedy.'

'I could have been married. But you stopped any chance of that happening.'

Her mother stops what she's doing and wheels round to face her. 'I beg your pardon.'

'You heard me.'

'And what's that supposed to mean? You didn't want to find Jasper. When you had the chance you did nothing,' she spits.

'You're right, I didn't, but only because I didn't think he wanted me. But you know differently don't you?'

'What do you mean by that?'

The question hangs in the air, mingling with foul cooking smells.

'You know exactly what I mean,' Sandy says, with tension in her voice as she struggles to be bold. She isn't used to challenging her.

A moment ago, she might have confessed, Sandy thinks, but she can see the shutters come down and her mother clamming up as she turns to take the chicken from the oven.

'Lay the table,' she orders in a brusque tone. 'You can see it needs doing.' And in that moment Sandy knows that she'll never admit to destroying the letters and it isn't worth pressing her. What was done was done and history couldn't remake itself. It's the future that counts.

When they're seated at the table, roast chicken, potatoes and veg on their plates, Sandy decides it's a good time for her big announcement. She needs revenge and while they have to know eventually, part of her wants to shock them and get one over on them. Her heart thuds in her chest as she puts down her knife and fork and looks from one to the other.

'I'm getting married.'

Her father colours and slams his fist on the table while he curses. Her mother is speechless and crosses her arms in that prim way of hers.

'Sorry?'

'You heard. I'm getting wed.'

'Who to? Are you pregnant again?'

'No. That's not the only reason people marry.'

Her father wipes his mouth with his napkin. 'Why don't we know him? If he's not decent enough to follow etiquette and ask me for your hand then I don't think much of him.'

'It's Jasper.'

'Jasper?'

Jasper's name hangs in the air like a bad smell.

'He never gave up on me, Mum. You know that but you didn't want us to be together otherwise you'd never have destroyed his letters. Why did you do it? Was it to punish me for getting pregnant? That was a cruel trick to play.'

Sandy has said too much. She didn't intend to be confrontational, but her emotions are all over the place. She scrapes her chair, places her napkin on the table and gets up.

'Why don't you sit down and finish your dinner?'

'I'm not hungry.'

'Sit down,' her mother snaps.

Sandy sits on the edge of the chair waiting to make her escape.

'So you've been back in contact with him?'

'He's moved back to London.'

'And have you told him about the baby?'

'There's no point. Why would I want to do that? It would only hurt him.'

Her mother huffs and resumes eating.

Anxiety grips Sandy. 'You're not going to tell him, are you, Mum?'

Her mother doesn't ask her for her father's opinion which is nothing new.

'Now why would I do that and have everybody know our business and the shame you brought on this family?' She says sternly.

Something snaps inside Sandy. She knows what she has to do. She isn't going to go into this marriage with a secret hanging over her. She'll tell Jasper when she can find the right words and the right moment and then nobody, not her parents or anybody else can hold her to ransom. Once it's out there, it's done and she won't have to spend the rest of her life waiting for her life to fall apart. It's a new approach to the way she's dealt with things up until now. He'll understand. In fact he'll be more interested given the fact that Toby was born deformed, because of the tablet she'd taken. He's been reporting on side effects of Thalidomide for months. This will alarm him but interest him too. She has to cling to this hope that she isn't risking their life together. She has nothing to feel guilty about. She only took a couple of tablets. And then she thinks about the tablets. Surely so few couldn't have caused his deformity? And how would she ever find out?

'And who's going to be paying for this wedding?' her father asks.

A thud of hurt moves across her chest. She's their only daughter and it's usual for the girls' parents to pay for the wedding. Why are they being so difficult and why haven't they spent years saving up like every other girl's parents? She's hurt but won't show it. She's got her pride. She doesn't need their money. Sneaking off to Greta Green for a low-key marriage suits her.

SANDY DROPS Jasper's hand and pulls her fur coat tight around her chest, shivering with anxiety. She's frightened about how

Jasper will react when she breaks the news. She considers when the best time might be to tell him. The sooner the better, but it's going to be such a bombshell she must choose her moment. She has a shaky breathless feeling, fearing her news will change everything between them.

He pulls her towards a bench by a bus shelter and they wait for the bus to take them the last leg to the cinema. Sandy blows air into her cupped hands and rubs them against the cold and her nerves. Various scenes play out in her head. She's scared of losing him and scared of him judging her but doesn't want to enter a marriage based on pretence and lies. Every time she sees him she's more convinced they belong together. He's ready for a future together and so is she. It was different back then. This will work, they are both ready for it, but I have to trust that this man loves me, he wouldn't have proposed otherwise, she reminds herself. This is going to take every ounce of courage she can muster.

'Oh look,' Jasper says, 'isn't that Eric and Pat up there. They must be heading for the cinema too. Why don't we catch them up and walk instead?'

It's hard to concentrate on the film. Nerves are dancing in Sandy's stomach and consumed by anxiety and fear she eats more popcorn that she intends.

'Didn't you eat before you came out?' Jasper laughs. 'It's not like you to break your diet.'

'Here, take the rest,' she hands him the tub, licking her fingers, 'before I polish them off. They're very moreish.'

AFTER THE FILM Jasper suggests a drink with Eric and Pat but Eric has to get up early in the morning and needs to get to bed. Sandy is relieved. She wants time with Jasper alone. He's away on business in a few days and she realises she must tell him tonight, even though it's getting late. She can't wait another week in the state she's in.

She's glad that the cafe is quiet and finds a table at the back where they can have some privacy. The nerves are returning and her gut twists. It's so bad that she realises she's chewing her nails—something she's not done since she was a child.

They exhausted discussion about the film on the way to the cafe, although Sandy didn't have much to say about it. With their coffee in front of them, Jasper is keen to talk about his work and an interview with Distillers that he's arranged. Sandy knows where the conversation is heading. Jasper will plunge into a talk about economics and business and soon her chance to tell him will be lost.

'Strange that Distillers, a drinks' company would sell medication,' Sandy ponders.

'I'll tell you how that all came about.'

Sandy glances at her watch, knowing that he will go into scientific detail. Her mind is made up. She has to tell him tonight. She grits her teeth and screams inside for him to stop. She doesn't want to hear anymore about thalidomide and be reminded about what she'd done. That wretched pill. Why was she marrying a guy who was investigating it? There would be many more conversations like this to come. She wants to forget she took it and move on.

'It's an interesting story of how Distillers took on thalidomide. They're the biggest drinks' company and one day, so I've been told, back in 1956, the chairman called a meeting to draw attention to an article that had been written in the *Sunday Times* by Aldous Huxley.'

She's no idea who Huxley is.

'The article talks about how popular valium had become and suggested that people might prefer a relaxing tablet when they got home from work rather than a whisky and soda.'

'But people like their drink. It's the taste more than

anything. You're not going to get the same pleasure from a tablet.'

'Distillers thought their business could be at risk if they didn't do something and so a year later they took on thalidomide, which was used as a mild sedative. It was supposed to turn their business around.'

He picks up that something is bothering her. 'Everything okay? You've been quiet all evening. You're not worried about my going away, I hope.'

'No...but I won't see you for a week and there's something that's bothering me. I need to get it off my chest.'

A group of loud teenagers shuffle into seats beside them, apologising as they brush their table. Sandy's heart sinks. The tables are too close and they won't have the intimacy they need.

'You're not backing out of marrying me?'

'Can we move tables?' She picks her coffee cup up and nods towards a quieter area of the cafe where a table is free.

'Sandy?' They're seated at the new table. He pushes a tray of debris away and puts his hand on her arm.

'No, nothing like that,' she smiles coyly. 'It's what I want.'

'It's not something bad I hope.'

There's a wariness in her voice. 'It is, it's something horrible and I'm worried how you'll react when I tell you.'

'Honey I don't want any secrets between us, you can tell me anything.'

'That night in Brighton,' she pauses, bracing herself, then blurts it out. 'I got pregnant. I'm sorry.' Her face is flushed. She wants to get up and run out of the cafe but has to see this through. 'I should have told you and I feel terrible that I didn't.'

Jasper takes her hands and pulls them towards him.

'I can't believe I'm hearing this.'

He's either shocked, Sandy thinks, finding the news hard to take in or is disgusted with her. She can't tell what he's thinking.

'I want you to forgive me but I'll understand if you can't.' Her voice is pleading.

A flurry of questions follow.

Sandy tenses at the questions. She explains what happened, but somewhere mid-sentence he reaches over to kiss her.

'You did what you had to do, I can't blame you for that. I just wish I'd been there to support you, my love.'

'You had your new job to focus on and I didn't want to ruin your life. Neither of us were ready for all that and we hadn't known each other long.'

'That's not the point. You suffered alone. I wasn't there when you needed me.'

She doesn't expect him to cry and is surprised when his eyes water. He pulls a hanky out of his pocket and blows his nose.

'I don't want you to feel bad.' She rubs his arm. 'I did what I thought I had to.'

'But it takes two to make a baby.'

'Do you think the baby was damaged because I took Distaval? I only took a couple of tablets. I didn't know. I feel so guilty.'

'Chemistry is chemistry, one tablet or fifteen. Now stop it. You weren't to know. Distillers should be held to account. The guilt should rest with them. They should be apologising.'

'My parents didn't think I should tell you. They said I should forget the baby and move on but it's hard sometimes.'

'Of course, it is. You carried a baby inside you for nine months.'

They fall silent.

'How do you feel now, my love?' He smiles and touches her face.

'That's the first time anybody's asked me how I feel... thank you.' Tears prick her eyes.

'Don't say thank you. I'm concerned for you, I love you and soon we're going to be married and I'm going to make everything alright, I promise.'

'I've gone through so many different emotions. Sometimes they come at me all at once. I've tried to put it behind me and not dwell. Bad things happen. What can you do? Finding out was a massive shock and an even bigger shock when I found out he had a problem. I felt as though I was defective in some way, that I couldn't produce a perfect baby and at the back of my mind I worry that it will happen again.'

'That's ridiculous. You mustn't think like that.' They are quiet for a few moments. 'I'd like a family with you but we don't have to rush into it.'

'I can't think about starting a family, not yet.'

'That's okay, I'm not going to put pressure on you. When you're ready.'

'That day in Brighton was so nice. But if the trains hadn't been cancelled things would have been different.'

His voice falls to a whisper. 'I should have used a condom. It was wrong of me. I got caught up in the moment.'

'It wasn't the most romantic of occasions.'

They hold hands and laugh. Relief washing over her. She feels loved and unburdened.

39

RONA

Rona's mother and sisters keep fobbing her off, claiming they're too busy for family get togethers but she's certain they see each other behind her back. They're excluding her and cutting her, Bill and Toby out of the family.

Rona tosses a mental coin in her head. She has two choices. She can hold her head high and force herself on them or bury her hurt and get on with life alone. The stand-off has gone on long enough. Rona must to rise above it; she needs to meet them, to clear the air. A heat of anxiety worms its way through her veins but this is something she must force herself to do for her own peace of mind. She doesn't want the years to slip by and her nieces and nephews to grow up without her in their lives. She will visit her mother, unannounced on Saturday. She knows she won't be turned away on the doorstep with the risk of the neighbours witnessing a scene.

Rona dresses Toby in his best clothes, a sailor suit and cap she made and wraps him in a hand-knitted baby blue blanket. On the doorstep, about to knock Rona loses her nerve and turns to go, ashamed of herself for ever thinking her mother

will accept Toby. But as she reaches the gate her mother opens
the door. She stops in her tracks, her heart banging in her
chest. Fear and apprehension melt away and she finds the
strength she needs to confront her.

'You'd better come in.' Her mother stands on the step, a
harassed look on her face.

Rona hesitates.

'Well, if you're coming in hurry up, you're letting the
cold in.'

Her mother glances furtively up and down the street as if
she's about to make a clandestine deal and with a sweep of her
arm ushers her up the path. But not before a neighbour sees
them and rushes over. Her mother is horrified. 'Get in the
house, quick. But it's too late.

'Rona, I heard you'd had a baby. Let me see him. I've got a
present for you at home. Drop by later? Can I hold him?' She
peers into the pram about to pull the blanket down.

Before Rona has the chance to reply her mother steps in
front of the woman and yanks the pram away.

'Not now Maureen, baby's asleep,' she snaps aggressively
and Rona throws Maureen an embarrassed look.

When the door is closed Rona says, 'You didn't need to do
that Mum, she was only being kind.'

'I don't want to scare her.'

'Scare her. What?'

'It's for your own good. It's private. Nothing to do with her.'

'Since when was having a baby a private matter?'

Rona wishes she hadn't come. But it's a hot day and she's
been on the bus— with her armless baby and nobody batting
an eyelid—for forty minutes and is desperate for a cold drink.

'You took your chance,' her mother sniffs. 'I might have
been out.'

'You're never out Saturday lunch time.'

'Well you might as well stay for lunch now you're here.' She sighs again and heads for the kitchen. The smell of lamb cooking in the oven makes Rona's mouth water.

'You can peel the carrots.' She passes her the peeler before Rona's had the chance to put her handbag down and sort Toby out.

Rona bounces the pram over the kitchen step and parks it in the shade outside, next to the outhouse, before she peels the carrots. The silence between them is only broken by the clinking of cutlery and the chink of crockery as her mother washes up. Now that she's here Rona can't think of anything to say and her mother is making no effort. Every few minutes Rona goes out to check on Toby, to get away from the tension building between them. Every time she does she finds his covers pulled up to his neck. It's a hot day, he'll overheat so she pulls them back. Every so often her mother goes outside too and Rona hears the clunk of the latch on the outhouse and imagines she's going to get something but she returns to the kitchen empty-handed. It happens several times and each time Rona finds Toby with the covers pulled to his neck, hotter and more uncomfortable. Irritation bubbles into anger and Rona can't take anymore.

'What are you doing, Mum? Are you trying to kill him? It's a hot day please don't cover him up. He's my baby for God's sake.'

Her mother tuts.

'You've never shown an interest. Your other grandchildren come first. You're ashamed of my baby. In fact, despite being the only one with a career, I bring nothing but shame on this family. First, I married Bill, now giving birth to a baby who isn't quite perfect.' She punches out her words in a long rant and slams the plates onto the table. She pushes the food to one side, sending a few splashes of gravy onto the white linen tablecloth.

'Now look what you've done.' Her mother's voice is raised. 'Ruining a clean cloth. You come here unannounced, expecting dinner. Where are your manners Rona? Is this how I've brought you up?'

'I wish I hadn't come at all, but one of us had to make the first move. It wasn't going to be you, was it?' Rona's face is red and heat prickles around her neck.

'Next time you decide to arrive don't come unannounced, give me some warning please. I won't have the neighbours knowing that cripple is my grandson, it's beyond embarrassing. And next time park the pram round the side where it won't be seen. It's as though you want to encourage them to come over,' she snaps.

Rona is hit in the gut by a torrent of emotion. Her temper is up in a second and she acts on impulse without thinking. With a grunt, she pushes her plate across the table. It crashes into her mother's plate, landing in her lap. Her mother screams, her face red and shocked. She pushes back her chair, rushing from the kitchen.

'Just get out, get out,' she screams as she thuds her way upstairs. Rona picks up her napkin and flings it at the plates resting on the floor, gravy and half eaten carrot and potato splattered across the spotless floor. She goes into the garden and swerves the pram round, bouncing it over the threshold, through the house to the front door. She stops at Maureen's house on the way to the bus stop, where she feels she might be welcomed.

Seeing Rona come up the path Maureen appears on the doorstep with a beaming smile. She's a slender woman with dark wavy hair in her fifties. Her three children are in their twenties and have long flown the nest but there aren't any grandchildren yet.

She frowns. 'You didn't stay at your mam's long.'

'Mum had things to do.'

'Oh. I thought she would have put her chores to one side to enjoy her grandchild.'

'I wasn't expecting to stay long. It was just a short visit this time.'

Rona stifles the tears that are threatening. It's tempting to open up and tell Maureen everything but she doesn't know her that well and it wouldn't be right to burden her.

'Leave the pram here and bring him in. I'm dying to hold the little nipper.'

Rona picks Toby up. Maureen hasn't seen him yet and she leads the way through to the small kitchen at the back of the house and the aroma of baking reaches her nostrils. Her stomach growls because she didn't eat much at her mum's house. Maureen fills the kettle and sets it on the stove before turning to Rona.

'Would you like a biscuit? I've just made a fresh batch.' She talks while staring at Toby's arms, seeing them for the first time, but she doesn't flinch or hesitate and is covering her shock with a cheerful tone.

'That would be lovely.'

'May I hold him?'

Rona passes Toby to her and she smiles down at him.

'Gorgeous eyes. What a poppet. He looks just like Bill.'

Rona almost laughs at that as the tension of the afternoon leaves her, but the statement catches her off guard. It's such a natural and normal observation to make that she forgets that Toby isn't hers or that he's different. It's not a forgetting, it's just that he's always with her and he's just Toby. He's a beautiful baby with red chubby cheeks, a sheen of blonde hair and corn-flower blue eyes and he's giving Maureen his cheeky smile as she pulls faces and laughs.

Maureen gives him back to Rona while she takes the biscuits from the oven. She hands Rona a plate and catches the sadness tucked behind her veneer.

'I'm so sorry, Rona. I didn't know. Your mam didn't tell me.'

'It's okay.'

'How are you are coping?' Her face has twisted into the pity she's seen on so many other faces. She was just relaxing and it makes her uncomfortable—there's always the pity.

'I'm lucky to have him, that's the way I look at it. Some couples can't have children. I fell pregnant really quickly. My child is a blessing so please don't pity me, he's my joy.'

Rona is used to spinning this lie and she's surprises herself with how it comes so easily.

40

RONA

The first three years of Toby's life are hard for Rona and everything is a matter of trial and error. She isn't assigned a social worker and there's nobody to tell her what she should and shouldn't be doing.

For a long time there's little mention of and information about prostheses or how to treat the deformed limbs. Rona's main concern is bringing up Toby as best she can. She encourages him to use his feet and mouth. She drops light toys near his feet so that if he wants them he has to grab with his lower limbs. She massages his feet and like all mothers, one of the first things she teaches her baby is how to wave. She takes her shoes and stockings off, waves at him with her foot and encourages him to wave back with his. She doesn't worry about how this will look to people and says to Bill, 'The feet are there while the hands aren't and something is better than nothing.' Rona is a positive person and her mantra is 'keep your face to the sunshine and you won't see a shadow.'

One day when he's six months old, Rona phones Bill at work to tell him some great news. 'He's sucking his thumb.'

'Is that all you've rung for?' Bill says, but to Rona it's an incredibly special moment.

As the months pass there is increasing mention of a government programme to fit prostheses as a possible solution to the problems the thalidomides face. The news portrays the prospect of artificial limbs as a magical dream, a chance for the children to function normally. When Toby is fourteen months old he's given his first pair of cosmetic arms which are like doll's arms made from plastic. They are strapped to his chest and manipulated with an attached canister of oxygen gas. From the minute they are fitted, Rona doesn't like them, but she had given in to the doctor and agreed for Toby to try them. She's being forced to give up her hard efforts to stimulate his feet and turn her attention to his hands. She's expected to put all her faith in the artificial limbs. The arms aren't so much arms as wieldy, unpleasant contraptions. They're a major disappointment, especially after she's listened to so many glowing reports about them. So much hope rested on them coming, but the biggest disappointment is that they end in steel hooks; how is that better than what he was born with? Rona calls Toby Captain Hook. She hates them.

When Rona and Toby visit the hospital for prosthetic adjustment the doctor says, 'You have to give them a chance otherwise when he grows up he might wonder why he wasn't given the opportunity.' She thinks they are cumbersome and Toby is uncomfortable in them. The cups chafe him and make his soft skin sore. She doesn't see the point in them and yet if she rejects them she knows she'll feel guilty, but they aren't making his life any easier and are weighty and awkward to use. She gives it two weeks to see how he gets on and then returns them to the hospital.

'I really think you need to persist, Mrs Murphy,' the doctor says.

'He doesn't need them,' Rona cuts in. 'He uses his toes for

most tasks - he can take his bottle, play with toys and he can hold a spoon between his toes.'

'I really would like you to try them for longer.' His voice has taken on a belligerent tone.

'His feet and legs are developing the grasping action. He's got two perfect legs, feet and toes. He uses those instead.'

The doctor is horrified. 'That's not practical. Maybe it is for the moment, but you've got to think long term. He'll spend his life putting shoes and socks on and taking them off. It's not going to work.' He frowns. 'Surely you don't want him eating with his feet in public. He'll be turned away from cafes and restaurants because they won't want him in their establishment.'

'He can walk with bare feet then. And if we get turned away I'll jolly well make a scene.'

The doctor rolls his head in laughter. Rona bristles. She doesn't like his condescending tone. It's getting to her. It's not ideal, but his feet will toughen up and he'll get used to it, or he'll wear slip-on shoes or flip flops if he has to.

'A fortnight isn't long enough. You need to actively encourage him and teach him how to use the arms. If you're positive, he will be. Give him lots of praise when he's learned something new.'

Rona sighs. The last words irritate her. She does nothing but praise and encourage Toby. It's as if she doesn't know how to treat a child. The doctor isn't getting it. All he seems interested in is promoting this wonder of technology as he likes to call it.

'In a few years he'll thank you for making the effort to teach him to use them, believe me.'

'He'll thank me for ditching them. With due respect you've only seen him wear them for a few minutes. You haven't seen the anguish and frustration like I have.'

'They'll be less embarrassing for you when you go out.'

'I don't get embarrassed, Doctor.' Her tone is laced with ice.

The doctor shuffles the papers on his desk and mutters, 'You might not be, but other people will.'

'Well that's their problem not mine.'

'That's where you're wrong, it's very much Toby's problem.'

Rona is in despair, she gives up. She's not winning so she resolves to take the arms as he's instructing but find the nearest bin to dump them in.

Back at home when Bill finds out what she's done, another argument breaks out. Since Toby Bill and Rona disagree about many things.

'Why didn't you give him the chance?' Bill asks over dinner.

'He manages perfectly well with his toes.'

'But we can't eat out.'

'Who says we can't?'

Bill sighs and shakes his head. There's the same resigned look on his face that's become familiar.

'Look. You have to give him a chance. When he grows up and sees his friends with arms he'll wonder why you stopped him having his own.'

'I didn't give up. He hates them.'

'He was doing well.'

'How would you know? You're never here.'

'I'm working, to support you both,' Bill snaps.

'I'm the one looking after him all day, I know what he needs.'

'You obviously know best.' Bill sighs and gets up even though he hasn't finished his meal.

'Where are you going now?'

'Out.'

This is hopeless thinks Rona as she hears the front door slam. She can't discuss anything with Bill. He has to take the counter argument and when he disagrees with her and she doesn't concede he goes to the pub. They argue about silly things that don't matter like who is supposed to put the bins out or change the cat's litter tray. He flares up so easily. He never used to be like this.

RONA HAS GIVEN up work to look after Toby, and Bill is always working. He has to work at the weekend to bring in enough money and he leaves Rona as Toby's sole carer. It took them so long to have a baby that when Toby arrived she thought, she would relish every minute, every cry and every sleepless night. But Rona realises Bill is intransigent. He is not the natural father and doesn't see why he should take on the dreadful night-time routine. Rona feels that if she grumbles or complains she will have it thrown back in her face—or he will leave. She does everything to keep him with them, bending over backwards to please him—and he works day and night and weekend. And when he's not working he's drinking. They are both physically and mentally exhausted.

Money is tight and her family don't visit. Bill's family don't visit much either. They make excuses that they are too busy but Rona isn't silly, she knows the reason. It's Toby. They can't cope, they don't know what to say and skirt around the issues she faces. Toby is the elephant in the room and they have nothing in common. Rona has given up visiting them too. If they can't accept Toby, they are insulting her and she finds it deeply upsetting. It isn't fair to her nieces and nephews, because they are missing out through no fault of their own. Her heart longs to see them again, but she'll have to bide her time and be patient, praying and hoping that all will be well one day. She becomes increasingly isolated. Her world begins and ends with Toby. Rona learns that many of the thalidomide children have things wrong with their internal organs, but Toby is lucky. It's only the parts of him that you can see that are damaged, like his teeth. When his teeth come through it's a shock to learn that they are weak and discoloured. It's a bitter blow because it's one more visual barrier for people to recoil from. He's an otherwise beautiful boy.

Rona doesn't go out much and feels like a prisoner in her home. There's no reason why she can't go out, apart from the way she is judged by other people. She's a woman who took the tablet that destroyed her unborn baby. She shouts from the rooftops that she doesn't care what people think, but how can she not?

In the summer she plays with Toby in the garden and if anybody calls unexpectedly she grabs him and rushes into the kitchen to put him out of the way. She's afraid of the stares and comments that will follow. When he is three she decides that enough is enough. She won't hide him. She'll take him to the beach, with her head held high and let him play on the sand with the other children.

Rona packs a picnic, sun hats and drinks before she can change her mind. At the front door she's hyperventilating, gulping in air and feels a wave of sickness. She reaches for the door handle and bright sunlight filters through the gap as she opens it. She will carry on and ignore the mounting fear. She has to get out otherwise the outside world will win, condemning her to a life of four walls until she goes mad. Toby deserves more than that life. She vowed when she took him that he would live normally and she hasn't lived by her convictions.

She ignores the buzzing in her head and prickles of heat behind her neck as groups of people stop talking and stare as she marches along the street, pushing Toby in his pushchair. She keeps her cool, determined not to make a comment. They can stare all they like, but they aren't going to stop her loving him. The fact that they don't have a thalidomide child isn't because they've necessarily done the right thing. It's purely about being in the wrong place at the wrong time, with a different set of pregnancy ailments. Each one of those mothers who stares, as she makes her way along the beach are lucky. It could have happened to any one of them. They have no right to judge.

Rona plonks herself on the cool sand and unclips Toby from his pushchair. She avoids the temptation to check if anybody is staring and focuses on Toby. But out of the corner of her eyes she sees two women she recognises from her street with their hands to their mouths in a whisper. She chats to Toby who is excited because it's the first time he's been to the beach.

Rona takes sandwiches from the basket.

'If I had something like that, I wouldn't bring it out of doors, would you?'

Rona puts the sandwiches on a plastic plate and stops. Had she heard correctly? She wheels round to face them. 'Do you want a photograph? Get stuffed will you?' Anger fizzes inside. How dare they? What gives them the right to think that their own children are so perfect? They might have arms and legs but if they are anything like their mothers they'll grow into horrible, judgemental human beings. 'If you don't like it go and sit somewhere else,' she snaps.

The two women are shocked by Rona's outburst and without saying anymore they gather their things and scramble away across the sand to find somewhere else to sit. Rona smiles at Toby who is helping himself to a sandwich with his feet. He's learned to use them to eat with and can hold what other people would call finger-food or by grasping a spoon or fork between his toes he can eat anything else. He holds a pen and paint brush and he is mastering the skill well, as if his feet are a pair of hands. It means that he doesn't want shoes and socks on most of the time but the chill of winter doesn't deter him. He wears flip flops because it's easier. It means that his feet are accessible when he needs to use them. Toby is far from helpless. From a young age he touched Rona and Bill with his feet and he can clean his teeth by holding the toothbrush between his toes. They developed the grasping action in the same way that arms and hands respond in any child. Rona knows that things will work out for him. And after all, she keeps telling the doctor, he still has two legs and two feet and there's a lot you can do with two limbs.

Rona feels stronger after she's spoken out. The women are sitting further away, but keep staring back at her in disgust. She notices that the crowd is thinning around her. People are moving to other areas of the beach. They move because of Toby. Her reaction to the two women is the start of a new and stronger Rona. She's learned to hide her hurt feelings under a hard shell. Eventually she'll grow tough enough to put up with all the unkindness without flinching. She has to be strong to make Toby strong. When he's old enough to be aware of his difference he has to know that when people are rude it's their problem; the boy has to be tough and it's down to her to lead by example. She isn't ashamed of Toby and wants to take him out as much as she can, now. She'll have to fight prejudice every day, on his behalf and prejudice is ignorance from people filled with their own insecurities.

Toby comes on better than she ever expected. He shuffles on his bottom before he learns to walk and when he can walk he runs instead. His lack of arms is no deterrent to getting most things done. Curiosity helps him solve problems. He always finds a way. Rona knows that his achievement lies in independence.

She finds it hard to watch him struggle with something, but she is determined not to do every task for him. She turns things into games and offers sweets as a reward. He is a bright and capable lad and by the time he is three years old he can dress himself with the aid of a dressing stick - provided by the team at Roehampton Hospital - and he loves drawing and uses his mouth to hold the crayon.

41

RONA

'Makes me so angry.'

Rona shrugs and looks out of the window of the cafe at the sea, mesmerised by the waves as they crash on the shore, under a lid of pewter cloud. Sheila's anger mirrors the fury of the waves. Rona isn't angry, at least not in the same way. She chose to live with thalidomide. Toby is a gift from God. He's made her life complete. She chose him and wanted to take him on, despite all the challenges that lie ahead as well as the battle with Bill to get him to show an interest in Toby. Other women had thalidomide thrust on them with no choice but to deal with it. She knows he'll find a way to overcome his disability and she'll help him, every step of the way.

'Anger's not going to get us anywhere. We have to get on with being parents.'

Rona is a fraud. Seeing the pain Sheila's suffers, she turns her attention to Toby who has chips filling in his red bib. Sheila picks up the spoon to feed Jim, but Jim still has a mouth full of battered cod.

Rona met Sheila in the doctor's waiting room when their babies were small and they've become friends, meeting regularly and sharing their experiences of parenting disabled children. Toby and Jim are three. Jim is in a far worse state than Toby. He has so much wrong with him. It's pitiful, Rona thinks to herself.

'Other parents are fighting for compensation from Distillers. They want to sue for negligence. I think we should join them.' Sheila is flustered with excitement. 'We need to fight together for justice. A lady came round the other day, did I tell you? She started mithering me to apply for financial help. There's money to help us if we need it. They've set up a fund called The Lady Hoare Appeal Fund.'

Rona can't imagine how the parents are going to get organised to do something, there's so many of them. It seems an impossible mission, given that there are hundreds of children in the country with varying degrees of thalidomide deformities.

'I don't want any help. Bill earns enough money.' Rona can't get involved, it would mean questions from authoritative bodies, but apart from that, she has her pride and wants to bring her son up without handouts or help from charitable funding. She has done her best to avoid attention for three years, something like this could blow it. It's too risky and complicated. She wants a simple, private life, away from the glare of the spotlight. She might be recognised as there is a lot of media attention on the thalidomides. She doesn't want to be a part of it. 'In any case, I'm not entirely sure that I did take Distaval. When the doctor showed me packets of pills I didn't recognise them.'

Sheila puts down her cup and splashes of tea pool in the saucer. 'You told me you had taken it.'

'Well yes,' Rona falters, 'but I can't be absolutely sure. Anyway, it's not in my nature to go moaning on about having a child with no arms. I don't like this pay-out thing, it feels like begging. I'm sorry, that's not to cast aspersions on you and the others, it's just that we're doing okay and don't need or want any outside help. And let's face it, don't hold your breath. Distillers is a huge company and they haven't admitted liability and they don't seem to be budging an inch.'

'Well, that's what the lady told me. She said my best hope was to apply for help with the appeal rather than have any pie-in-the-sky ideas about taking Distillers to court.'

'You should take their help if it's on offer. God knows, if anybody needs it, you do,' Rona encourages Sheila, but her tone is flat. She wants the conversation to move on to something brighter. Maybe she'll suggest a walk in a bit, but the clouds are threatening rain and any minute there'll be a deluge. It's as if the grey world outside is wrapping them in its sadness.

Sheila is quiet. There's a moment of dithery throat clearing before she sits up tall and a thread of steel slips into her tone. 'I've written a letter, to the Minister of Health, Enoch Powell.' She's fiddling with a napkin and waiting for Rona to encourage her.

'Whatever for?'

'I got back from the hospital after Jim's eye operation and that night I woke up angry. I can't describe it, I felt overwhelming anger. I went downstairs at three in the morning, wrote the letter and walked to the post box in my nighty and slippers before I had the chance to change my mind.'

Rona's interest piques. She can understand Sheila's anger. Poor cow, Rona thinks. She's been through so much and is so strong - it's a wonder she hasn't had a nervous breakdown. And poor little Jim. He's sitting quietly in his pushchair about to drop off to sleep. He has an eye patch because he's been in hospital to remove a growth on his right eye. One of his ears is tiny and undeveloped with no hearing and he has only slight hearing in the other one. The poor boy is missing all four limbs. Rona readjusts her expression in case it's revealing any pity. Rona is sick of being on the receiving end of it herself and knows what it's like.

'You know you can always call me, day or night. I know it's so hard for you, being alone.'

Sheila was abandoned by, Peter, her husband, soon after Jim was born. The day after his birth he'd come to the hospital to visit, blurting out that it was horrible and he'd been throwing up all night. He doesn't have any emotions for Jim and hasn't asked how Sheila is coping. All he was concerned about was wanting to know what she was going to do with 'it.' Sheila was made to feel guilty for what had happened and Peter asked her to sign consent forms for Jim to be taken to an institution. When she said she was keeping the baby, he was horrified. 'What on earth are people going to think?' She told him she didn't give a stuff what people thought, she was bringing Jim home and that was that. He was angry and bent towards her face and in a stony lowered voice said, 'If you bring that thing home, I'm leaving.'

'Leave then. Get out of my life,' Sheila had replied. It was a courageous thing to say given that Sheila has no family to help out as her parents passed away long ago. His decision to have nothing to do with Jim remained as firm and he's never been back. Sheila didn't blame him for not sticking by them. She didn't have a bitter bone in her body; she saw Jim as her baby and her responsibility. She took those tablets and she made him what he is—she may not blame Peter for anything but she carries her own burden. Rona doesn't understand how she's supporting them? Rona knows that she doesn't ask Peter for maintenance. They never go without but maybe, Rona thinks that's because she's a proud woman. Sheila doesn't have a job and Lord knows how she would have the time anyway, as looking after Jim is a full-time job in itself. Even running back and forth for appointments at the hospital is time-consuming, she's never away from the place. Recent medical reports are full of the word thalidomide and Jim has become a guinea-pig for doctors from all over the world to analyse. They come at him with their clip boards and endless questions. And at every clinic visit she gets asked the same thing. 'Are you sure you don't want to send him away? Are you coping on your own?' But Sheila is adamant, Jim stays at home. At least Rona has Bill. He works hard to support them even though Rona gets frustrated and feels let down by him because he still doesn't show much interest in Toby. She's no idea whether or when that will happen. She's tried to engage Bill with the daily routine, she hasn't nagged and she's praised him all the way, but he's detached as though he doesn't belong to the family and it makes Rona sad.

'Thank you, love.' Sheila rubs Rona's hand and smiles warmly. 'I know I can rely on you if I need to and I want you to know I value our friendship. Sometimes I don't know what I'd do without you.' Tears glisten.

'Tell me about your letter. What did you say?'

'I explained my situation. I told him I'd taken Distaval and that within hours my hands and legs went numb. I told him about Jim and his conditions and asked him to imagine how he would feel if it had been him. I said, why should my baby and the hundreds of others out there have to spend a lifetime of pain, with no financial support because a company was allowed to market a product which hadn't been properly tested? I asked him what he intended to do about compensating the families.'

'Good letter. Wow. Well done. I wonder what he'll reply. The thing is how can anybody trust medication again? We have no idea what's in what we're being told to take. Social conditioning presents the doctor as the man you can trust. We've never questioned what we're prescribed because he wears a white coat, and white is the colour of trust and peace and safety. We pay our taxes and put faith in the doctors, but after this— well it all beggars believe.'

'Exactly.'

42

SANDY

'One of the thalidomide mothers has written to our newspaper.'

Jasper is polishing his shoes in the kitchen as he gets ready for work. He likes to look smart, in a shirt and tie, even though many of his journalist friends dress down. Standards are slipping he tells Sandy. Work clothing straddles between formal and casual. Culture has moved away from the post-war rationing and the way people interact with fashion has changed.

He has moved work. He's the science reporter for a national newspaper and loves it.

'Why's that?'

Sandy is still modelling but they are trying for a baby. As soon as she gets pregnant she'll give up work and concentrate on home life. She's not without worry though. Jasper is keen to have a baby, but she has doubts. She's scared. What if she gets morning sickness again and it's so bad that she needs to take something? And what if the baby's problems were caused by a genetic issue and not Distaval? Until a child is born will she be sure?

'She wrote to Enoch Powell. He's the Minister for Health.'

'I know who he is.'

'Yes well, I know you don't like listening to the news.'

Ruffled by his comment Sandy snaps, 'Carry on.'

'She wants to know what the government plans to do about compensating the thalidomide children. She said it's a disgrace and she's right, it is. The government should be doing something. All that unnecessary suffering that should have been avoidable. The children are the innocent victims in this. We need to remember that.'

Sandy prickles with irritation. He never considers the suffering I went through, she thinks to herself. I deserve some compensation. 'So what did Enoch Powell reply?'

'He didn't. That's why she's written to us, to take up the story. Honestly love you're a bit slow at times.'

'Don't be patronising. I was only asking.'

'She's planning a court test case.'

'Sounds complicated.'

'Our article came out last week. I'm speaking to the woman this morning to see whether my article has prompted Powell to reply to her. I'm fully expecting it will.'

JASPER PICKS up the phone to call Mrs Edwards. The poor woman he thinks as he dials her number, she's been through so much with her baby. And it didn't stop with the shock of his birth and his ongoing care—now he's in and out of hospital trying to rectify problems with his eyes. *This should not be happening. It's a medical disaster and nobody is listening to the plight of the families.* He can't begin to imagine the suffering and he feels a burning sense of anger on her behalf.

'Mrs Edwards? Jasper Kenward here.

'Jasper, do call me Sheila.'

'Any news, Sheila?'

'I've had a reply, just like you said I would. Not from Mr Powell himself. It's from someone in his department, apologising for the delay in replying.'

Jasper rolls his eyes to the ceiling and balls a fist. Bloody typical. He hates the Conservative Government and their lack of compassion on social issues.

'Would you mind reading it out to me.'

'Yes of course. One minute.' Jasper waits for her to get the letter and hears rustling as she takes it out of the envelope, clearing her throat. She speaks slowly and enunciates every word, as if she's speaking to him through a crackled line from Australia. He sits up, a chill washing through his body as she reads on.

'"... The horrible side effects from the use of thalidomide has caused the Minister deep concern: he is keeping a close eye on the situation and is seeking advice."' Jasper's irritation mounts.

'It says that the Minister was advised that thalidomide was subject to the usual laboratory tests and there was no reason to suspect that the drug could have side effects. It was tested on small animals and that didn't highlight any issues either. He says the NHS has specialised support and care for babies and children with deformities.'

Jasper leans back in his chair, digesting the implications of this letter, realising that it sets out the Government's official view on the issue. My God, he thinks, we have a big battle ahead.

He comes off the phone and stares at the notes he's made, trying to make sense of it when a leading broadsheet newspaper is slapped on his desk. His eyes are drawn to a piece of news on the front page. The headlines read 'Thalidomide tests showed no sign of danger.' He wonders if Mrs Edward's letter has prompted this article. He casts an eye over the article. It's written in the same vein as Mrs Edward's letter.

'Before being put on the market in Britain, the drug was subject to rigorous tests with no sign of danger reported. It was tested thoroughly by Grunenthal.' But what about tests to detect birth malformations? Jasper wants to know. He reads on.

'The need for tests to detect birth defects has been made evident before.'

Jasper is deep in thought, the words swimming before his eyes when another broadsheet whacks onto his desk covering the article.

The office boy smiles.

'Hey,' Jasper says, 'I was in the middle of reading. Do you mind?'

'Sorry sir.'

A similar headline catches his attention. He reads. 'Neither the British manufacturers of the drug thalidomide, nor the doctors who prescribed it to expectant mothers who went on to give birth to deformed babies were in any way to blame for the present epidemic of congenital abnormalities.' It suggests that the problems could not have been foreseen.

Jasper's mind is in overdrive. The letter to Mrs Edwards and the two newspaper articles are on Distillers side.

He reads the article again. 'Before thalidomide was available in Britain it was tested thoroughly. There was no sign of danger. It was tested extensively by Chemie Grunenthal.'

Jasper is outraged. He stands up with his hand on his forehead not knowing what to do. The articles draw a veil around any controversy, exonerating Distillers and attempting to hush a national outcry about to erupt. He can see Distillers getting off scot free for the greatest national disaster of the century. He can't believe it. A public enquiry is needed. He can't understand why, in the face of a big increase in the number of abnormal births during the late fifties and into 1960 and 1961 why nobody noticed that this coincided with an increase in the use of thalidomide.

But what about tests on pregnant animals, to see if the drug produced birth defects, he wants to know. He reads on. 'The need for such tests,' the medical correspondent of the leading paper says, 'has never been made evident before... the manufacturers of the drug and the doctors who prescribed it cannot be held responsible for the epidemic of birth defects.'

Jasper gets up and heads for his boss's office. He bangs hard on the door.

'Come in. What's up. You've got a face like thunder.'

'Have you read the articles? They're in all the leading papers!'

'You'll have to be more specific, I'm not a mind reader.'

'About thalidomide.'

'Yes, very disturbing.'

'I'm glad we agree.'

'Their source of information is Distillers.'

'The Government needs to hold a public enquiry. We have to push to make this happen. As a newspaper, we are the voice of the people and have a moral obligation.'

His boss hesitates.

'That's quite a speech, boy. A Labour MP, Maurice Edelman, who's a personal friend of mine, has already asked Enoch Powell to set up a public enquiry. He's got some support in the House of Commons, but word's out that Powell has no sympathy with the affair. He said that no one can sue the Government.'

'This tragedy is like the worst train crash in history and it needs to be taken seriously.'

'A delegation has been to see Powell asking for the setting up of a drug-testing centre to make sure that the tragedy is not repeated. The bastard replied that anyone so much as taking an aspirin puts himself or herself at risk and have to accept personal liability. They also suggested he launches a publicity campaign to warn the public to check their medicine cabinets in case they still have thalidomide and to destroy it. He refused, saying they were scare-mongering. His attitude stinks.'

'Well, I've never heard of a single word of compassion from that dreadful man.'

'With no official examination of the tragedy and no public enquiry, the parents themselves, all those Sheilas out there, are going to have to take the law into their own hands. They have to trust the law to help them. I don't hold out much hope of that happening.'

'And where will the parents find the money to finance legal action? They'd have to rely on legal aid and that's not going to be handed out. They'll need a decent firm of personal injury lawyers—the best. It has to be somebody who will take on every instance as a single case and hit the courts in the biggest civil suit of all time.'

'It'll be difficult to show that Distillers has been negligent in marketing a drug that maimed unborn children. This is going to be an extremely tricky situation. I'm glad I'm not a lawyer.'

'Their best line of attack is the fact that Distillers knew there were problems with the drug but they didn't withdraw it earlier. I've done a lot of research on this. Drug regulation is my pet subject. I've long been suspicious of any drug my doctor dishes out. Not everything the doctor gives you is beneficial. It's a shame that more people aren't suspicious. We trust doctors but sometimes they're just guessing when they dish out something new.'

'God, you really are Mr Cynical.'

43

RONA

'Just go.'

'You sure you can cope?'

'Of course, I can.'

It's the first time Rona has left Bill with Toby. She's going out for the evening with friends and the guilt she feels at leaving Toby is killing any excitement she feels about her first night out in five years.

He's five and has just started at the local primary school. She goes in to help, because they only agreed to take him at the school if she's prepared to assist. They said they didn't have the facilities for a handicapped child and that he needs to be in a special school. The headmaster said that there was no specialised equipment and that having him in class would hinder Toby's physical, emotional and intellectual development.

'What I'm most worried about is Toby becoming a burden to the other children. I have to take into consideration all of the children, not just what's best for Toby.'

She knew it wasn't going to be easy getting him into the mainstream school. She'd spent five years keeping a low profile and not wanting to draw attention to herself. Whatever he said, she wasn't going to complain to the local authority even though she'd probably win, because the way he was treating her was outrageous. She'd prepared herself for this.

'He's a self-sufficient kid, more than you're giving him credit for.' He was making judgements without really seeing what Toby could do.

'I'm worried he might be bullied. We've got some difficult children here that might target him.'

'How do you normally deal with bullying?'

'We discourage it of course.'

'Can I make a suggestion?'

He nodded. He's hoping I'll go away, Rona thought, but she stayed, determined to win this battle— but with the minimum of fuss.

'I'd like to come in and give a talk to the children about disability before Toby starts. I'll tell them about thalidomide and how it affected Toby and how he gets by. Mr Bradley, children are sponges. And sometimes it's the chipped teacup that's the best one. They'll be curious and eager to learn about him. This is positive for your school. It will show that you're open minded.'

Mr Bradley was defeated; he'd rolled the dice and lost. He'd taken another stab from a different angle. 'We'd be financially stretched.'

'He uses his mouth and feet for everything—tell me, what do you need to buy him? I can't think of a thing he needs that other children don't. You won't have to buy any equipment for him or make any changes to school life.'

The head was calculating. 'And toileting... how does he use the toilet?'

Rona was expecting this. 'Like anyone else. He opens the door and he goes in.'

'And how does he use the toilet?'

Rona felt intimidated. A rising tide of embarrassment washed over her but she was determined not to show it. 'And how do you use the toilet, Mr Bradley? Let me ask you, are all of your five year-olds able to use the toilet on their own?'

Mr Bradley hesitated. 'Well, no, not exactly, some of them still need help.'

Rona sat tall with a look of triumph on her face. 'Well then.'

Mr Bradley had no choice but to relent. He couldn't be seen to be guilty of discrimination. He agreed to take Toby on a trial basis. She didn't like the way he handled the situation and was glad to be able to go in to school to help out. It was her way of keeping an eye on things.

Rona leaves Bill and Toby alone in the house. She has to trust him even though he shows little interest in Toby. She doesn't want to miss her friend's hen night. She's turned down so many evenings out. She'll have no friends left if she doesn't make an effort.

She puts her coat on when she hears a car horn outside at eight. Trisha, an old friend from her nursing days, is picking her up. She gets in the car and is met by a cloud of Trisha's heavy scent. They're wearing pencil skirts but Rona's is longer because Bill didn't want her going out 'all tarted up.' They're going to a pub first and then on to a dance venue.

A wave of beer and smoke hits them as they make their way to the bar. The pub is long overdue a refurbishment. Peeling candy-striped wallpaper adorns the walls and the ceiling is nicotine yellow. Shelving groans under the weight of dusty shire horse ornaments and an array of copper objects. Rona is surprised they've chosen to meet in this seedy pub on the corner of Roxworth Road. But it's convenient and on the way to the dance hall. Sheila lives along Roxworth Road, she never gets a night out. Rona visualises her, a few doors away from the pub tucked up in bed after a tiring day with Jim. She feels a tug of guilt that she's enjoying herself when poor Sheila never gets to go out. She can't imagine what it must be like for her to bring a handicapped child up alone.

'So Doris,' Trisha asks when the four women are settled in a snug at the back of the pub with bags of Walkers' crisps and shandy.

Doris is dreamy as she goes into detail about her boyfriend. 'The minute I first clapped eyes on my Charlie in that bus shelter, I knew he was the one for me.'

'You big softie,' Trisha laughs.

'I'm just nipping to the loo,' Rona says when they've finished their drinks, 'before we head on to the dance.'

The toilets stink like a subway and Rona holds her nose as she closes the door. A small window is open above her head and she welcomes the breeze. There are hushed voices beyond the window. She recognises one of them but can't immediately place who it is. It's only when she's standing up to flush the chain that she realises it's Sheila's voice. But it can't be. Sheila will be in bed by now, it's past ten and there's nobody to look after Jim. But there's no mistaking her Brummie lilt and the dreary nasal tone. What's she doing here? She's talking to a man.

Rona leaves the toilets, passing crates of beer lined along a tiled corridor until she comes to the back door. She pushes it open, pins herself against the wall, to peer round into the dimly lit empty car park until she locates the voices. From her vantage point she makes out two figures. The woman is dressed in clothing that Sheila would never wear; a tight short skirt, fishnet tights and high heels. Her hair is piled high on her head into a bouffant and a whiff of lacquer. Cheap perfume drifts in Rona's direction.

Her heart bangs in her chest. What on earth is Sheila doing out here? But she doesn't need to ask, she knows, because it's plain to see. No wonder Sheila is never short of money, she's raking it in. Who's looking after Jim, Rona wants to know and

where is she going to take this man? Rona's worried and terrified for Sheila's safety. She's risking everything to bring in a
living for her son. She'll have Jim taken from her if she's not
careful. Stupid bloody Sheila, Rona says in her head. She can't
stand by now she's seen and heard what's going on. She has to
do something. They move away from the light. Sheila's giggling
and the man loops his arm in hers, guiding her across the
carpark to a black car. He opens the door and as she bends to
get in, he slips his hand up her skirt and she giggles. Rona
watches the car speed off up the hill in the opposite direction of
Sheila's house.

The door behind Rona swings open and Trisha comes over
to Rona, putting her hand on her shoulder.

'There you are. We were worried. What are you doing out
here?'

'I don't feel very well. Came out to get some fresh air.'

'You've only had one drink. What are you going to be like by
the end of the evening?'

'Actually, Trisha, I hope you don't mind but I'm going to get
off home.'

'No, really?'

'I'm sorry, I'd be no fun.'

'I'll get the barman to order you a taxi.'

'Thanks.'

44

SANDY

Sandy's waiting for the taxi to arrive. Her body feels trembly and effervescent as if her blood has been replaced with carbonated water. She checks her watch. Jasper is away for the night attending a meeting of thalidomide families. He won't be back until late tomorrow. She'll spend tomorrow in bed recovering and hopefully by the time he walks through the door she'll be out of bed and will have a meal waiting for him. She'll kiss him on the cheek with a smile, the adoring and devoted wife, acting as if nothing has happened.

Jasper is passionate about wanting to help in the fight against Distillers. There's still hope for the parents to win compensation from them, even though at this stage everything is stacked against them. The Government is unsympathetic, none of them have the money to finance the case themselves and they will have to rely on legal aid, which, it has been made clear is going to be meted out cautiously. It's not helped by a bunch of pessimistic lawyers who don't believe they can win. They think the parents have a poor case for a number of reasons. Mainly they believe that the pharmaceutical companies could have done nothing to avoid the disaster. They didn't know about the risks of medicating pregnant women.

Sandy is dressed in pink slacks and a smart blouse. Despite a cloud of perfume, fresh minty teeth and hair lacquer, she feels dirty and ugly on the inside. She hates lies and deception. She should never have agreed to a baby. It's too soon. The memories are still there and the fear at the back of her mind that it might happen again is overwhelming. Maybe the time will never be right. She might never heal. A dark curtain of guilt has encircled her ever since she walked out of the doctor's surgery last week with the appointment booked at the clinic. The doctor was disapproving and when he'd listened to her worries he'd told her coldly and matter of factly, 'Your only option is a termination.'

She picks up the bag containing spare underwear, sanitary towels and a nighty and the secret she's hiding from Jasper. She chastises herself for wearing pink and not black. It'll only attract looks and attention, twitching net curtains and questions from neighbours. 'Where did you go yesterday? We saw the taxi.' But pink distracts her from the awful thought of what's about to happen. She's going to have an operation. Pink glosses over the truth, it's an innocent colour and it returns her to the glamorous person she is.

The taxi driver doesn't speak. They slow for red traffic lights and as they speed past shop windows Sandy longs for the day when she can get back to being mannequin slim. There's an alien growing inside her and if she changes her mind and asks the driver to pullover and let her out, she would become a mother. A role that she didn't want last time and doesn't want this time. The transformation into motherhood would be a huge mistake.

'What is this place?' the driver says as they arrive. Sandy's certain he knows but is asking to embarrass her, rubbing salt into the wound. She pays the fare without replying. The clinic has recently opened and was the site of a bombed pub. There are signs all over the carpark but the entrance isn't immediately obvious. Anxiety mounts and she has to ask for directions. As she walks into reception she catches the disapproving looks of a few women in the waiting area. They are younger and she suspects unmarried. They have no right to throw her looks. They are lower down the pecking order of women waiting for an abortion. Their pregnancies are unplanned, the result of stupidity, forgetfulness and sex with too many partners. She has a wedding ring and a home to bring up a baby, a freshly decorated nursery, and a loving husband and father to be. Her pregnancy was planned and wanted— just not anymore. She's allowed to change her mind. Jasper hasn't changed. He's always wanted to replace the baby they lost. She had gone along with it, hoping her muddled head would clear and she'd come to want a family.

There are three older women with grey hair behind the reception desk, in frumpy clothing and in all probability sex is a distant memory in their lives. Sandy gives her name and she feels as though she's being judged for something wicked.

'You're here to see...?' Asks the one with her hair tied in an unflattering bun. Her tone hints at disdain but her rigid face gives nothing away.

She's taken into a room by a nurse to provide a urine sample. The nurse asks questions about her decision. She gets the impression that she's going through the motions and not really wanting to change her mind but going along with what the legislation requires her to do.

'You're married?' The nurse is surprised.

'Yes. I don't want my husband to know that I'm here.'

'I see.'

Sandy catches the hint of an imagined scandal. She realises

that the nurse is putting two and two together and assumes she's been having an affair. She doesn't want to have to explain why she can't go through with the pregnancy—fear at not trusting herself to grow a normal, healthy baby and trusting herself even less to be a normal, doting mother. But she knows that she must give a reason in order for the two doctors to sign the form to allow the termination. It's an intrusive requirement of the procedure. She explains how she suffered from the worst morning sickness imaginable and how this affected her mental state. The nurse seems satisfied and scribbles some notes.

As she pees into a bottle behind the closed door of the toilet she can hear the nurse discussing how many terminations have been carried out since the law came in, in April 1968, allowing it. They're turning it into an achievement to be bragged about.

She changes out of her clothes and into a white gown and is ushered into a holding bay where twenty other women, all identically dressed sit along a bench. They look like members of a choir, dressed in white robes. It seems to be an unwritten rule not to connect with each other and each minds her own business. Yet they are sharing one of the most heartrending and traumatic experiences of their lives.

The first woman is called into a room at the end of the bay and everybody shuffles along. Nobody speaks. It's as if talking is strictly forbidden. There's a low table with a fan of magazines to read, but nobody does. There's so much they could discuss; what brought them here, how they feel and if they have any regrets but everything has already been said. They are lambs to the slaughter in the abortion mill.

When it's Sandy's turn, she enters the small room where the operation will take place. The ceiling and the walls are stainless steel and implements hang from hooks, the way they are displayed in a butcher's shop. The needle is inserted in her arm.

When she wakes she's in bed in a ward with other women.

A member of staff is asking if she can eat a chicken sandwich. She just wants to sleep. She can't eat. She doesn't want to open her eyes. She feels groggy and could sleep for England, but the woman is asking her to sit up, insisting she must eat and drink before she can go home. She doesn't want to go but doesn't feel welcome and it's as if they are trying to hurry her along. She's reached the end of the conveyor belt, a can of baked beans ready to be packed off and put in a lorry to begin its journey to the supermarket. A punched in the stomach feeling of fear takes hold as she thinks about Jasper for the first time since leaving home and a new secret she must keep locked in —forever.

She slips into bed at home, nursing her sore tummy. Period-type pains stretch across her abdomen. She doesn't know what she feels. She isn't feeling emotional or tearful. She doesn't feel guilt or a smidgen of regret. She feels nothing and yet she knows she should feel something because the campaigners against making abortion legal threw up so many issues and made it appear a terrible thing to do. They say it has devastating consequences for women. She drifts in and out of sleep, searching her soul and willing herself to feel something. The only thought she has is that it's a quick and easy procedure. One day of her life and only a ten-minute operation. Does that make it a good thing or a bad one? Is it too easy? But why can't it be easy, it's every woman's prerogative?

She's in bed the following evening when Jasper gets back.

'You're in bed early love. Feeling alright?'

He pulls his tie from his neck and unbuttons his shirt. She knows she should pat the bed and give him the come on if she wants to keep him happy and in love. But sex is the last thing she wants. She feels like crap and she's bleeding heavily.

'No, I've got a heavy period and pains.'

'I was hoping you might be pregnant this month.' He gives

her a cheeky grin. 'Next month maybe. We'll just have to spend more time in bed.'

Sandy is afraid to connect with him. She feels like a fraud. She bites her lip and tries to press down her emotions. He mustn't see how she is. She's frightened that he'll guess what's happened although there is no reason why he would.

'Can we wait for a baby, do you think? I don't feel ready.' This is enormous, she's telling him she doesn't want to have his child.

He sits on the edge of the bed and leans in to kiss her, a puzzled look on his face as he waits for her to explain but she doesn't want to. She shouldn't need a reason.

He rubs her arm and the puzzled look changes to disappointment.

'Just a few years. There's plenty of time. We don't have to rush into it,' she hears herself whining.

He accepts what she says. He doesn't contradict or counter her but gets up and goes through to the bathroom as if they've just had a minor disagreement over what to eat for dinner.

She looks at the swaying branches of the oak tree in the middle of the lawn. Such an old tree, she thinks, witnessing change over so many years; buildings going up and down around it, people scurrying, coming and going, and yet it stands quietly observing, growing leaves, shedding leaves, adding extra lines to its bark, for years going through the motions of life. It's easier for a tree she muses. It doesn't have to think.

Jasper brings her a cup of tea and stands at the window.

'Good meeting?'

'Yes, kind of.'

'What do you mean?'

'It was a sobering experience being in the same room with so many parents who've suffered this appalling tragedy and hearing their different stories.'

'Did you tell them about our baby?'

'No. I didn't think you'd want me to.'

'I don't mind if it helps. What do you think their chances are, if it goes to court?'

'They'll have to show that Distillers have been negligent. There's no authority in our law that a child injured before birth has a claim for action.'

45

RONA

When Rona gets home she finds Bill crashed out on the sofa, the handle of an empty mug of tea looped around his finger and the radio blaring in the background. She looms behind him unbuttoning her coat and gives a throaty cough to wake him. He grunts and glances at his watch.

'You're early love.' Dazed, he rubs his face.

'Toby go to bed okay?' She flops down beside him.

'We played football,' he says flatly. 'But he was disqualified for a handball.'

'In the front room? I hope you didn't break anything?' She ignores his sarcasm. Safety is swept away when she registers what he's just said. Bill has been playing with his son. Her heart lifts. 'That's good though.' But all she sees is the same dead expression when he's talking about Toby.

'Is it?'

'What's wrong Bill? You're a great dad.' He isn't but she needs to boost his confidence and make him believe he is.

'I'm not an ogre.' He takes her hand and squeezes it, pain etched across his face. 'Every time I look at him, he reminds me of my biological failings. I watch him eating, playing and I'm aware that I wasn't able to get you pregnant.'

'You mustn't blame yourself. We don't know why we couldn't have a child. It might be my fault, not yours.'

' I'm doing everything I can to connect with him but it's just not happening. After five years he feels no more mine than he did on the first day.' His words ebb into a sad silence that floats through the room. He buries his face in his hands and leans forward with his elbows on his knees.

Rona's mouth gapes in frustration. She doesn't know what to suggest. It feels as if they've come to the end of the road. She feels flat. She thought taking Toby on was the right thing to do, but now she's questioning herself. She realises that Bill wasn't prepared emotionally and she was wrong to act alone.

'In all this time Toby still feels like a stranger. I just go through the motions.'

Rona knows this but stays quiet.

'I can't love him the way he deserves, I can't fix him or change how things are for him. I carry a guilt for how he is but I shouldn't feel guilty because he's nothing to do with me. It makes me angry with myself for feeling this way.' He shouts at her in frustration, 'It wasn't me that took that bloody pill but I'm paying for somebody else's mistake. I work day and night to support him and it's not even your mistake—just some random stranger and I'm left paying for her kid. I'm sorry but you want honesty—that's how I feel. You call him my son—and I've tried, Rona, God knows, I've tried—but he isn't mine; I see him as a drain on us and if the truth be told he disgusts me.'

'I'm sorry you feel that way. I feel guilty too.'

'Really?' He puts his arm round Rona. 'But you always seem so strong.'

'Most days I muddle through.' She leans towards him and kisses him on the cheek. 'What are we going to do? Are you saying that you want to leave me?'

'God, no. I'd never leave you.' Alarm skitters across his face. 'You do know that don't you? I'd never break my marriage vows. My gut is telling me to walk away but my head's telling me to stay. You'd never cope on your own with a handicapped child.'

'We've got to find a way to make it work love, and we don't do so bad. If only you could feel differently about him. I'll tell you someone who isn't coping.'

'Who?'

'Sheila.'

'It must be hard for her all alone. I wouldn't want that to be you. That's why I have to stay. I wanted the fairytale marriage, but I promised in sickness and in health and all that and I'm sticking by my promises.'

'I love you, Bill.'

'And I love you too.' She pauses before delivering her news. 'Sheila's on the game.'

'What?'

'It's true.'

He looks puzzled. 'How do you know?'

'That's why I'm back early. I saw her go off with a fella at the back of the pub. She was dressed like a tart and I saw her doing business. I felt sick to the bone. I wouldn't have enjoyed myself if I'd stayed.'

'Surely not? She's not the type.'

'That's what I thought. What are we going to do?'

'It's not our problem. Why do you have to take on everybody else's trouble?'

'She's a friend.'

'You can't help every friend.'

'She's only doing it to support Jim. She must be desperate. Please can we help her?'

'Rona, you're pushing me to the limits. I can barely cope with Toby and now this. What do you suggest we do for Christ's sake? I'm not taking her damaged kid on as well.'

'Don't swear.'

'You drive me to it.'

'He could stay over, in the spare room.'

'What she's doing is illegal and you want to drag us into it.'

'No, it's not like that. She leaves her son in the house alone while she goes out on the game. I'm worried about Jim, can't you see that?'

'It's not just about Jim though. She's putting her life at risk doing what she's doing. She could get another job. He needs to be in care. She doesn't have to go sloping off into the night.'

'A shop job isn't going to pay the bills. What she does probably pays well. In any case don't forget she needs to be available for hospital appointments.'

'Thinking of doing the same are you?' Bill says, with sarcasm streaked through his voice.

'Don't be stupid. You know what I'm driving at.'

Bill flings his arms in the air in defeat. 'Well go on then. You'll do it anyway, when have my feelings ever come into anything? Suggest to her that Jim comes here. Things can't get any worse than they already are,' Bill says in a stroppy voice and with a resigned sigh.

She leans into him, planting a kiss on his cheek before getting up to go to bed.

'I knew you'd agree.' She gives him a beaming smile.

'I've got mug written across my forehead.'

RONA TAKES a nerve-steadying sip of tea. 'Sheila I was at the pub on Saturday evening. You were talking to a fella in the car park. I'm not judging you, but I know what's going on.'

Rona sits opposite Sheila in the cracked leather chairs in Sheila's front room. It's dowdy but the midday sun bounces the colours of the swirly carpet across the Artex walls and ceiling giving it a note of cheeriness. Rona folds and unfolds her legs in embarrassment. This is one of the hardest conversations she's ever had but she's determined to confront Sheila and offer her help.

'What are you going to do? Dob me into the social and have my kid taken away? I knew I shouldn't get drawn into a friendship with you, I feel ashamed and scared every time we meet. Well, now you know, so go on, do what you have to. You can't make me feel any worse that I already do—but please Rona, I'm begging you, don't have my son taken off me, he's all I've got.'

'No of course not. I want to help.'

'I know you mean well Rona but I can cope.'

'You can't leave Jim on his own.'

'He sleeps through. Don't judge me.'

'That's not the point. One night he'll wake up and wonder where the hell you are. You don't want that to happen?'

'He can't go very far.'

'Sheila this isn't right. You're not being responsible. This isn't the person I thought I knew. It's like there are two Sheilas. The one I got to know and love; sensible, clever, law abiding... and this. Please Sheila wake up. You've got your safety to think of. Do you want Jim to have no father or mother because that's what could happen?'

'I don't like leading a double life, but it's what I have to do for Jim. Promise you won't tell anyone.'

'Your secrets safe with me, but let me help.'

'I don't enjoy what I do but it pays the bills. I'm not proud of it. I use protection and I make rules about no kissing and no oral.'

Rona blushes. 'Spare me the gory details.' Rona's cup and saucer wobble in her hand. She stares into the dregs of her tea before placing the cup and saucer beside the hearth.

'How can you help? I don't understand.'

'You've got no family Sheila. Look just drop Jim round to

ours before you go out. At least that way, you know that one of you is safe.' Rona can't believe how easy she's making this. 'I can't condone what you're doing but if you're determined not to stop, I just want Jim to be safe. We've got a spare room. But it's just till you've sorted yourself out. You need to get a proper job.'

'As Jim gets older, I'll be able to do something else.'

'I don't know how you can trust these men.'

'It's not easy. I find it hard to trust anybody after the thalidomide and Pete. I'm more wary and distrustful of people in general. I have my wits about me, don't you worry.'

Rona expects this arrangement to go on indefinitely.

RONA SAYS GOODBYE AND LEAVES. Sheila has to keep hold of the house otherwise she'll be out on the streets with nowhere to go. Rona has heard about money grabbing rogue landlords kicking out tenants and reletting the property at much higher rents to large families. Over tea she'd focused on having Jim overnight and the thought of Sheila selling her body had sickened her but it's only now, as she boards the bus and shows the driver her return ticket that she thinks about Sheila's rent. She'd admitted that she owes several weeks. How on earth will she pay it and why hasn't the landlord put more pressure on her to cough up? Something isn't adding up. But surely, Rona muses, they can't kick her out. A law has been passed to stop this sort of thing happening. But at the back of her mind anxiety brews. Sheila's house is too big for her and Jim. The landlord will seize the opportunity to make more of such a big property and it doesn't look as if Sheila's husband will be coming back, not now. Too much time has passed.

46

RONA

R ona carries Jim in and settles him. They've got into a routine. Rona has Jim on Thursday, Friday and Saturday nights. The arrangement works well although Jim needs to be carried to the toilet when he wakes in the middle of the night. She doesn't mind. If she can stop her friend from getting evicted, she's willing to help and do what she can. Bill goes along with the arrangement. It's as if he's resigned to Rona's surprises, wondering what will be next.

Rona goes through the motions, doing what she needs to do and chatting to Sheila about Jim and everyday things, blocking from her mind Sheila's circumstances. They don't talk about it or refer to it. Prostitution. It's the word they don't mention.

There's urgency to Sheila's knock. Normally it's a single tap but this morning it's a loud rat-a-tat-tat and Rona senses something's wrong. She opens the door and although the hallway is dark Rona can make out the purple bruises on Sheila's face and a black eye. Her chin wobbles and her voice cracks as she opens her mouth to speak, collapsing into Rona's arms in fitful sobs.

'Who the hell did this?'

Sheila pulls away. Snot trails down her face and mascara

mingles with tears. 'We've got nowhere to live.' There's a large bag at Sheila's heel.

Jim fidgets in Rona's arms, breakfast still around his mouth and although he loves coming to Rona's house he's crying because he's pleased to see his mum and wants her to hold him.

'We need to ring the police. Whoever did this mustn't be allowed to get away with it.' Rona's glad that Bill has left for work. He would worry about her getting involved.

'No.' Sheila grabs Rona's sleeve, alarm written across his damaged face. 'I don't want the police involved.'

'I think you've got some explaining to do then. Here, take Jim and go through to the lounge. I'll make us a brew.'

Rona pours the tea and feels helpless. She wants to be the rescue package but doesn't have any of the answers and can only do so much. They're battling against disability, poverty and a broken society.

'My landlord,' Sheila stutters through tears. 'He threatened to cut off the electricity and water and break all the locks if I didn't give him sex.'

'Oh Lord.'

'To start with he was nice. He seemed so understanding when Pete left. He was my friend, looking out for me. And when word got out about, you know, what I do, he said as long as I was discreet and kept myself to myself, it was ok, he'd turn a blind eye, but then things changed.'

Rona claps her hand to her mouth. Tears prick at the corner of her eyes. She reaches for Sheila's hand and gives it a squeeze.

'He said he'd let me off paying now and again in return for favours.'

Sheila pauses, sips her tea and her face is set like stone. Rona allows her silence to fill the room as Sheila gathers her emotions. Jim's on the floor with Toby and Rona thinks about their innocence and the world they are growing up in. Usually she's optimistic but her positive outlook is waning.

'He got nasty last night. He's never been like this before.'

Sheila's eyes are pleading with Rona to believe her. Rona listens but says nothing. She doesn't want to know all the details. It's painful for both of them and so she focuses on searching for a way forward. Sheila's life is spiralling downward through no fault of her own. Circumstances have conspired to make it a living hell, but out of everything that's happened she has Jim whom she loves with all her heart and she'll fight to keep him.

'He told me I had to leave. He needs the house. Says he needs to put the rent up and can get a lot more by filling it with immigrants. He says I'm unprofitable.'

'Oh God I'm so sorry, Sheila. What did you say?'

'I offered to give him sex every day and if that's what it took I would do it, to keep my home.'

'You can't do that. It's horrible.'

'What options do I have?'

'It's intimidation. You could take it to court.'

'I'm not doing that. It's my word against his, there's no proof. He's a reputable landlord, married and he sits on the church council.

'Bill was talking about the rental market the other day. Something about rent controls being relaxed a few years ago. It's bad in London. Some landlords are getting rid of tenants by whatever means they like and re-letting their properties at higher rents.'

'Can we stay here, Rona? Just till I've fixed something up.'

'Of course. But long term what are you going to do?

'Will you help me look for a room? That's all we need.'

47

RONA

Sheila and Jim are shopping. They've been at Rona and Bill's for a couple of weeks and now that the bruising has faded it's time to look for a room. Rona is going with Sheila to look at rentals. Bill has been badgered into looking after Jim and Toby for the afternoon. He doesn't kick up a fuss because it's in his interest that Sheila finds somewhere. Her bags and boxes line their hallway and he's constantly asking Rona, 'How long is this going to go on for?'

'If she carries on, she'll get caught,' Bill snaps. He's on a chair in the front room changing a light bulb.

Rona hands him the bulb. 'I know and I'm doing my best to come up with an idea. She doesn't have any family. There's nobody to help. We're all she's got.'

'I don't see why it's down to us.' Bill clips the bulb into place and gets down from the chair. 'Look, love, I know you always want to help everyone but sometimes it's not possible. It's affecting us and we were already at breaking point. I don't know how much more I can take.'

. . .

A WORRYING THOUGHT sweeps through Rona's mind as they trawl the streets in search of vacancies. Up and down street after street of red-brick Victorian housing splashed with soot and dirt, it's easy to get lost because they all look the same. Has Sheila even thought this? Rona takes a gulp of air, bracing herself for the difficult suggestion she needs to make.

'I know this is hard for you, Sheila, but you can't survive on your own. Better to send Jim into residential care than have the authorities take him from you.'

'That's not going to happen,' Sheila says sharply.

'There's a nice residential school in the countryside around Liverpool. Honestly, it's the best thing for him. I'll get Bill to drive you over there to visit. I'm sure they'll let you see him whenever you like.'

'I've told you I can't do that.'

'It's the right thing to do and you know it.'

'I'm not listening.'

'I know it's not what you want to hear.'

'I'd miss him.'

'Of course you would, but you're not alone. Other thalidomides are in residential care. He can come back in the holidays. It'll give you time to sort yourself out. You're trying to do too much.'

Sheila is pensive and doesn't respond and Rona wonders if she is giving the idea some thought or blocking it out.

'Most of the time it's okay, being on the game.'

'Who are these men anyway? You don't know them. You're putting your life and Jim's at risk.'

Sheila comes to a halt in front of a notice in a window. 'No children, no coloureds, no Irish.'

'That's no good.'

They walk on. There's wasteland to their right and they comment that it should be used to build more housing.

'I know you don't believe me when I say that most of the

time it's okay, but it is. Most of them are decent ordinary men who play golf on a Saturday, go to church on a Sunday and take their wives on holiday to Butlins. But they don't get sex and they're frustrated. I've got a few regulars that treat me really nice and pay a cut above the rest. There's this bloke called Neil.'

She stops to read another notice in a window.

'No Irish no coloured. Doesn't say no children.' She raises her eyebrows to Rona and knocks.

The landlady opens the door. She's younger and prettier than Rona expects and as she smiles warmly Rona feels hopeful.

'Do you still have a vacancy?'

'I do.'

'Do you take children? I've only one child.'

'I do,' the woman says looking doubtful, 'but it'll cost you. I ask for a deposit of a hundred pounds in case of damages.'

Sheila frowns at Rona, as if she's hoping for Sheila to say something to get her out of paying this extortionate sum, but Rona is embarrassed and leaves Sheila to do the talking.

'This is the tenth house we've been to. I don't have that kind of money. My child is no trouble, he's crippled and we've nowhere to go.'

'I'm sorry, I can't help you.'

'It's as if children are a bloody crime. If I had a giraffe you'd probably say yes.'

But the door is shut in Sheila's face by the time the words are out and they turn to head up the hill, scouring more notices.

'You said something about a bloke called Neil.'

'Yes. He's my best client. He knows I'm only doing it to support Jim. He owns a club in town and now and again he takes me there and treats me like his girlfriend. He gives me money to buy nice dresses and I'm companionship more than anything. They aren't all like that though. Some knock me down in price and tell me to come back when I'm more experienced. The punters are a mixed bunch. But I earn good money. I don't want to give it up. I don't have much option. Until this happened with the landlord I was beginning to enjoy my success and the money it brought in.'

Rona stops walking. She has no option, she's got to offer her spare room to Sheila and Jim permanently. Maybe in time Sheila will meet a nice man who'll take her on and bring Jim up as his own. It's perfectly possible; there have to be decent men out there somewhere and the thought fills Rona with hope.

'Let me see what Bill says. I can't promise anything, but you can stay a bit longer, providing Bill agrees. I need to clear it with him first.'

Sheila stops walking and gives Rona a hug through teary eyes. 'I knew you wouldn't see us out on the streets.'

Rona sighs and wonders what on earth Bill will say. She knows she's pushing her luck this time.

48

RONA

Rona is so engrossed in her thoughts that she doesn't hear Bill turn the wireless off and come into the kitchen behind her. When he wraps his arms around her, she's startled and turns with a distant smile to rub his cheek with her finger.

She calls Toby for his breakfast. His pyjamas are inside out but it's amazing how much he's come on and he's trying to do so many things for himself. Her inability to grow a baby inside her womb had made her feel a horrible failure. It was the one thing women were supposed to do effortlessly. But she doesn't feel like this anymore. Little chinks of elation fill her as she watches Toby flourish.

They sit down to breakfast. It's the weekend. Afterwards he can't wait to get down to play with his cars in the lounge. Rona washes up. Bill picks up a tea towel and dries a plate.

'What's happening Rona?'

'Sheila's gone down to the council and left Jim with me. She's putting her name on the waiting list for a council house. Although the waiting list is long I think she'll jump the queue because of Jim. Surely she'll be a priority.'

'I meant what's happening to us?'

They are suspended in uneasy silence as Rona concentrates on scrubbing a saucepan, moving the scouring pad hard across the surface and wishing she could scrub out the bad parts of her life. She feels trapped between the need to help Sheila and a sense of duty towards her husband. Her problem has always been trying to please all people at all times but she's learning that it doesn't work.

'How do you mean?' she asks tentatively, but knows what his answer will be.

'Bit by bit I'm losing you to all of these other people. It used to be just you and me.' Bill doesn't sound angry but Rona detects hurt tucked behind his words.

'Then it was you, me and Toby. Now it's Sheila and Jim too. It feels as if you don't care about me anymore. I don't come first. This isn't how it was supposed to be.'

He's right Rona thinks, although she's not going to admit it. She'll just have to try harder to please him and talk to Sheila again about residential care. Something can be sorted but she doesn't see that Sheila has much option as a single mother.

'I'll try to broach the subject of residential care again.'

Bill puts the tea towel down. Rona is rinsing a bowl under the tap.

'Stop washing up, love. Come and sit down, I need to talk to you, before they get back.'

A shaky feeling comes over her. She knows there's a huge conversational bomb coming by the tone of his voice. Her heart misses a beat.

Rona folds pleats in her apron as he pulls out a chair, anticipating the worst.

'I've got a solution.' He pats her on her hand. 'A friend of mine...'

This is typical of Bill, he's always calling in favours from friends. Whatever is it this time she wonders.

'There's a residential place in Sussex called Chailey Heritage. It's a school for the educationally subnormal I think or a school for the physically handicapped, I'm not sure exactly. But it's also a hospital and they have workshops where they make aids for the handicapped to help them overcome their difficulties.'

Rona is doubtful. 'There's a place near Liverpool and she won't send him there so she's hardly going to say yes to going down south.'

A smile sweeps across Bill's face and he pats her hand again. 'Let me finish love.'

'Go on.'

'I met a builder who's been working there and he said what amazing work they are doing for thalidomides. He put me in touch with the head and Jimmy has a place if she wants to send him there. But not only that, he's willing to take Sheila as well, to work as a live-in cook and cleaner. It's free board and lodgings.'

'No way. That sounds amazing.'

'The only other idea I can come up with is a ten-pound passage to Australia as a mail-order bride for a lonely sheep farmer—and I tell you, love, I'd happily pay the tenner to get rid.'

There's a beat of silence, then they laugh. It's as if the tension bound up in the Sheila situation has been released and leaves them more relaxed than they've felt in a long time.

Through splutters Rona says, 'Can you honestly see Sheila rounding up sheep?'

'Bit of a career change I'd say.' Bill's face is flushed.

'I'm sure there must be a Bible story along those lines.'

The relaxed atmosphere breaks when they hear Sheila come home. The strain returns to their faces, realising that they'll need to discuss their thoughts with her and knowing that it won't be easy.

Sheila blunders in huffing, she takes her coat off and unstraps Jimmy, leaving the pram in the hallway. There's barely any room because Sheila's belongings fill the small area but Rona is patient and knows it won't go on forever. Sheila wanders into the lounge and puts Jimmy on the mat to watch Toby play cars.

'Any luck?'

'The waiting room was crowded. Jimmy was fidgety. When I arrived the man on the counter was having a right go at some poor woman, telling her the whole country is gripped in a housing crisis and the Government are trying to clear thousands of slums and that she stands no chance of getting to the top of the queue. Jesus, Rona, I nearly gave up but then it was my turn and he said I could have a room in a council-run hostel.'

'If it's all they can offer...'

Sheila goes to fill the kettle and Bill and Rona exchange wary glances.

'I'd rather sleep on the streets,' she calls from the hallway, followed by a huff.

Rona and Bill follow her through to the kitchen.

'Let me make you a cuppa,' Rona says taking the kettle. 'Sit down. Bill's got an idea.'

Bill opens the discussion. Sheila gives a morose shake of her head, a wall of resistance growing around her.

Rona puts a hand on Sheila's shoulder. 'Let him finish.'

Bill deftly circumnavigates around all of the issues he foresees that Sheila will raise as objections as he explains the proposition. When he finishes he pauses to gauge her reaction. Her face is alight with interest. Rona puts the milky tea in front of her with a rich tea biscuit.

Sheila lets out a small inaudible sigh and raises her eyes to the ceiling.

'Doesn't look like I've got much choice.'

Rona hovers over her in a nail-biting moment. She thinks it's a great opportunity but can see that Sheila is begrudgingly going along with it. She feels sorry for Bill because he's gone to a lot of effort making phone calls and sticking his neck out. Sheila's not showing much gratitude and it niggles her.

'The ethos of the founder of the school, Grace Kimmins was to give handicapped children a purpose and to focus on what they can do, not on what they can't. She didn't want them to end up on the scrapheap of life. They have workshops for carpentry and apparently they build a small ladder as a symbol of how every handicapped person can overcome their obstacles. It's got its own chapel. They take groups to the sea. They play football on crutches. They've had royal visits. Grace's philosophy was, 'do not be defined by your disability and be happy in your lot.' The thalidomide children are still very young but there are quite a few living there. What do you think?'

Rona and Bill wait in anticipation.

'Well yeah, sounds good.'

'We'll take you down there, see if it's suitable.'

Rona wishes Bill would sound more decisive rather than giving her the option to back out.

'It's a long way.'

'We'll make a small break of it and visit some places while we're down there,' Rona entices.

The conversation snaps to a standstill and Rona gets up to peel potatoes for dinner.

Sheila has a bath and later over dinner she says, 'Anywhere's got to be better than round here. I'm beginning to think that hiding away in a special community is the answer. I went in a cafe this afternoon and the bleeding owner turfed me out.'

'What?' Bill is dumbfounded.

'Why?'

'He said Jim was ugly and he didn't want ugly people in his cafe.'

Bill and Rona stare at each other in disbelief.

'God's honest truth. He said Jim was a misfit and he can choose who he serves because it's his cafe.'

'What cafe was it?'

'Rumbolds on Earl Street.'

'That's dreadful,' Rona and Bill say in unison.

'I'm not going in there again.'

'Oh yes we are,' says Bill. 'Tomorrow we'll take Jim and Toby and let's see him throw my boy out. In fact, how many thalidomides can we round up? Let's have a tea-party and let him see what these kids are made of. We'll show him, the bigoted bastard.'

Despite the bad language Rona has never been prouder of her husband.

49

ALSDORF, GERMANY, 1968

I t's a chilly, grey morning in May and the late-rising Heinz wakes with a splitting headache and a sharp pain in his mouth. For days he's refused medical help for his toothache. Other things are on his mind, like the accusations mounting against him and his board of directors.

A crowd gathers outside the club house belonging to the Eschweiler mining association in the small town of Alsdorf. It's the only building in the area with enough space for the six hundred people—judges, jurymen, lawyers, stenographers, witnesses, defendants, co-plaintiffs, press, radio, television reporters and spectators attending the trial against Grunenthal each day.

Heinz is escorted to the trial. He and eight others at Grunenthal have been charged with intent to commit bodily harm and involuntary manslaughter. He sits in the back of a police car, awaiting his fate.

As they round the corner, a sense of dread washes over him when he sees mounted guards and a battalion of state police troops outside the building. Hundreds of people are thronging the street. He's terrified about being mobbed by this huge crowd. He's done nothing wrong as far as he's concerned. Mothers huddle on the pavement holding children with missing limbs. One of them waves her fist at him and spits at the car. He reads her emotions and turns his head from her child. In a flash Heinz feels like a bus driver who has run over a group of children, unwittingly, killing and injuring many of them. But he is resolved about one thing. He will not be admitting guilt in this trial. He must be resolute.

The trial is expected to run for months. It will take its toll on him, but be resolved fast, he is sure of that. But God knows, he's been through six years of hell already. When he and his board of directors made the decision to withdraw thalidomide in late 1961 he thought that would be the end of it. But those bastards at the public prosecutors office had given them a bloody hard time of it. To think of everything his poor wife went through in those six years. No wonder, Heinz reflects, that she left. The stress had taken its toll. He'd turned to drink and staying out all night sleeping with women in brothels to get some sort of release from the pain he was suffering. And when he'd admitted what he'd been doing she couldn't take anymore. He was disgusted with himself; not because of the thousands of crippled children but because he'd taken to slapping his pretty wife around. She hadn't deserved that. She'd been woken several times during the night with the thud of police fists on the door, demanding they search the house to look for important documents. The police were stupid. He'd made sure at the very outset that the critical documents they needed to draw up a bill of indictment were locked away in a secret bunker.

And then, like a pack of wild animals a group of hooligans rush forward and pelt the car with stones and eggs. Heinz is terrified. He's never been in more fear of his life. Something black is put over his head and he's told that they are driving the car to the rear of the building where he will be ushered in to safety.

His lawyer waves him into a quiet room where they can talk. They're allowed twenty minutes together. Grunenthal have a battery of forty lawyers in total.

'The Ministry of Justice have planned for every eventuality. They're bringing in standby judges and jurymen in case anyone falls ill,' his solicitor tells him.

'Jesus fucking Christ. Is that really necessary?'

'I'm sorry I can't comment.'

'Well at least we've organised our own news agency so that we can send our own version of the trial's progress.'

'I can't comment on that either but I can update you on what's going on. The case against two of the defendants has been dropped because of their ill health.'

'Good.'

'If I can run through the basics of what you are on trial for, before we go into the courtroom.'

'Go on,' Heinz sighs with irritation etched across his face.

'You put on sale a drug that even when taken according to instructions caused an unacceptable degree of bodily harm. You failed to test it properly. You went out of your way to advertise it as safe when you could give no guarantee that it was. It caused those who took it to itch, sweat, vomit and suffer peripheral neuritis. You suppressed reports of reactions as they were reported to you. And the drug caused an epidemic of malformed babies.'

'They'll have to prove that thalidomide caused birth defects. Our doctors will see to that when they're called as witnesses.'

'And they'll have medical witnesses of their own.'

'We'll slam them down.'

'We'll argue that you've done no wrong under German law because an unborn baby has no legal protection apart from in connection with criminal abortion.'

'And there's the argument too that a variety of other factors might be responsible including food additives, nuclear fallout and even television rays. It will be very hard to establish that thalidomide is the cause. Yes, I think we're going to win.'

50

SANDY

Pressure is building in Parliament and in the press against Distillers with little effect. It looks as if the court battles will go on for years.

In 1972 Jack Ashley MP gives a speech that is met with silence by a packed House of Commons. 'Adolescence is a time for living and laughing, for learning and loving,' he says. 'But what kind of adolescence will a ten year-old boy look forward to when he has no arms, no legs, one eye...How can an eleven-year-old girl look forward to laughing and loving when she has no hand to be held and legs to dance on? ...Yet the powerful Distillers Company has had no compunction in fighting these children for the last ten years.'

Sandy can't imagine being responsible for another human being. She isn't broody. 'Motherhood isn't a hobby, it's a calling and I'm sorry but I don't have that calling,' she says to Jasper. 'And I'm not going to be like some of the other mothers of thalidomides, giving birth to a replacement child. Our son was unique and can't be replaced.'

'You've got the same calling as me though. We work well together. You helped put the posters up didn't you?'

Sandy gives a mischievous grin.

'I'm sorry. It's my feisty side coming out. I'm doing what I can to help the campaign.'

'I'm really proud of you and if our son had lived he would have been proud of his mother for fighting his corner.'

'What you've helped to do is great, but Scotland Yard are searching for the originators. The posters are putting people off buying Distiller's drinks, but the newspapers can't reproduce the posters by merely reporting them as news because we've got to consider contempt.'

Thousands of posters are plastered all over the country making savage attacks on Distillers and calling for a boycott of their products. They contain a series of different slogan images. Sandy is a member of the campaign which aims to hit Distillers where it hurts—in its pockets. Beyond home with Jasper, life for Sandy is fulfilling and has a purpose. Being involved in the campaign makes her feel good about herself in ways she never imagined.

Sandy's modelling career is behind her and she realises that it was about vanity and glitz and that it wasn't real. It was fun in the glamour industry, she reflects, but time to move on to bigger projects, like this one which has become her vocation.

51

RONA

The match finishes, Bill blows his whistle, jumps up and down and shouts for joy.

'Three nil,' he says with an arm around Toby. 'We showed 'em, eh son.'

Rona smiles from the crowd of spectators lining the pitch. It's the only time Bill shows physical affection towards Toby and this makes her happy. Bill is the referee and when Toby became interested in football he volunteered to help in the under tens' team.

It's a cold winter's day and she's come to watch Toby play. She doesn't usually come along because it's Toby and Bill's special time together but she likes to show an interest once in a while and join them for fish and chips in the cafe afterwards. Playing football gives them space away from her and fresh air to run about and have fun. She calls it their male bonding time and it happened because of their shared love of footie. In fact when she thinks about it she realises that football has saved their marriage and broken the ice between father and son. They share the highs and lows of the game and at home they follow Manchester United on the television, screaming when a goal is scored and doing a jig. She knows that Bill gives Toby a sip of lager as they sit on the settee together. That's part of being a father-and-son team and she turns a blind eye.

Toby's lack of arms doesn't matter because the other boys are in awe of his skills. He learned to dribble the ball skilfully and can find his friends, passing the ball from a long way off. He's one of the best players in the team.

All in all, Rona is happy with the way things have turned out. She's giving Toby every opportunity to thrive and develop a range of skills from painting to running. And after ten years Bill is happy to call him, Son.

She wouldn't swap him for the world.

THE END

If you enjoyed this book, please would you kindly leave a short review on Amazon. Reviews are always appreciated. Click here to post your review: My Book

FIND OUT WHAT HAPPENS NEXT... "Every Father's Fear." My Book

Only a handful of people know what really happened on a London maternity ward in February 1961 when a thalidomide baby was born and a shocking crime committed. Those involved will pay a heavy price for their secret.

That baby, Toby, is now a teenager. Rona, the woman he thought of as his mother, is dead. Left to raise Toby alone and run a business, grieving Bill soon discovers the demons his wife battled with, as he battles his own.

Living with his disability and coping with the appalling attitudes of those around him, Toby, not wanting to burden Bill, faces his tormentors alone, with disturbing and heart-wrenching consequences.

Meanwhile, a young journalist, keen to publicise the plight of the thalidomide families across Britain, finds out more than he bargained for.

This is a powerful story of revenge, lies and secrets and the enduring power of love. And a triumph of fatherhood. Loosely based on true events in 1970s Britain this is the standalone sequel to Every Mother's Fear.

This is the stand-alone sequel to 'Every Mother's Fear'.

POSTSCRIPT

The UK distributors of thalidomide, Distillers (now Diageo, successor to Distillers) agreed to compensate victims in 1973 and the Thalidomide Trust was set up. Fifty years on hundreds of victims have never received any compensation for their life-altering conditions. Grunenthal has always maintained that it is not liable because it met contemporary industry standards for drug testing. It argues that back in the 1950s no-one tested the effect of drugs on foetuses.

In 2012 survivors in England received £80 million in compensation from the Government to help with their on-going needs. The Government expressed its "sincere regret and deep sympathy for the suffering caused."

Grunenthal, the German manufacturer of the drug set up a fund of 50 million euros for victims mainly on the Continent and unveiled a memorial in 2012 when it expressed its "sincere regrets." It has never compensated British victims.

Made in United States
North Haven, CT
11 August 2024

55909943R30189